NIGHT OF PASSION

Kieran's words echoed in Margaret's head. *Sometimes not taking the chance is the biggest chance of all.*

He looked at her steadily, his eyes dark as dusk in the low light. She knew she could never do what he urged her to, and yet she couldn't bear to have him see her cowardice. Finally she pushed away from the table and went to stare out the window in the guise of checking the weather.

The wind moaned, as if in agony. Transparent veils of snow sifted like smoke over the ground, the moon slicing cold light over knife-edged drifts.

"It looks like it should be clear tomorrow. Good for traveling."

He came up to stand behind her shoulder. The solid bulk of him was almost familiar now, his sounds, his scents.

"It sure is one lonely night," he said at last.

She looked up at him over her shoulder. The moonlight cast him in silver and black, that beautiful face with its lines of pain and living. And suddenly she saw her life after tomorrow, endless empty days and empty nights and empty beds and not even any memories to fill them, until she'd wither up like an unwanted flower and blow away and nobody would ever notice the diff—

She took a deep, sh_____
have to be."

Books by Susan Kay Law

Journey Home
Traitorous Hearts
Reckless Angels
Home Fires
Heaven in West Texas
One Lonely Night

WITH LORI COPELAND AND CASSIE EDWARDS

Baby on the Doorstep

Published by HarperPaperbacks

ONE
LONELY
NIGHT

 SUSAN KAY LAW

HarperPaperbacks
A Division of HarperCollinsPublishers

HarperPaperbacks
A Division of HarperCollins*Publishers*
10 East 53rd Street, New York, N.Y. 10022-5299

This is a work of fiction. The characters, incidents, and
dialogues are products of the author's imagination and are not to
be construed as real. Any resemblance to actual events or
persons, living or dead, is entirely coincidental.

ISBN 0-06-108475-1

HarperCollins®, 🔥®, and HarperPaperbacks™
are trademarks of HarperCollins*Publishers* Inc.

Cover illustration by Jim Griffin

First printing: August 1997

Printed in the United States of America

Visit HarperPaperbacks on the World Wide Web at
http://www.harpercollins.com

❖ 10 9 8 7 6 5 4 3 2 1

*To my comrades from Lester Prairie High School,
class of 1980:*

*Colleen Radtke (Jon, you too!), Julie
Hawkinson (who tells more people about my
books than anyone short of my mother), Merri Lea
Kyllo, Sheila Jilek, and Sherri Ruesink.
With deep thanks for your enthusiasm about
my books, and great joy that our paths in life
brought us all back together again.*

*Special thanks to Merri Lea, who, when we
were in junior high, shoved a copy of* The Flame
and the Flower *in my hands and said, "You gotta
read this!"*

And I did. I guess I owe it all to you!

Acknowledgments

Big thanks to the always-brilliant Connie Brockway, for plotting above and beyond the call of duty;

and to the inimitable Krissie Ohlrogge, for giving me *Redemption*.

1

1884

  "Redemption, Dakota Territories." Kieran McDermott murmured the name to himself, testing it out. It seemed a strange place to find a murderer, a town called Redemption. He'd look there all the same, for the instincts honed over two decades of hunting urged him on.

  The small rented room on the outskirts of Chicago was dim, sparsely furnished with battered furniture and ragged curtains. Outside, a train rumbled past, clouding the air with smoke and harsh sounds.

  Kieran ignored it. He occupied the cheap room not because he couldn't afford better, but because it simply didn't matter to him at all. He'd learned to disregard such trivialities years ago.

  A map was spread out on the lopsided pine table in front of him. Pins stabbed through the thin paper, indicating crime sites, their scattered arrangement holding no pattern that he could discern.

If there was one thing that marked his quarry, that was it. The man had no pattern, no favorite methods at all. He was as likely to invest months posing as a colleague or employee, gaining access to vast company funds before quietly absconding with them, as he was to recruit a gang and stage a bold, bloody daytime holdup of the largest bank in Milwaukee. Years of crimes, all over the Middle West, without coming close to being captured. Crimes that wouldn't even be linked together, if it weren't for his single, signature habit—he sent notes thanking his victims.

So he had pride, Kieran thought, pride and arrogance enough that he couldn't stand his successes going completely unnoticed. There'd be no reason to send the notes—indeed, much safer not to—other than to claim his work.

It wasn't the sort of job that Kieran would normally accept. The wealthy businessmen and profitable enterprises that had been robbed could well afford it. They could command dozens of law officers to catch the Uncatchable Man—as the newspaper writers had recently dubbed him—and hire detectives of their own, as well.

But then there'd been a young girl drawn in, a lovely fifteen-year-old girl—sixteen now, Kieran reminded himself. And a broken and distraught father had begged him to help, and the hunt had begun.

Kieran mentally sifted through the bits of evidence

he'd collected, a witness here, a train record there. The hotel chambermaid who'd taken note of the strangeness of the young girl being found in her "father's" bed one morning. The experienced Minneapolis detective who'd chased a lead all the way across Minnesota before being found, stabbed to death, in the Big Sioux River.

For nine months Kieran had followed the trail. Longer than he'd chased anyone, except the first.

That one had taken him ten years.

Despite his work, the trail would still seem pitifully thin to anyone else. It didn't matter to Kieran; he felt it, the razor-sharp focus of his attention, his senses, and the rising churn in his blood that always told him when he was narrowing in on his prey.

He reached forward and placed his finger on the tiny dot on the map, just east of where the Missouri River snaked its way through the southern half of the Dakota Territories. "Yes," he whispered.

It would be Redemption.

Margaret Thayer lit the tiny stub of candle—saved from last year for just this purpose—that was carefully pushed into the exact center of her birthday cake. The cake was small, thinly frosted in white icing, an indulgence she'd earned by prudently drinking her coffee unsweetened for the previous two weeks.

Her thirty-fifth birthday. And she was entirely alone, just as she had been for the past three.

Outside, the wind raged and battered her small

house. An unusually vicious late-April snowstorm drove needle pricks of snow through the air with a whistle like bullets. After a week of mild temperatures and clear days, the sudden storm was a shock, as if mocking anyone foolish enough to believe that spring had come to Dakota. Though Margaret had stuffed every crack she could find with rags, the wind still forced its way in, fluttering the small candle flame.

Thirty-five years *old*. When so many of those years had seemed to pass so slowly, how in the world had she gotten here so fast? At church services, just last Sunday, Martha Ann Perkins—who Margaret knew full well was three months younger than she was—had confided she was soon to become a grandmother. A grandmother!

Margaret's goddaughter Carrie, whom she still thought of as a tender, towheaded six-year-old, had married, known a man, conceived a child. And here it had been almost twenty years since Margaret herself had been so much as kissed. Even then, only once, a quick stolen mashing of lips that was so long ago she could no longer conjure up even the slightest memory of the feeling.

A loud thud made her jump, her heart race. Was she now to become a foolish, fearful woman, too, who jumped at every stray sound? For surely it was nothing; likely the wind had just ripped a loose board from the shed and flung it against the house.

The candle's flame wobbled, diminished, threatening to extinguish itself before she even had a chance to make a wish. Best to be quick about it.

Margaret had long ago given up wishing for things like love or fortune or even happiness. Now, her dreams were more modest.

Please, I just want something to happen.

And, with a quick huff of breath, she snuffed the meager fire.

This time there was no mistaking the sound for a wind-borne object. The thudding was steady and hard, a heavy fist against her door.

For a brief, ridiculous instant, she thought that perhaps someone had remembered her birthday after all. But none of her acquaintances would come out in this storm; it would be sheer stupidity. The stupid did not survive long in the territories.

What, then? The banging grew slower, weaker. For a moment she considered ignoring it. Certainly that would be the wisest course; a woman living alone two miles from town couldn't be too careful. And everyone in the area had more sense than to go out in weather like this. Still, what if there was an emergency, a desperate need for her assistance?

Well, she could hardly let whoever was out there die on her doorstep. Surely there was not that much danger. Far more likely that someone had merely been lost in the storm than they'd deliberately gone out in it to find her and do her harm. Still, she checked the loading of her shotgun and propped it up against the wall within easy reach before she opened the door.

Cold and snow blasted her, stinging her face. A tall figure swayed in the doorway, long dark coat flapping stiffly in the wind. Not a slice of skin showed between the battered, ice-coated felt hat pulled low and the turned-up collar hunched high around the ears.

"C-cold. Din' 'spect . . ." The words were slurred. He moved forward a shuffling step. "Storm," he said, and toppled over.

"Oh no, don't do that!" He pitched straight into her arms, a heavy, frigid weight. She valiantly struggled to keep them both upright, but she was not a large woman and she slowly sank beneath the burden.

Oh, dear, she thought, as the hard plane of the floor painfully met her hip. Perhaps I should have been a bit more specific with my wish.

Something *good*.

Had he simply died right on top of her, just like that? He didn't move, and his weight made breathing hard. She squirmed, easing herself from beneath him until he rolled to one side with a thump. She was free.

Margaret scrambled to the door and leaned against it, forcing it shut against the wind. She dropped to her knees beside the still form, tugged off the hat, and turned down the stiff fabric of the coat's collar.

She'd never seen this man before. For surely if she had, this face she would have remembered. Cleanly sculpted features, not marred a whit by the lines bracketing his mouth and eyes. A fall of heavy dark hair, thickly iced with silver. Skin pale as the blowing snow outside, a stark contrast with the dark stubble of a few day's beard.

Strange to think of a man as beautiful, but there was no other word for this one.

And he was still alive.

Beneath her fingertips, where she'd placed them against the curve of his neck, she could barely detect his pulse. Faint, and far too slow, but there just the same.

"Can you hear me?" When she got no response, she grabbed his shoulders and shook hard, nearly shouting this time. "Wake up! We've got to get you up."

The hard, driving bits of sleet had scored his eyelids with tiny cuts, leaving them swollen and red. When he blinked his eyes open, she found the purest blue she'd ever seen.

"Sorry," he mumbled "Din' know . . . I . . ."

"Not now. We've got to get you warm, and the floor's too cold. I can't get you up myself, and you have to help me. Do you understand?"

"Unnerstan'." He didn't move.

She lifted his limp arm and looped it around her shoulders, locking her own arms around his chest. "Come on," she urged him. "Get up!"

He moaned—not a pained sound, she judged, but one of exhaustion and protest. How long had he been caught in the storm?

He tried; she had to give him that. But it seemed as if his limbs weren't entirely under his command, and she had to pull and tug and shout, taking as much of his weight as she could, dragging him to his feet.

They stumbled toward the bed together, once bumping hard against the wall—of course *she* was the one nearest the wall, and took the brunt of it— and twice nearly pitched to the floor. Finally, they made it, and, relieved, she simply released her hold and let him tumble onto the bed. It creaked and shuddered beneath him, and for a moment she regretted dropping him like that, concerned the old frame would break beneath him.

His face pressed against the straw mattress, he mumbled something she couldn't hear. Perhaps he couldn't breathe, with his nose buried in the bed like that. She climbed up beside him and crouched down, working her hands beneath him, positioning her shoulder at his side, and gave a heave. He flopped over.

Legs next. She scrambled off and grabbed his feet, dragging them up on the bed so he finally lay full upon it. Despite the biting air that rushed into the room while the door had been open, sweat dampened her forehead and back by the time she finished. Who would have thought a man would be so dad-blamed heavy?

Unfortunately, the exertion hadn't warmed him at all. He shivered so hard the bed quaked, his teeth clicking together.

First, she decided, she had to get him out of those cold, wet clothes.

His boots had probably once been expensive. The leather was very fine, the stitching even and small. But they'd had hard use, the heels worn down, the leather scarred and scratched. They were easily dispensed with; she just grabbed and yanked.

Machine-made socks, she thought in disgust, thin, knitted things that probably wouldn't keep a toe warm in August. Had none of the women in his life enough sense or care to knit him some good sturdy ones? She stripped them off, too, throwing them in the direction of the boots. The flesh beneath was white and cold, hard as marble. His feet needed tending, but it would have to wait.

Best to worry about saving his life before she set herself to saving his feet.

He wore a duster of heavy gray glazed cotton that reached his ankles. It didn't matter how long it was, though. Dakota required skins, and anyone with half a brain knew it.

Her fingers fumbled on the buttons of his plain white shirt. Stop that! she scolded herself. This was no time for maidenly nerves. Surely she should have left such useless conceits behind years ago.

She moved faster, attempting nurselike efficiency. But she couldn't keep her gaze from sometimes brushing the skin she bared, any more than she could pretend that she didn't feel a bit of . . . curiosity. It was foolish, but she was a thirty-five-year-old spinster who'd never seen a bare-chested man—not even her father. And she'd never expected the fascination of it, the way that skin—just plain human skin—could seem so much more *male* than hers.

The wet heaviness of his denim pants made the metal buttons stubborn. Margaret found it hard to force them through their holes and even harder to ignore where her fingers worked and pressed. The heat in her cheeks shamed her, for there was nothing at all prurient here. It was only about saving a man's life.

Still, she tried looking away, focusing on a strip of wallboard that showed through the plaster instead of the sight of her work-roughened hands against a man's bare belly and denim-covered crotch. But trying to unfasten his pants without sight only made her flounder all the more. She squared her shoulders and concentrated on her task, finally freeing the last button. She tugged the denims from his hips and his long—very long—legs, eyeing the drawers that twisted low around his hips, and decided that would have to be enough. They were still fairly dry, and she'd done as much as she could bring herself to.

He lay, still trembling with the cold, sprawled on her old sheets, his hair dark and mussed against the creamy white of her pillow. She piled blankets over him until she feared the weight would hinder his breathing, and stacked several more next to the stove to warm.

What next? His cheeks, his fingers, his feet; all showed signs of frostbite, but she thought she should try to get something warming in him first. She bit hard on her lip, wishing there was someone to tell her if she was doing the right thing. The man—the stranger—could easily lose his fingers if she chose wrong. She wasn't accustomed to responsibility, to having others dependent upon her decisions.

Hot water from her supper still simmered in a pot on the stove. She grabbed a mug, dropped in a pinch of cayenne and ginger, and scooped in a healthy dollop of tinned milk. She debated only a moment, then added a heaping spoonful of sugar, sighing as she consigned herself to a few more days of black coffee. He needed it more than she did.

Steam rose as she poured hot water into the mug. It would probably have been better if she'd had some whiskey to add, but she never kept spirits around. This would have to do.

Stirring, blowing ripples across the surface of the mixture so it wouldn't burn him, she hurried across the room, surprised, once again, by the sight of a man in her bed. She thought it rather sad that it was such a shock to her, that she couldn't seem to prepare herself for the look of him there.

She'd assumed he was asleep, but at her urging he opened his eyes and struggled up. She sat next to him, hip hard against his side, and slipped her arm behind him for support.

"Here, drink this," she said, nudging his lips with the rim of the mug. "It will warm you."

He shook his head, his hair, surprisingly soft, brushing against her cheek. Scent filled her nostrils, cold and soap and something so alien and surprising in her house that it took her a moment to identify it—the smell of a man.

"My . . . horse." His speech, though still slow and careful, as if the words came hard, was more coherent than before. That was good. "Outside. Take . . . care of him?"

Margaret sighed. Of course he had a horse; how else would he have gotten here? She didn't relish the thought of going out in the bitter cold, and now she had little choice. "I'll take care of him soon. Let's worry about you first."

He turned his head to face her. His chin bumped the mug, sloshing a little over her hand. He frowned, blue eyes holding her gaze, demanding.

"Now."

"Soon." She brought the cup toward his mouth. "Drink this, and then we'll see about the parts you froze, and then I'll take care of your horse. Okay?"

He pressed his lips together, set his jaw, making it clear she wasn't getting any of her concoction down his throat without his cooperation.

"Now."

"For heaven's sake." Weren't people supposed to be grateful to the ones who saved their lives? Obligated to do whatever they asked without protest?

Oh, better not to examine that thought too closely. Too many dangerous possibilities there.

"All right, then. You drink this first, though, and then I'll go out and look for your horse."

He nodded and bent his head to the cup. He drank deeply, quickly, his shoulder pressing hard against her breast. The cup drained, he looked at her, his mouth gleaming moist, and repeated: "Now."

"Fine." Obstinate man. She settled him in, blankets tucked around his stubborn chin, and dressed for going out in the storm.

She hated to leave him alone. His frozen flesh wouldn't thaw properly without attention, and she wasn't sure how much time they had. She thought he was in no immediate danger, but what did she know of it? And she felt another reluctance, an odd, foolish one, to leave her house when he was there. An impatience to stay inside—with him—when, all winter long, she'd longed to leave and had snatched any excuse to get out of that confining space.

A knotted rope led from her front door to the shed that housed her own animals. Thank goodness she hadn't taken it down in last week's good weather.

Snow churned the air. Wind caught the bits—couldn't really call them flakes, when they were so small and hard—before they hit the ground, whipped them in a straight line across the empty spaces. Not all that much snow, she judged, but enough to blot out any vision when it flew like that. And the cold was fierce, making her eyebrows and her teeth hurt.

She'd hoped the horse had stayed where it had been left, near the door. Unfortunately, as she expected, it wasn't there. Likely it had wandered out into the endless white, where it would be found only after the weather warmed and the snow melted.

But she had promised him, and so she worked her way along the rope, shouting for the animal, even though she knew the wind's scream would blot out her voice almost completely.

She'd nearly reached the shed, and the end of her determination, when she found him. The horse stood still, waiting, at the front door of the shed, as if he fully expected her to come and let him in.

"Well, there," she said softly. "Find it, did you?"

She led him inside and quickly unsaddled him, checking her own elderly mare and cow before giving them all handfuls of straw. Water was solid in the tin bucket, but they'd drink little while the storm raged, anyway. Impatiently she turned for the door, pausing at the last moment to grab the bag she'd found lashed to the stranger's saddle.

The warmth of her small house welcomed her back inside, and she rushed toward the bed, tugging off her mittens and coat as she went, carelessly tossing them over a nearby chair. No one in Redemption would have believed it, she thought, that Margaret Thayer was scurrying to get to a man in her bed.

He'd stopped shuddering, she saw immediately, lying still and large against her pillows. She lightly brushed his forehead and he opened his eyes.

"Is—"

"Your horse is fine," she promised him, and bent to her work.

Too much to do; she needed more hands. His feet had seemed in the worst shape, she decided, and tugged the quilt from the mattress and peeled it back.

To her shame, her stomach gave a silly little lurch. What was so intimate about a bare foot that would make her react like that? She tried to recall the last time she'd seen one. This one seemed so much larger than hers, with its pale skin and little bit of wiry black hair. Undeniably male.

Get on with it, Margaret. You have no time to stare at the poor man's feet.

She lifted his knees, placed his feet in a pan of alum water, and let them soak while she turned her attention to the other parts of him that had been marked by the cold.

To prevent as much damage as possible, the flesh needed to be warmed slowly, carefully. She probably shouldn't have left his hands and feet under the blankets for so long as it was. Margaret fetched a bucket of snow, sat on the edge of the bed, spread a towel across her lap, and took his hands in her own.

She rubbed them with the snow, her own fingers aching with the cold. She glanced up once, checking to see if the treatment pained him, and found him watching her. Her hands fell still.

His steady gaze was assessing, unwavering, as if taking in everything about her while giving nothing of himself away. Unused to such close regard, she quickly looked back down and returned to her task.

Muffling silence lay heavy between them. She'd never had the taste or the talent for useless chatter. She had questions, certainly, many of them, but now wasn't the time for them. Fierce exposure to cold tended to blur the mind temporarily, and it would be a few hours before he'd think clearly again. He needed rest.

But she was constantly, acutely conscious of him watching her as she worked. She focused instead on his injuries, alternating between his hands and his cheeks, rubbing first with snow, then flannel, then simply her own hands.

Once her discomfort faded, she found herself unwillingly fascinated. By the feel of frozen fingers taking on her warmth, by watching white skin flushing pink and then red. By seeing his flesh come to life beneath her palms, and an answering heat sparked in her.

She was working witch hazel into his fingers when she dared to look up at him again. "I know it hurts," she said. "But that's good. It means it's thawing out."

"Don' matter," he said, but she thought she detected pain lurking deep in his eyes.

"You should rest," she told him.

In answer, he turned his wrist, curling his fingers until he cradled her hand in his own. Good strong fingers, ones she'd likely saved. Hoped she'd saved, for the thought of him losing them was more than she could bear.

"Thank you," he said softly, and drifted off to sleep, holding her hand as he would a lover's.

2

❦

The gentle light from the oil lantern cast deep shadows beneath his eyes, his cheekbones. His mouth was relaxed, parted in sleep. Margaret eased her hand from his grip—and no, she told herself, she had not for one second considered leaving it there for a little while longer—and held her palm an inch from his lips, checking to be sure he still breathed properly.

Moist, warm air flowed over her skin, making her heart skitter shamefully, and she snatched her hand away.

Ah, but he was lovely. There was nothing boyish or pretty about him, nothing studied or blandly handsome. His looks were harsher than that, sharper, as if the cruelties of life had pared away at him, honed him down to the essence of a man. His eyes were hidden from her now, but she remembered them well, their clear blue color and

17

what she'd been almost certain was a shadow of loneliness.

But she doubted that could be, for why would a man like this be lonely? He was strong and free and, if not young, certainly not old. And he was a man, not bound by all the ties and rules and expectations that chained a woman.

People tended to see what they wished to, Margaret reminded herself. Perhaps she'd imagined loneliness because it gave them something in common, something that bound them together.

If she was a more fanciful woman—or a foolish one—she might have thought that the fates had just delivered a most intriguing birthday present to her door. But she was neither, and so she turned away, hand pressed to the dull ache that pulled at her lower back.

The weariness she'd not noticed until now made her shoulders and eyelids droop. She nearly stumbled over the leather saddlebag she'd taken from the stranger's horse.

Everything she'd been taught since she was young told her to leave it alone. Prying into another's business was always a risky proposition, her mother had said. Keep to yourself and keep safe.

But she'd still feel better if she could pour a few shots of whiskey down his throat, to get his blood running again. A man like that probably toted along his own bottle, just in case. And it was safer, wasn't it, to know who she was dealing with before he woke up? There'd be clues among his belongings, maybe enough to know if she needed to take steps to protect herself.

It had nothing whatsoever to do with curiosity, she assured herself. It simply made good sense. She sank into the nearest chair and tugged the bag into her lap, unwinding the thin leather strips that held it shut.

He traveled light. Two shirts, good cloth, very well made. Another pair of denims. Three balled-up pairs of those worthless machine-knit socks. She stacked his clothes carefully to one side, automatically smoothing the creases, as she had done so many years ago for her father. Funny how quickly the habit returned, fussing with a man's clothes, neatening them up.

Next came a bundle of laundered drawers. Blood rushed to her face at this blatant reminder that she was trespassing on another's privacy. Guilty, she glanced at the bed, where he still slept on. Hastily she set them aside.

A book rested just beneath the clothing. She ran her fingers down the spine, over the fine dark leather that bound it. Gold letters stamped into the cover spelled out *Journey to the Center of the Earth*. The temptation to skim just a page or two was strong; it had been a long time since she'd had anything new to read, and, reluctantly, she laid it on the growing stack of his belongings.

She pulled out a razor, wrapped and tied in a scrap of toweling. A strop, a cup stuffed with a brush and a sliver of soap whose scent she could already recognize. A deck of playing cards—was he a gambler, then? He had the look of it. But nothing about Redemption would draw a gambler; there were few with much money, and those who did weren't the type to relinquish it on the turn of a card. And there, tucked beneath a pair of leather gloves, she found a fat roll of bills.

Slowly, she turned the money in her hand. More than she'd ever seen in one place in her life, she'd be willing to bet. *Who are you?* she silently asked him, and got only the faint rumble of a snore in response. No possibility she came up with made the slightest lick of sense. Before she was tempted to count it, she crammed it way down in the toe of one of his boots.

The bag was nearly empty now. She rummaged around in the bottom, her hand bumping against a hard lump beneath the leather. A pocket, like none she'd ever seen, sliced into the side of the bag, opening both inside and out. She undid the fastenings to find what it held.

A gun. Of course, a gun. An obviously well-kept one, too, without so much a smudge on its gleaming barrel, the stock oiled and smooth.

It meant nothing. A man would be a fool to wander around in the territories unprotected.

It was a million times more likely that he was simply a lost traveler accidentally caught in the storm than a stranger who'd braved the weather because he had designs on her precious virtue— even if the second theory was slightly more flattering. Still, her heart beat hard in her chest as she contemplated the weapon.

Well. She clicked open the chamber and dumped out the bullets. She gathered the rest of the ammunition, went to the kitchen shelves, and buried all the bullets in the bottom of a half-full sack of flour.

Her forgotten birthday cake still sat on the kitchen table. The candle had long ago melted away, coating the top of the cake with thin streamers of hardened wax.

What a waste. She flipped the cake over, dug out a few bites with a spoon, but it smelled of wax and burnt sugar, and she finally dumped it into the dishpan that held other scraps. Perhaps the animals would like it better.

After slipping the revolver back into its special pocket, she repacked the stranger's bag and propped it against the wall near the bed where he'd find it when he woke up. As the storm battered her house, she watched her uninvited guest, the way the blankets rose and fell with the movement of his chest, the sound of his breath sighing evenly.

She longed to crawl into her nice soft bed. If only she dared . . . but that was utterly, completely impossible, so much so that she was faintly shocked the thought had even occurred to her.

It would be warm from his body, the shallow impression in the center of the mattress tipping them together. Even through her thick wool slippers, she could feel the chill from the floor.

It shocked her even more that the idea appealed to her.

Instead, she went to spread a quilt on the floor next to the stove.

Her bed tonight would be very hard. And very, very cold.

*   *   *

When Kieran first awoke, he'd no idea where he was. There was the softness of a feather pillow beneath his cheek, the scent of clean bed linens and a coal fire. Quilts lay heavy over his chest.

Bits and pieces of the night before drifted back to him. Hazy, swirling, disconnected images of low dark clouds racing over the sky and the jolt of brutal, almost instantaneous cold. He'd given Charlie his head, hoping the horse's instincts would function better than his own through the sudden, impenetrable whiteness.

And then there'd been a faint light, there and gone and back again in the swirls of snow.

And then the woman.

He eased up slowly. His head spun, and he stilled, half sitting, half slumped, until it started to clear.

She was only a few feet away, curled up in a tight ball in a pile of blankets on the floor. A skein of hair lay over her shoulders, gleaming against the dark blue of a quilt. Harvest colors, hair halfway between brown and gold. Her eyes almost matched, he thought; he had a distinct memory of gold-brown eyes looking directly into his.

She sighed in her sleep, shifted, her small fist tightening around a wad of blanket. Even her complexion held a hint of gold, as if she'd gained color from the sun last summer and her skin had been reluctant to give it up. Near his own age, he judged. Perhaps a little less; prairie life was hard on a woman.

He'd been lucky, extraordinarily so, to stumble across this place. Though he knew he couldn't be all that far from Redemption, he'd lost all sense of direction once the storm kicked up, and had been pretty damn sure he was going to be found when the sun came out, frozen stiff as a preacher's widow. Though he'd always known death would catch up with him sooner or later, he'd expected his end would come fast and violent, at the hands of someone who desperately wanted his death. Not a slow, cold fading away at the mercy of something as impartial as the weather.

He swung his legs over the side of the bed and tried to push himself up. The instant he put a little weight on his feet, pain, hot and cruel, shot through them. He groaned and plopped back down on the bed.

The woman sprang up immediately. "Oh! You're awake." She dashed over to him, placed a hand on his forehead. "I'm not sure you should be getting up."

"I have to."

"I really don't think that's a very good idea—"

"No, *I have to.*"

"Oh." She colored immediately, red nipping at the tip of her nose, the tops of her ears. "Well." Her chin lifted. "You'll never manage by yourself," she said briskly, as if determined to be thoroughly unaffected.

And if that wasn't an opening, he didn't know what was. If he said what instantly occurred to him, wouldn't she really blush then? But he figured he owed her a favor—for saving his life and all—and so he remained silent.

She stuffed him into a buffalo coat that she said

had belonged to her father, and piled him under so many blankets that he staggered. Then she dressed herself in what seemed to him to be completely inadequate outerwear, considering what she'd swaddled him up in, draped one of his arms around her shoulders, and guided him to the outhouse.

He felt utterly idiotic, needing this small woman's help to get to the necessary and back. But by the time they made it back inside, he admitted to himself he never could have managed it alone. The floor dipped beneath his feet, and he wove across the room before sinking gratefully back onto the bed.

She stood over him, hands on her hips, while a smile flirted with the corners of her mouth. "Well, sir, I suppose I should ask this while you're still so weak. Are you planning to do me any harm?"

"What happens if I say yes?"

"I could tie you to the bed."

It came from nowhere, a sudden image of himself tied widespread upon her bed. And then, from the haze that was last night, came the vivid memory of her hands upon his skin. Small hands, made rough and strong from work, enough so that a man could be certain of feeling them on him. "Go right ahead."

"Excuse me?"

"Nothing." Unwilling to remain at such a disadvantage, flat on his back, he eased himself to a sitting position, propping his back against the pillows. "If I say I mean you no harm, would you believe me? Nasty outlaws bent on rape and pillage aren't really known for their honesty."

She studied him intently, as if trying to make up her mind. Ridiculously, he almost reached up to smooth his hair, check the growth of his beard, before he caught himself. What did it matter? Though it surprised him that she'd even allowed him into her house, considering what he must look like.

"Yes," she said finally. "I'd believe you."

A long time since anyone had believed him so easily. And her faith was so badly misplaced.

"But it would be good if you told me your name," she added.

"Since I already spent the night in your bed, you mean?"

There it was again, that immediate pink glow. Amazing how easy it was. He'd have to watch himself; it would be much too entertaining to set himself to luring out that color as often as possible.

"Kieran McDermott."

"And I'm Margaret Thayer."

"It seems I owe you my thanks, Mrs. Thayer, I—"

"It's Miss."

Damn it, this time he hadn't meant to make her blush. Hadn't meant, either, to make her look so miserably uncomfortable. But trying to allay her discomfort would probably only make it all the more obvious. "I don't think I would have lasted much longer out there."

"It was remarkably foolish of you to travel without the proper supplies."

"The weather was fine when I left Yankton. Warm, even."

"In the territories, that's good enough reason to be wary."

"You've lived here long, then?"

"Long enough."

Under any other circumstances, it was an opportunity he would have followed up on. She could tell him about Redemption and the people who lived there. Perhaps even give him a hint of the right place to begin searching. But behind her he could see the tumble of blankets where she'd slept on the floor. Her clothes were rumpled, hair straggling out of its knot. Fatigue brushed blue shadows beneath her kind eyes, and he couldn't bring himself to use her just yet.

"How are you feeling?" she asked. "Really. Don't give me any of this 'everything's fine' when it's really not. I'm told men are very fond of pretending such things."

"A little woozy," he admitted. "If you decide to tie me to the bed after all, I doubt if I could put up much of a struggle."

"Are you hungry?"

"Maybe a little."

While she fussed in the kitchen, he automatically took a good look around her home, gathering all the information he could.

It didn't take long. There was only one small room. A corner served as the kitchen, holding an old black stove and a few shelves stacked with dishes and pots. She'd nailed a crate to the wall to serve as a cupboard, draping it with faded gingham curtains that matched the ones at the windows. A jar stuffed with dried wildflowers centered the rickety table, its one short leg propped up with a piece of wood.

She'd tried to brighten it up. A braided rag splotched color in front of a dark wood rocker. A brick-red knitted throw softened a straight-backed chair. Pale-tinted sketches of flowers, obviously torn from some magazine, were tacked to walls badly in need of fresh plaster.

But the bright quilt that spread over him couldn't hide the fact that the bed frame was old and cheaply made, any more than her womanly touches could hide the truth. Valiantly battled poverty was something he recognized, because once, a long time ago, he'd known it himself.

She rattled around in the kitchen some more, scooped something into a bowl, and thwacked a big spoon on the side of a pot. She rushed across the room and thrust the bowl at him. "Here. There's no milk, I'm afraid—not until Daisy drops the calf, should be fairly soon now—and it's just oats, but—"

"I'm sure it will be fine."

Now that they didn't have the bowl to clutch, her hands fluttered at her waist. Strands of hair bobbed around her flushed face as she shifted back and forth.

He tried to remember the last time he'd so disconcerted someone. At least, not without trying. And he had no idea how to set her at ease, any more than he did why he wished to. What others thought or did was usually a subject of extreme indifference to him, as long as they had nothing to do with whatever task engaged him at the time.

But then, being indebted to someone was extremely rare for him, too. There was no way around the fact that, however accidentally it had happened, he probably owed this woman his life.

"I'm keeping you from your work," he said. "Please go ahead."

"Oh, no! In this weather, there's little enough that can be done. You're no trouble at all."

"How long do you think the storm's going to last?"

"Hard to say. Another day or two." Her voice was carefully neutral. "I suppose you're in a hurry to get going again."

"Once I can stand under my own power again." Bits of dried apples studded the cooked oats; a drift of cinnamon and sugar sparkled over the top. He hadn't realized he was so hungry. But it was awkward, to have her standing there, watching him shovel it in. "Have you eaten?"

"A little, while I was cooking. I'm not terribly hungry."

He studied her carefully, trying to gauge whether she'd told him the truth or given him all the morning's rations. Her eyes showed nothing but kindness and weariness and nerves. Not so surprising, he supposed; a stranger had dumped himself on her doorstep. Why shouldn't she be nervous? She had no way of knowing just how dangerous he could be.

He was half-tempted to tell her the truth—that he could be very dangerous indeed, but he intended none of it for her. He doubted that knowing precisely what he was capable of would improve the situation, however.

"If you've nothing pressing," he said, "why don't you sit and keep me company? Lying here staring at the ceiling all day will probably drive me mad."

She dragged over a chair and perched on the edge of it, tucking her hands between primly pressed together knees. "I don't suppose you're used to doing nothing."

"No."

Her knees jiggled. Her eyes looked everywhere but directly at him. He couldn't decide whether it amused or annoyed him.

"I'm not sure I'm going to be very good at it," he added.

"Well . . . perhaps you would like to read?"

"You have books?"

"No, not really, just a Bible and a few old magazines. I . . ." Her voice trailed off and the flush started immediately, creeping up her neck. He found himself wondering whether the color made her skin heat, too, enough for the warmth to be perceptible to a man's touch. "I"—she studied her thumbs—"I looked in your pack, while you were sleeping," she admitted, shooting him a guilty glance. "I thought maybe I could find out who you were, in case . . ."

Such honesty. He never would have known she'd poked in his things, never even cared either way. He was accustomed to people who chose their words for effect, for what those words could gain them—as he himself did. Sometimes, when he'd been from home too long, he forgot people like this existed.

"I don't mind." He didn't. He never carried

anything in his pack that might give him away. He'd made sure of it. She, however, looked at him doubtfully. "I'd like the book. Could you get it for me?" he asked, giving her permission to touch his things.

She let out a relieved breath and smiled at him. It transformed her, threw glints into her eyes, brought a dent—almost but not quite a dimple—to her cheek. He found himself scouring his brain for something he could say to make her smile at him like that again.

"Certainly." She bent and carefully removed the book, her fingers brushing almost reverently over the dark leather and the gilt-brushed edges of the paper. She thrust the book at him, a look of almost transparent longing on her face.

"Why don't you read it to me?" he suggested.

"But—"

"I'd really appreciate it, ma'am. I'm much too . . . weak to do it properly myself."

"All right." She settled herself, carefully cracked open the book, took a deep breath, and began to read. At first, her voice was halting, tentative. She stumbled over the words. But then, as the story took hold of her, she read with rapt absorption, the words flowing out of her, smooth as fresh cream.

He'd asked her to read for her sake, because he suspected that books were few in her life and that she longed for the words. But, surprisingly, there was much for him there, too, the fascination of the expressive play of emotion across her features, the novelty of having someone read to him.

He should be preparing himself for what lay

ahead. He faced a difficult task, a worthier opponent than he'd chased in many years. He should be marshaling his strength, plotting his opening moves, sifting through different possibilities.

But right now, the world he'd lived in for so long seemed very far away from this small warm house sealed off by the storm.

Tomorrow would be soon enough. He lay back against the pillows that still carried a hint of her scent, and listened.

3

Her needles clacked together, the stream of deep blue knitting growing steadily. Beneath the familiar sound, and the howling protest of the storm, she thought she could detect the even rhythm of his breathing.

He'd fallen asleep while she read, although, lost in the story, she couldn't have said exactly when. Such a book! The wildly imaginative places it described were no more alien to her than the people in it, people who took extraordinary risks simply for the adventure of it. She recognized the stupidity of it—why leave safety for so little reward?—even as the characters fascinated her.

But no more than he did.

Kieran McDermott—even his name seemed new to her, something entirely out of her existence. Perfectly polite, oddly attentive, he gave little of himself away, in many ways as much a stranger as when he'd first stumbled through her door. And yet she fancied she detected something familiar in him, that he was a person who lacked having many others close to himself, who spent much time alone, even as she did.

Though perhaps his isolation was of his own choice, and that made all the difference.

She couldn't deny it was pleasant to have him here. Oh, he made her nervous, unsettled, uncomfortable. She'd never fussed and stuttered so much in her life, and was determined to get over it. What else could she expect, though? Having a handsome man closeted with her was something she'd not only never experienced but never considered; no wonder she was unable to handle it calmly.

But simply having another human here with her turned her dreary and isolated house into something cozy and content. Only a day earlier she'd been restless, wild for the winter to end so she could get out and walk into town. Now, she didn't think she'd mind if the storm went on for days.

And if she had the sneaking suspicion that it was this particular man that made all the difference, she refused even to consider it.

Margaret Thayer was nothing if not a practical and cautious woman. Practical, cautious women did not spin fantasies about unknown drifters, no matter how fascinating they were.

Even as her fingers automatically flew through the stitches, she looked over at him and wondered if, when he was gone, she'd ever again crawl into her bed without thinking of him there.

*　　*　　*

"Show me what you got."

Kieran paused in the process of scraping the small pile of beans toward him on the bed. "You don't want to know."

"Yes, I do." Margaret frowned down at the fan of cards in her hand—the ones she'd just decided were not good enough and that had caused her to "fold." "How am I supposed to know if I made the right decision or not? How else am I going to learn?"

His expression carefully blank, he flipped over his hand.

"But you—you —" Outraged, she riffled through his cards, certain there must be something there she'd missed. "You have nothing!"

"Well, now, I wouldn't exactly say I have nothing—"

"I had two pair. Two pair!" She pounded the mattress in frustration.

"Then you should have kept bidding."

"But you kept going up . . . and up . . . and you looked so sure, and—oh!"

He'd lured her into playing with him by claiming that his feet were hurting him and he needed something to keep his mind off his pain. It had worked beautifully—she'd clearly grown more comfortable with him as the afternoon, and then evening, wore on. She'd started out sitting primly on the edge of the bed, as far away from him as she could manage. Now, shoes off, her feet tucked beneath her, she sat with her hip almost bumping the side of his out-stretched legs.

The change in her fascinated him. Watching her

expression shift from wary control to intense concentration on the game, her manner with him soften from stiff nerves to friendly ease—it was . . . fun? Strange word, not one he'd ever thought to use in relation to himself, but it was fun. He enjoyed seeing the little gold lights come up her eyes, and the lines on her forehead ease. Even more, seeing if he could make that shy little dent peep out on her cheek.

But right now she was glaring at him.

"I'm not going to play with you anymore."

"Aw, come on—"

"You cheat."

"I do not!"

"Well, maybe not cheat, exactly." She eyed the heap of dried beans in front of him, and the tiny—and rapidly shrinking—hoard neatly arranged in front of her.

Margaret simply could not figure out what had happened. Oh, she was new to the game, but he'd explained it clearly enough and scribbled what combinations beat what on a sheet of paper that he let her refer to every time she needed.

She'd played carefully, deliberating over each decision. Making prudent bets, never committing to a move until she felt certain it was the correct one.

But him! He played wildly, recklessly, with no pattern at all that she could discern. Carelessly betting huge sums on what he *might* draw next—and, more often than not, the card he needed came to him. And, if he didn't, he merely won all the more on the next hand. Now this—running up the betting on a nothing hand until she gave in.

She didn't understand it at all, how those brash tactics could possibly have been successful. Even more, she didn't understand one little bit how she could have *lost* to him.

"You promised I would have beginner's luck."

"You did." He grinned, shuffling the deck for another round in his big, quick hands. "You would have been busted a dozen hands ago if you hadn't a little extra luck."

"I thought a good sportsman was supposed to take it easy on a new player."

"No. He's supposed to win."

"Easy for you to say," she grumbled. "You've stolen all my beans."

His bark of laughter startled her enough to make her jump. As annoyed as she was, though, she couldn't help but smile, for she suspected that he didn't laugh like that very often, and she was glad—probably too much so—that she'd been the one to spark it.

"Well," she said, snatching the deck of cards from his hands and gathering up the beans, "I've had enough for one night. And you should really get some rest, give yourself plenty of time to heal."

"I'll take the floor tonight."

"No, you won't."

"I've imposed on you enough."

"It was no imposition." She would never tell him how very far from an imposition he was. "Besides, which one of us is the patient here? You're supposed to follow orders. How can you convalesce on the floor?"

"I've slept in worse places."

"You did as you were told last night."

"Now that's not fair. I was too groggy to protest last night."

"And tonight you're still recovering." Some of the beans had rolled away, hiding in the rumpled folds of the quilt, and she plucked them out. He reached over, covered her hand with his, and she froze.

Dear Lord. The sensation, almost painfully acute, burned itself into her skin. Each callus, each ridge of skin, each swell of his palm was distinct.

Remember this. She closed her eyes, trying to fix in her mind the exact temperature, the precise pressure.

"Miss Thayer," he said, "I really couldn't sleep well if I knew I'd put you out of your bed."

"All right." She inhaled, trying to force the breathlessness from her voice. She did not want him to think her a foolish spinster who was ridiculously moved by the bare touch of a man's hand.

Even if it was true.

"I could put down my father's coat," she suggested. "And perhaps a few more blankets."

"That would be fine."

"You must promise to tell me if it's chilly or too hard. If you're unable to sleep for any reason at all, I need to know so we can make other arrangements," she said severely.

"I swear."

"All right, then." He gave her hand one last squeeze and released it. Margaret's breath shuddered out of her. It was over, then. Perhaps he would shake her hand when he left. Other than that, he would never touch her again. And the deep regret of that hurt, deep inside, in a way she never would have imagined.

She efficiently bundled him into the makeshift pallet near the stove, adding three more blankets than she herself had used the night before, and once more pried out his reluctant assurance he would call her if he was cold or otherwise uncomfortable in any way.

The idea of spending another night in her rumpled clothes held little appeal. But the complexities of getting into her nightclothes, much less having him see her in that drab garment that should have been consigned to the rag basket years ago, was more than she could bear. For now, fully dressed, she crawled between the covers. Before he woke up, she'd have a quick wash and change.

And discovered that, where he'd stretched out as they played, the old muslin sheets still held the warmth of his body. She swallowed heavily and carefully laid her head in the shallow dent he'd made in her pillow.

"Ready?" he asked.

"Yes," she whispered. He snuffed the lantern and the room went black.

A day and a half. That's all the longer he'd been in her house. She lay in the thick darkness, listening to the steady thrum of another human's breath—a sound she'd become accustomed to all too quickly—and wondered how many months it would take to stop straining to hear him in the night.

*   *   *

The snow quit by four o'clock the next day. Margaret, mixing bread on the table for the next morning while Kieran read another chapter to her, glanced outside to find she could see clear to the shed and stopped stirring the stiff dough.

"It's stopped snowing," she said.

He glanced up, cocked his head as if to listen for the noise of the storm. "It doesn't sound much different."

"It's still blowing some."

"Oh?" Carefully, he marked the page and slowly closed the book. "Much?"

"A fair amount." She dropped her gaze to the bowl, poked at the sticky pale mounds of dough. "You're not familiar with the area."

"No."

"And it still gets dark pretty early." She swallowed. "It might be best if you waited until the morning to leave."

What is that, she wondered, lodged up there in the base of my throat that makes it hurt like that?

"Perhaps," he said at last, "I *should* wait until the morning. Though I've surely imposed too much already."

Her throat eased, air flowing out in a rush. "It's fine." She peeked up at him, comfortably slouched on her bed across the room, and thought: a reprieve! One more night. "It would be worse for me, worrying about whether you made it into town all right. This is much safer."

"The morning, then," he agreed.

An hour after sunset, they sat down to the table she'd set with mismatched dishes and a steaming pot of stew. Kieran had shaved before dinner, and the masculine smell of his shaving soap mingled with the domestic scents of cooking food and the coffee simmering on the stove.

"Are you sure you wouldn't rather eat in bed? After tomorrow, you won't have me to wait on you anymore."

"I'm sure. I'm a little sore, here and there, but if I lie around anymore I'm going to get so jumpy you'll wish you'd tied me down after all."

"You probably wouldn't be quite so sore if you hadn't insisted on sleeping on the floor last night," she scolded him.

"And I'm sleeping on the floor again tonight, so you can just drop the subject."

"All right." He'd sounded downright grumpy about it. Likely men didn't much like having their gentlemanly gestures questioned, she decided, and then smiled at herself for the thought. Have a man in her house for two days, and here she was, already thinking she understood them!

She lifted the lid off the pot of stew and dished him a bowlful, wishing she'd had something more to put in it than withered potatoes and hairy carrots and a little bit of salt pork. Several weeks, maybe not much more than a month if it warmed up quickly, and then—then there'd be peppery new radishes and bright tender pea shoots and young thistles for stewing. As much work as the growing season entailed, she vastly preferred it to the winter, when she had only a few chores to occupy her time and the days, and the food, were always blandly the same.

But tonight, at least, was nothing like any other night in her life. "There's nothing but coffee to drink, I'm afraid. I don't keep any spirits around the house, and you had nothing in your pack."

"It's fine. I don't drink much."

"You don't?"

"What, do I look like a man who drinks?"

"Yes, I guess you do."

He set down his spoon and tipped back his chair, folding his arms across his chest. "What's that supposed to mean?"

"I don't know." She contemplated him through the hazy, unclear light cast by the oil lamp. "Just that I can picture you in the corner of a saloon, with a glass of whiskey and a hand of cards. Maybe a pretty woman draped over your shoulder."

"Well." His chair fell back into place with a thunk. "I'm not quite sure whether to be insulted or flattered. You've seen the inside of lots of saloons, have you? That you know just how to see me there?"

"Well . . . no," she admitted.

"Known lots of drinking men, then?"

The sparkle left her eyes as quickly as if he'd snuffed a candle. "It only takes one."

"Look," he said quickly, "you don't have to answer that, I didn't mean—"

"No, it's fine." She gave her attention to arranging her napkin across her lap. "My father, he . . ." She shrugged. "It was a long time ago. It doesn't matter now."

Doesn't it? he wondered. But it was hardly any of his business. "Anyway, I'm not much of a drinker."

He wasn't. He'd learned years ago that drinking slowed his reactions, muddled his thinking. And, though he'd long accepted that the risks he took would eventually kill him, there was always some-body who depended on him. Someone who needed his help too much for him to die this time, on this particular job, and who he couldn't bear to have suffer simply because he'd gone too deeply into a bottle of whiskey. And so he left the stuff alone.

"What *do* you do, then?"

"I travel, mostly." He dipped into the stew, chewed while he considered what to tell her. "Sometimes I do people favors."

Do people favors—that covered an awful lot of ground, Margaret thought, a good part of it illegal and much of it dangerous. She remembered the thick roll of money packed away in his things. But he'd not seemed at all concerned that she found it, and she didn't want to think about him like that. He'd been nothing but charming and respectful with her.

"Why Redemption? It's hardly on anybody's grand tour."

"Maybe I just took a fancy to the name." He shrugged. "I go a lot of places for no particular reason."

A perfect opening. Kieran suppressed the small, and totally unfamiliar, twinge of guilt that said he owed her too much to use her. Asking her a few deliberate questions about her hometown in no way harmed her. And there was a stronger guilt, lurking beneath that mild one. A guilt that said he wasn't that far from Redemption, that he should have left two hours ago, and there was a young girl's life to consider.

She'd been there nearly ten months already. What difference could one more evening make? But then, who knew what hell Melissa Dalrymple was in right now? "Tell me about Redemption."

"What do you want to know?" She cupped her coffee mug in her hands, traced the rim with her thumb. "It's not so different than anyplace else, I suppose. It's grown a lot in the last several years, though we all persist in thinking of it as a small town."

The tentative oil light softened her skin, blushed the golden shade to apricot. The high lace collar of her blouse was worn, turning limply down on one side, but the ivory looked nice against her neck. He suspected that maybe his lack of urgency to get on with his job had less to do with sore feet and bad weather and still slightly numb fingers than the fact that, though she wasn't exactly pretty, he liked looking at her just the same. Liked listening to her even more, and liked making the color bloom in her cheeks most of all.

"Why is that? That it's grown so much?"

"Since the mill opened."

"There's a mill?"

"You really don't know anything about it, do you?" she asked, clearly curious.

"It's better that way." He knew a great deal about a missing girl, however, and not as much as he would have liked about a mysterious man. He'd spent little time learning the town itself, but perhaps, in telling him about Redemption, Margaret would reveal something about the people there that could point him in the right direction. "I get to discover things as I go along."

"Oh, well, it's . . . maybe six or seven years ago now. When Benjamin Lessing moved in. He founded the bank, and then he built the woolen mill." Margaret had been hopeful, at first, that the influx of new people and excitement in Redemption would spill over to her. But her mother's health had been at a low point then, keeping Margaret close to home. About the only difference the changes in Redemption had made in her life was the availability of cheap yarn. Knitting at least gave her something to do during the long monotonous winter, and sometimes she was even able to sell a few of the items she produced.

"Of course, not everyone's all that thrilled about the mill," she went on. "Lots of workers coming and going, all those girls who work the machines. He brings some of them in from orphanages, I know, and rumor has it some of them might even come from prison."

Damn! Kieran had assumed, in an isolated town in the middle of the Dakota Territories, any newcomers would stand out like a tree on the plains. Instead, there were probably dozens of unattached young women floating around.

Still, it didn't seem all that likely that Melissa would be working in a mill, a young woman raised in comfort and wealth. More likely her outlaw lover had installed her near him, keeping her handy for his pleasure. Perhaps even in his own house, passing her off as a niece or much younger cousin.

"The mill people are kept quite separate from the town," she told him. "And we are, I'm afraid, fairly careful with newcomers. You might not find it a terribly friendly town."

"So are there many other newcomers? Visiting relatives?"

"Not that I know of. Of course, I don't really go into town that often in the winter." She balanced her spoon on the edge of her bowl, giving him her full attention. "Why so interested? Are you planning on staying?"

"No reason." He shrugged, as if he cared not a bit, even as he warned himself to be more careful. He'd gotten too comfortable with her, and had asked too much, too soon. "Just curious. But no, I won't be staying. I never stay."

"Where will you be going then?"

"No idea. Wherever I feel like."

"Do you know," she said slowly, a note of wistfulness shading her words, "that, since we moved here, almost twenty years ago now, I've not been more than fifteen miles away?"

"Really? Why don't you go, then?"

"Just like that?"

"Why not, just like that?"

She gave a small laugh, spread her hands as if it were obvious. "There's the land, the house. Who'd take care of them?"

"Sell it."

"You're not serious." With the food she grew in the summer and the small rent she received for leasing the rest of the land to her neighbor, she had enough to survive. Not an ample income, perhaps not even an adequate one, but a safe one. "And then what, when the money ran out?"

"Who knows? There's a whole world of possibilities." He leaned forward, bracing his arm on the table. He couldn't have said why this mattered to him; he only knew that he did not like to think of her here, alone, in this drab house with her meager dinner and her small duties.

He was asking too much, too fast, making light of the challenges she'd face. But he had no time to nudge her thinking along more slowly, and he knew if he made changing her life seem like a bigger gamble she'd never take it. "Just go. Take a chance."

"Take a chance," she repeated, the words as strange on her tongue as the idea. Margaret Thayer did not take chances. Her mother, Eleanor, had taken a handful in her life. All of them had failed, and she'd wasted no opportunity in using them to warn her daughter.

Eleanor had taken a chance in marrying a young and charming drifter, who'd soon proved to be more fond of the bottle than of his new wife. And she'd risked following him to Dakota, only to find out that their problems had followed them, he was no better farmer than he'd been a businessman, and the harsh Dakota climate did not agree with her frail heart. And, finally, Eleanor had allowed her husband to go off to Deadwood in search of gold. In return, six months later she received the letter that said he'd found another woman, and in two more years they got word of his death.

Yes, Eleanor had taught her daughter well the price of risk.

"I couldn't take a chance like that."

"Why not? Sometimes *not* taking the chance is the biggest chance of all."

And what had being careful ever gotten her? Margaret wondered. All alone on her thirty-fifth birthday, that's what.

But alive, she reminded herself. And safe. As her mother had been, until she died three years ago, not of her dicky heart after all but a chill she picked up when she risked a trip into Redemption for church on a lovely October Sunday. The cold had quickly settled into her chest, and she'd died without a fight, her daughter by her side.

He looked at her steadily, his eyes—dark as dusk in the low light—searching, coaxing. Expecting. And she knew she could never do what he urged her to, and couldn't bear to disappoint him, to have him so clearly see her cowardice and dullness. She pushed away from the table, went to stare out the window into the night in the guise of checking the weather.

The wind moaned, as if in agony. Transparent veils of snow sifted like smoke over the ground, the moon slicing cold light over knife-edged drifts.

"It looks like it should be clear tomorrow. Good for traveling."

He came up to stand behind her. The solid bulk of him was almost familiar now, his sounds, his scents.

"It sure is one lonely night," he said at last.

She looked up at him over her shoulder. The moonlight cast him in silver and black, that beautiful face with its lines of pain and living. And suddenly she saw her life after tomorrow, endless empty days and empty nights and empty beds and not even any memories to fill them, until she'd wither up like an unwanted flower and blow away and nobody would even notice the difference.

She took a deep, shuddering breath. "It wouldn't have to be."

4

He'd known there was an attraction between them, of course, simmering strong and steady just below their polite veneer. He'd chalked it up to their situation—to being holed up together, out of time, out of the world. And to that clear memory of her hands on his skin. But he'd ignored it—something he was very good at—because he'd assumed she was simply not the kind of woman to act on it.

But her words ripped away that thin barrier of control, leaving him raw and wanting and instantly, violently aroused.

Even worse, it left him unsure of exactly what she meant. If he assumed wrong, he was going to be painfully disappointed.

In the shadowed edge where the cool moonlight from without blurred into the warm lamplight, she looked pale, her eyes dark and shimmering.

"I'm not sure I understand, I—"

"Please don't make me say it again," she whispered, her fingers twisting into a tight knot.

"All right." He brought his hands to her face and she thought: *Yes, touch me. Please don't make me talk, don't make me think, just make me feel.* "But I must know," he went on. "You . . . want me?"

Want him. *Want* did not seem a big enough word for this thing that churned inside of her. She wanted spring and fresh vegetables and a new dress. This was larger, stronger, a hundred times more powerful than mere want. "Yes."

His thumbs stroked her cheekbones. "There's something I have to tell you—"

"I don't want to know," she said quickly.

"You have to. I . . . my . . ." Damn. How was he to explain this? After Cynthia's death, it was years before he touched another woman, before it felt like anything but the worst sort of betrayal. Once he'd avenged her—even then it seemed unfaithful to what they'd shared to be with a woman he didn't feel at least a vague affection for. As his life seldom allowed affection, his relationships were infrequent. And, perhaps because of their relative scarcity, they were almost blindingly physical and extremely . . . energetic. "I am not . . . easily sated."

Emotion blazed through her eyes. Shock, excitement, fear? He couldn't tell. Wasn't sure he even wanted to know, in case it was something that would compel him to pull back, to end this before it began. Because he doubted he could do that now, any more than he could wait one more second to kiss her.

He bent his head and found her mouth with his

own. An exploration, a promise of what was to
come. Her lips were soft and pliant, asking for
nothing, allowing him everything. He moved his
hands to cup the back of her head, to urge her
closer and deepen the pressure.

Yes, she thought, *at last.* She gave fleeting consideration to the dirty dishes that cluttered her
table before forcing it from her mind. She knew if
she stopped this now for even a second she would
never find the courage to begin again. She would
come to her senses and, ah, her senses were so
well pleased by this, by the smell of his shaving
soap and the feel of his fingers rubbing her scalp
and the sound of his ragged breath sighing past
her ears.

It must have been quite some time for her, too,
Kieran decided. For she stood stiffly, unmoving,
giving him few hints as to what pleased her.
Obviously out of practice at making her desires
known. He stepped closer, letting his body brush
hers, giving her time to become accustomed to his
nearness, his heat.

He nudged her lips open with his tongue and
came inside, learning the taste of her, a hint of
coffee and the dark sweetness that was her own.
He had to lure her into the play, to tease her into
response, but even that excited him, for when
she finally rubbed her own tongue shyly against
his he nearly groaned aloud in pleasure and tri-
umph.

Gasping, he found other places to taste, her jaw,
her throat, the small depression beneath her ear.
She wore no scent and he found that surprisingly

erotic, for the faint clean hint of soap did not cover up the richer, complex scent of woman.

"Tell me what you like," he murmured against her mouth.

"I—" What she liked? She liked this, the close press of his big hard body and the feel of his thumbs stroking the cords of her neck. More? There should be more? She knew there would be, longed for it, but could not imagine giving up this in order to seek it, even if she'd had the least idea how to ask for it. "Everything. I like everything."

"Everything?" he repeated, startled. And then a grin spread slow and wide across his face.

Oh, my, she thought, what did I just let myself in for?

She'd wanted it all. Wanted not to be alone tonight. If she only had one night when other women had entire marriages, why not take all there could be? But nerves skittered in her stomach, threatened to mute the pleasure of discovery.

"What about you?" she asked hastily, determined not to be distracted by conscience, to experience this to the fullest.

His hands were moving on now, sweeping down her back and around her waist, grazing her ribs, coming up to nudge just at the lower curve of her breasts and her breath stuttered.

"You could touch me," he suggested.

Hesitantly, she rested her palms on his shoulders, pressed the swell of warm muscle under thin fabric. Encouraged by his sigh, she explored further, testing his arms, his back, the smooth corded column of his throat.

Ah, the heady luxury of it, to delight her poor battered hands with such textures. Fingers accustomed to rusty tools and dirt and scratchy wool yarn instead got the thick fall—so soft!—of his hair. Even after his recent shave, the stubble along his jaw pricked her fingertips.

Too much to feel, to know. How could she concentrate on any one sensation, when there were so many at once? His urgent mouth, on her lips and brow and neck. The brush of his leg against her thigh. And, soon, the shocking bump of his knuckles nudging her upper chest as he worked the small buttons of her blouse. Involuntarily, she jerked away.

His hands stilled. "Something wrong?"

"No." *You wanted this,* she reminded herself. *Asked for it. Did you think that your clothes would stay on the entire time?* She managed a wobbly smile. "Nothing's wrong."

"You're sure?"

She wasn't sure of anything, except that the idea of going on as she had before, of letting what was probably the only chance for passion she would ever have walk out the door, was more frightening to her than anything that might come. "Yes. I'm sure."

He quickly undid the rest of the buttons, brushing aside the fabric. He looked down at the upper curves of her breasts revealed above her shift, while she, rigid, stared over his shoulder, afraid he would find her lacking as he surely must. His quick intake of breath reassured her; somehow, miraculously, she pleased him.

The air was cool, dappling her exposed skin with gooseflesh.

"You're cold," he murmured. "I'll warm you."

And he did, bending down, his mouth and breath and tongue warm on her, the contrast between heat and cold acute.

He cupped one swell in his palm, kneading softly, his forefinger sliding inside the fabric to find her nipple and rub it with his knuckle.

So sensitive. She got dressed every day, dragging cloth across her breasts without ever expecting that they could feel like this, a strong, near-painful excitation with each touch.

He slipped an arm beneath her thighs and lifted her.

"You shouldn't," she protested. "You've been ill, and I don't want to hurt you."

"You weigh nothing." Her concern touched him, and her shy delight in this small service. He strode to the bed, glad that he could perform this easy chivalry for her, a little disturbed that no one had bothered before. He'd worried that he could not read her well enough to please her; her reactions to his touch had seemed carefully contained. And yet, her heart had beat heavily beneath his kiss, and now she laid her head upon his chest with a sigh as he carried her.

Perhaps it was simply that they still knew each other so little; surely she was accustomed to building to this moment over weeks and months, to knowing her lovers' thoughts before she knew their bodies.

But in some ways he knew her so well. He knew

the little half dimple that hid in her cheek, and how to make it show itself. That her skin blushed pink at the slightest provocation, and that she thirsted for new stories. He knew her kindness and concern for a lost stranger, and how her hands flashed quick and steady, over her knitting or his frozen flesh.

He knew that she took great care with every thought and word and action. And, because of that, he was terribly certain that, if she'd known him any more than she did, she would not be in his arms preparing to become his lover.

If he were a better man, he would have stopped and told her all those things. But he was not a good man—maybe he never had been—and his blood ran thick and hot for need of her.

He lowered her to the bed.

His hands moved faster now, stripping her blouse off her shoulders, making quick work of the knots that held her corset snug.

The mattress rustled beneath their weight—the bed she'd shared with her mother, and then slept in so many nights alone. Musn't think of that, she told herself again. Couldn't think at all, of the scandalous things he did to her, for when she did think a whisper of trepidation and something that was too close to shame chilled her.

She wanted the heat instead, the glow that started inside when she looked at him and outside where he touched her, that grew and swelled together until she felt she might burst from her own skin.

Don't think. Feel.

And remember.

Naked to the waist, she fought the urge to cross her arms over the torso that she knew full well was too thin, her breasts too slight.

But she could not hide from him this night. He reared back to look at her, reaching out to place one finger on the very tip of her breast. "Ah, Maggie," he said, his voice hoarse, his eyes . . . she would almost think he was fascinated.

"Maggie?"

"No one calls you that?" He circled her breast, drew a line down the center of her stomach. "Miss Thayer seemed a little formal, considering."

She sucked in a breath as his finger bumped up against the barrier of her waistband, then found its way beneath.

"No, no one calls me that." Not that casual, friendly name that her mother had forbidden her decades ago. "I think I like it."

His gaze riveted on her nakedness. "Me, too."

She sought any remaining shred of bravery, wondering if she'd used it up in that first, frightening move. But, surprisingly, there was more. Plucking at a small bone button over his breastbone, she said: "Your turn."

He grinned. "You don't want to help?"

"I've already undressed you."

"I don't know that that's entirely fair. I was almost unconscious for all the good parts that time." He worked fast, stripping off his shirt and tossing it aside. He paused, hands resting at his waist. "Everything?"

"Everything." It was more of a croak than a

word. He didn't seem to care, just went ahead and undid the fastenings of his denims.

It amazed her, that she had only to ask and he would do it. The power thrummed through her, twined with the desire until she could barely distinguish the two.

When she took his clothes from him that first day, she'd tried hard to politely keep her eyes away. Now, to be free, even *encouraged* to look her fill, to take in all these new and masculine sights . . . she could hardly believe it.

His buttons undone, pants gaping in a V low across his belly, he hopped on one foot, lifting the other to tug at his boots.

"This is always the awkward part," he said. "Undressing. Never seems to be a smooth way to do it."

It gave her a pang, to hear him admit out loud that there'd been other times and other women for him. How foolish of her; she should be grateful that at least one of them knew what they were doing.

His boots hit the floor with a clunk. He tore off those ridiculously insufficient socks.

She caught her breath as his hands returned to his waist. Taking off his pants—it seemed such a finality to her, that once his pants were gone there was no turning back.

He shucked them quickly, pants and drawers together, giving a flash of shadows and muscle and round pale buttocks.

She knew vaguely what to expect from this evening. She lived on a farm, after all. And, many years ago, when Martha Ann had been a giddy and ecstatic new bride, she'd confided perhaps more than was proper to Margaret about her new husband and the joys of wedded bliss.

Still, nothing in that hazy knowledge prepared her for what the sight of him, naked, could do to her.

He grabbed one of her feet, propped it against his naked thigh—right *there*, so close to his . . . Nimbly, he untied the laces of her boot, slid it off her foot, pausing to massage the deep hollow between her heel and her ankle before he moved on to the other one.

"There." He gently laid her legs back on the bed. "Are you still cold?"

"Cold?" she repeated numbly. How could she know? It was all so much, sights, sounds, smell, the feel of his hands on her, that her senses seemed confused, unable to distinguish anything but him.

But the covers, at least, held some possibility of modesty. She couldn't imagine being without her skirts and drawers, laid open to him on top of the quilt. "I . . . guess so."

"Let's get you in, then." He drew back the blankets for her to crawl beneath. The sheets were cold and smooth against her bare back, and she watched with some regret as he prepared to clamber in next to her. Too bad there wasn't some way to tactfully suggest he stay above the covers. She wanted the shelter, a place to hide, but she really would have liked to keep looking at him.

But then he slid beneath the bedclothes, pulling her close so her nose almost met the hollow of his throat, and the chill warmed up quickly. He put out such heat, so much so that she was distantly amazed that the storm had been able to freeze him; he seemed to hold the warmth of the sun beneath his skin.

Everything was new. She felt the angle of his arm across her bare back, and the little prickles of hair against her breasts where she pressed against his chest. How was she to feel, to remember it all?

And then he kissed her again, soft and gentle. A kiss that made no demands but lured her in, had her shifting closer, her tongue seeking deeper, her hips tilting, searching.

His fingers brushed at the back of her waist. "Lift up," he said, and, unthinkingly, she did, scarcely even noticing as he swept her skirts away. Just knowing that there was now, thankfully, *less* between them, only the thin fabric of her drawers, and he could press, hard and hot, against the juncture of her thighs.

Groaning, Kieran reached down, cupping her rear to drag her tight, thinking, Who would have known it?

Who would have thought that this bit of a woman with her rough hands and easy blushes would make him so crazed? But she did; his heartbeat thundered in his ears, and his always well-controlled hands struggled with the fastening tapes of her drawers, nearly knotting them before they, at last, came free.

Her body was slight, made small and wiry from too much work and too little food. He found that surprisingly erotic, this evidence that life had not been easy for her and she had survived it, even as he felt the familiar urge to make it right. To take her somewhere safe where she could rest and he could feed her cream cakes and oranges and beefsteaks.

But he had another that needed rescuing first.

Now, he only wanted to make Maggie cry out, to sob his name with the pleasure he gave her.

Assuming he could make it last long enough this first time, and, at the moment, that seemed a very dicey proposition indeed. It had been a while, and he wanted her very much.

If only there were more light. The oil lantern, half a room away, was too dim. He longed to see her, to find out if the rest of her skin blushed as easily as her cheeks. For now, he'd have to make do with touch and taste, and he slid down to take her breast in his mouth.

The contrasts fascinated him, the feel against his tongue of the smooth softness of her skin and the firmer, bumpy texture of her nipple. She arched, allowing him to take her more deeply inside. Her hands came up to burrow through his hair and hold him firm.

He dared not take off her drawers, not yet, in case it tempted him to do too much, too soon. Instead, he slid his hand inside the opening, searching, finding her sleek and hot, and he knew it was a very good thing she wasn't completely bare to him yet.

Margaret whimpered, twisting into his touch. She knew she should be shocked. But his mouth felt so *good*, the gentle tugs like that, and she'd needed something *there* and now his hand was, and she let her legs fall wide so he could stroke her more fully.

"Please, Maggie," he said, his voice urgently strained.

Please what? She would have done anything he asked—anything!—if only she knew what it was. His thumb was lightly rubbing, his fingers deep inside . . . oh! She'd known he would come inside her, of course, but not his *fingers*, and they kept sliding in and out, and she was terribly afraid that, if it got any better, she just might burst into tears.

"Dear God, Maggie, now!" he pleaded desperately. He had to get inside her, he just had to; the command thrummed in his head, throbbed low in his belly. But he had to see to her first, before it was too late. He couldn't return her generosity and care with his selfishness, but, Lord, how long did he have to wait? He pressed the heel of his hand firmly against her, slid one more finger inside. She went still in his arms, and then, oh, thank you God, she began to shake, sweet little cries coming from the back of her throat.

He waited—how did he ever manage to wait?— until she quieted and sank down into the bed, her limbs soft, her smile pleased and surprised and blissful.

"Why don't you slip off your drawers now," he suggested. If he were to try it himself, Kieran thought, it was unlikely they'd survive in repairable shape.

"Hmm?" Maggie asked, sleepily blinking at him. He wanted her to move? She wasn't at all certain she still had bones. What was that? What Martha Ann had called a "woman's pleasure," she supposed, but, dear Lord, Maggie had never expected it to be anything like that. There'd been those long seconds when it seemed nothing else existed in the world but those waves of strong sensation. She arched, reveling in the deep relaxation.

"For God's sake, Maggie, would you get those off? If I do it, I swear I won't be responsible for their condition."

"What?" She focused on him slowly, wondering what he was mumbling so insistently about.

"Take off your drawers!"

"Oh." Poor man. She realized that, while she was feeling all good and warm and loose, he must still be in that state before, where the yearning had almost made her scream at him to finish it because she couldn't take it any longer. "Sorry."

She reached down to tug off her underclothes. Kieran was leaning over the side of the bed, rummaging around in one of the side pockets of his bag, where she hadn't bothered to search after she found the gun and the money. "What are you doing?"

He rolled back to look at her, one hand fisted. "It's a . . . device."

"A device?"

A dusky flush crept up his neck.

"To keep you from . . ." Until this moment, she would have said it was impossible for him to look so uncomfortable. "It catches my seed," he said quickly. "So there'll be no child."

"Oh." She fixed her gaze on his chin.

"I never knew my father. I won't let that happen to a child of mine." Unless . . . could that have been what she wanted all along? To bind him to her? Or, even, to capture another man with his child? It explained why she would bed him so quickly, when he never would have expected it from her.

But, no, he could not envision it. He would not believe that she was capable of such deceit. The shame that he would even consider such a thing of Maggie surprised him as much as it disturbed him.

"Does it bother you?" he asked.

"No. I just . . . I hadn't thought of it." She'd been trying very hard *not* to think. And how utterly foolish of her that had been, what a huge disaster she might have created by letting herself simply get caught up in the moment. She glanced up, giving him a tremulous smile. "I'm glad you did."

He reached down and swiftly covered himself. He levered over her, nudged her legs apart with his knee, and pressed himself against her.

Finally. She was wet and hot and oh, so tight as he pushed himself inside her. So tight, and so unbelievably good, and then it was difficult to go any further.

"Sweetheart, you have to open for me a little more."

She spread her thighs wider, and he slid in a fraction more. Maggie's eyes went wide, and she gave a little whimper that sounded more like pain than pleasure, and he realized what it must be.

Well, damn, he thought. I sure didn't see that one coming.

But it was too late. His hips flexed of their own accord, he went deep inside Maggie, and surrendered.

5

❦

When he'd finally, reluctantly, slid from her body and rolled to one side, when he could finally gather enough breath to speak, he asked, "Why didn't you tell me?"

Facing the ceiling, she flicked a wary glance at him out of the corner of her eye. "Why didn't I tell you what?"

"That it was your first time."

Her arms were sealed along her sides, the covers tucked high over her breasts. "What makes you think it was my first time?"

"Maggie—"

"Did I do it wrong?"

"No." She had the sheet stretched so tightly across her chest that it dented the soft flesh. He traced the edge with his forefinger. "No, you didn't do it wrong at all."

"How could you tell, then?"

"There's a barrier, inside you, that I had to . . ."

"Oh," she said quickly, still contemplating the darkened ceiling.

"Why didn't you tell me?"

"I was afraid it would matter to you." She gave a deep sigh. As if determined to see it through, she flopped onto her side, propped her head on her arm, and studied him as carefully as she'd avoided his gaze a moment ago. "*Would* it have mattered to you?"

"I . . . I think so, yes."

"Then that's why I didn't tell you."

What was he supposed to say to that? That he wished he'd taken more care of her, made certain that she knew what she was getting into? Been more tender, more special, more . . . something? His relationships with women had always been simple. This should have been, too.

"Does it . . . matter to you now?" she asked slowly.

Did it? It shouldn't. He'd not pushed her into this in any way, hadn't seduced her into giving up her virtue to a stranger, and surely he wasn't foolish enough to be bound by any stupid preconceptions and societal codes about virginal women.

And yet—yet he worried about her. Wondered how she'd feel tomorrow, after he was gone. Wanted to know if she felt disappointed or pleased, if she regretted anything.

"I think maybe it does."

"It's not really your concern," she said stiffly.

And, as much as anything else, he was curious. "Maggie . . . why?"

She shrugged. "You were my last chance."

Well, hell. He guessed he deserved that one, for being idiot enough to ask.

What did you want her to say? he berated himself. That she'd never met a man who tempted her as much as you did? That she was overcome by passion for your manly form?

Yep, that pretty much covered it.

"I didn't mean that the way it sounded," she amended quickly.

"It's okay."

"No, it's not." Gently, she laid her palm against his cheek and, at even that simple touch, his pulse began to hammer again. "If it had been anyone but you, I don't think I would have cared that it might have been my last chance."

"Did I . . . hurt you?"

"Not really."

"Did you bleed much?"

"I . . . don't know." She dropped her lashes, veiling her eyes. "I don't think so."

"Let me check." He made a move to tug the quilts away, and she clutched them frantically.

"Kieran McDermott, don't you dare!"

"I'm going to get around to looking at you there sooner or later tonight. Might as well let me check now."

Her gasp mingled shock and embarrassment. She tried to cover it up with an indignant sniff. "I would have thought by now, after all these years, a useless bit of flesh like that would have dried up and disappeared."

"How old are you, anyway?"

She scowled at him. He wondered if it even

occurred to Maggie that she could choose not to answer him—or could tell him something other than the truth.

"Thirty-five," she admitted.

"Oh, my God! Ancient. And I'm past forty. Amazing either of us can totter across the floor."

The corner of her lips quirked, as if a smile wanted to peek out and she wouldn't quite allow it.

"Sometimes I feel old."

"Do you? Let me see." In a move so quick she never once anticipated it, he closed his hand over her breast, squeezing lightly. "I don't know. Doesn't feel all that old to me."

"Kieran!"

"Do you know, that's the first time you've called me by just my first name? Do it again." He rolled swiftly atop her, pressed the full length of his naked body against hers. "Nope, I don't know about you, but right now I don't feel old at all."

"Kieran," she whispered, softer, as passion crept into her eyes.

"I knew you could do it again." His sex brushed against the curls that covered hers, still slick from their last loving. "Come to think of it . . . can you do it again?"

Trying to accustom herself to the sharp, sudden newness of passion, Margaret had lost the train of the conversation. "Hmm?"

He pulled her arms up, linked them over her head. "Tell me the truth, now. Are you sore anywhere?"

Why was he still *talking*? she wondered. "I don't think so."

"Stop me if it hurts." He bent and took her breast in his mouth.

"Kieran!"

"You can't say I didn't warn you."

Kieran awoke the next morning to the smell of fresh bread baking. He stretched slowly, his body content and relaxed, if not precisely sated. That, he suspected, would take far more time than he had.

Maggie stood over the stove, spooning coffee into a big enameled pot. She'd obviously been up for a while, for the mess they'd left from supper the previous night had all been cleared away; surprisingly her rustling about hadn't woken him. Her hair was now relentlessly scraped back into a knot, and her blouse buttoned tight around her neck and wrists, making her look like that prudish maiden lady that she, very decidedly, was no longer.

"Good morning," he said, voice gruff with sleep.

She shot him a glance before quickly returning her attention to the stove. "Morning." She stooped to poke at the fire, and the fabric of her blouse curved nicely against the slope of her waist and the small mounds of her breasts.

He could so easily get used to this, a woman to sink into every night and wake to every morning. For a moment, he debated the wisdom of calling her back to bed, to bring in the morning properly. The idea of loving her in the bright, strong light appealed to him, discovering the exact shade of rose her nipples took on when he licked them.

Aroused, he shifted in the bed, reluctantly deciding against tempting her into another round.

For—other than that he'd enjoy it immensely— no other good could come of it. When all was said and done, though she'd tried to pass it off casually, he'd been Maggie's first lover. It would be only natural for Maggie, like any other woman, to pretty it up a little and make it more than it was. Maybe even to start thinking about the prospect of a less perfunctory relationship.

He fully intended his stay in Redemption to be as brief as he could possibly make it. It would simply be cruel of him to give her the wrong impression.

In the kitchen, Margaret flipped up the curtain that covered the cupboard and rummaged deep. There was no butter, and she felt the need to serve something to him more than plain bread or cooked oats. It deeply mortified her to have so little to offer.

One more jar of last summer's chokecherry jelly hid behind a canister of currants. She grabbed her find, turned, and nearly dropped her jelly.

Kieran clambered out of bed, totally naked and apparently quite unconcerned about it. He gave a big, allover stretch that somehow seemed typically male, then shivered. The light was clear and unyielding and completely revealing, and need hit her with the all-encompassing force of this week's storm.

Last night . . . last night she'd become a woman she hadn't recognized. She'd lost count of the number of times they'd come together; it all blurred and blended in a seamless quilt of purely physical release.

Along the way, Kieran had surely explored every inch, every secret corner of her body, places she'd only been vaguely aware of up to then. And she— she'd cried out and moaned and begged. She had a horribly clear memory of, once, even dissolving into noisy sobs, when all those feelings had swamped her with so much sensation she'd simply been unable to hold it back. Dear Lord, what he must think of her!

Even now, with parts of her undeniably sore, she wanted him. She tingled and dampened. Deep inside, she felt a tremor, as if someone had plucked a harp string that resonated in her womb as it readied itself to receive his seed.

She'd wanted only to see what it was like. To have a memory of the most attractive man she'd ever met to warm her through the many cold, lonely nights ahead of her.

Instead, it seemed, she'd made a wanton of herself.

She *craved*.

And he was going away, soon, and she would never see him again.

"Brr." Kieran dragged a quilt from the bed and wrapped it around himself. "It's cold."

"I'm sorry," she said automatically. "I forgot to get up last night, and the fire went out."

"You were rather occupied." He shuffled over to her, a corner of the quilt flapping between his knees. "It was worth it."

He debated how to handle this. Too light,

consigning what had happened between them to insignificance, or too heavy, making more of it than it could or would ever be; both seemed dangerous. One might hurt her now; the other would certainly hurt her later.

He thought he might kiss her. Just a friendly little peck, something that conveyed friendship, appreciation, and good-bye in equal measures. But she wouldn't look at him, just kept her chin tucked down around her chest while she carefully set a jar on the table.

"Will you be leaving soon?"

Was she so anxious to get rid of him? She'd had her little experiment and now she wanted him out of her house? And why the hell did he care, either way?

"Soon as I can get out of here," he said, too harshly. She flinched visibly, her shoulders hunched.

Oh, now, that had been unfair of him, hadn't it? He'd just assigned her unflattering motives when he really understood nothing of them. He didn't know her nearly well enough to read things into her comments and expressions. And he certainly had no reason to think anything but the best about her.

"I didn't mean to be sharp," he said. "I've just already lost more time to the storm than I really could afford to spare."

The excuse sounded weak, even to him. But he'd always gone into an affair knowing how it would end. He'd no practice in smoothing the bumps of taking his leave of a woman who'd never said good-bye to a lover before.

Her back to him, she wrapped a cloth around her hand and bent to slip a high brown loaf of bread from the oven. "Of course. I didn't realize you were on such a tight schedule. I somehow had the impression you simply went when and where the spirit moved you."

"I do, usually. But sometimes I have promises that must be kept."

Promises, he'd said. That could be anything, to anyone, she thought. Even to a woman. She'd not asked, and now it was too late, and she was terribly afraid she didn't even have the right. He'd made her not one pledge, and she hadn't asked for one. And if all those things he'd done to her body had somehow felt like promises, well, that was her problem, wasn't it? Not his. "You're welcome to stay for breakfast." She tapped the top crust of a loaf, testing for doneness. "I'd planned for you to be here, and I've made plenty."

"I'd like that." He'd like it even more if she'd look at him, at least once. But he hadn't earned the right to ask anything of her.

Perhaps she was simply self-conscious. Morning-afters were always awkward, sometimes brutally so. Particularly when the night before had been entered into and enjoyed without clear expectations on either side.

And when that enjoyment had been maybe a little more powerful than either one had expected.

When, not to put too fine a point on it, they'd downright wallowed in it.

He briefly touched her elbow. "Are you all right?"

"Of course. Why wouldn't I be? I'm just fine," she said crisply, shaking out the warm loaves onto a clean cloth.

"I'll just get dressed before we eat."

She refused to watch him while he packed up. This was difficult enough without forcing herself to watch him prepare to leave her.

She simply had not thought this far ahead. Nowhere in all the curiosity and loneliness and just plain boredom that had prodded her into last night's frighteningly risky behavior had the reality of the next morning occurred to her.

For in the morning, there was no hiding in shadows or moonlight. There was no losing oneself in sensation and blinding, mindless release.

No more pretending that she was a brave and daring woman. Or that she hadn't thrown aside every moral, every rule she'd been taught for the sake of a handsome face and a strong warm body.

Reality mocked her as readily as the pleasant sunlight that would make his day's travel easy.

The truth of it was that Margaret Thayer was a drab thirty-five-year-old woman who'd thrown herself at the first attractive stranger who'd wandered by, and now she must send him on his way pretending that it didn't matter.

Kieran sat down to slices of fresh yeast bread slicked with jelly and a dish of stewed apricots fragrant with cloves. It bothered him to know that once again she'd gone out of her way to make him a meal that she couldn't really afford and would never have prepared for herself. What had he done for her but take her food and bed and virginity?

She seemed more uncomfortable with him than at any time since that first day. She picked at her breakfast, breaking off bits of bare bread that would hardly have fed a mouse. Her fingers drummed the edge of her coffee cup but she never bothered to drink.

At first, he attributed her pale color and shadowed eyes to simple exhaustion. He hadn't allowed her much sleep last night. Strain drew harsh lines around her mouth and eyes—eyes that stubbornly refused to meet his.

This was more than mere embarrassment.

It looked like shame.

It shouldn't have hurt him. It was no concern of his what emotion she chose to have over a night she'd not only accepted but instigated.

But it did hurt. More than he ever could have guessed.

They'd come together in pleasure last night. What was so wrong about that? Held back the howls of a lonely, storm-whipped night. But he knew that, when he thought of this, he wouldn't be able to simply enjoy the memory of their passion; he'd also remember that, afterward, she'd been ashamed. And it would always bother him, though he had no clue what he could have done to change it.

Except to have not bedded her at all. And, from the moment he'd known that she would welcome him, that she wanted him, he wouldn't have been able to deny her. Still wouldn't, had she given him the slightest encouragement.

"Are you finished yet?" she asked.

Darn it, that had come out much more

unfriendly than she'd intended. It sounded as if she meant to hurry him on his way. But, though there were a thousand things she wanted to say to him, there were few that she dared, because they made her sound needy and alone.

And so she could not ask *if*. If he ever wandered this way again, whether he would stop to see her. If he would remember her fondly, more so than all the many others he'd undoubtedly met on his travels.

Nor could she tell him that he'd been . . . magnificent last night, that if that was all the pleasure she'd have in her entire life it was undoubtedly more than many women would ever know.

But if she said any of those things, asked any of those things, she was terribly afraid he would pity her. And even more terrified that, if he pitied her, she might begin to pity herself.

"I guess so." His chair scraped back and he got to his feet. She stood, too, her hands laced together so she wouldn't be tempted to touch him. He slung his coat over his shoulders and grabbed his saddle-bag. "There's just one more thing—"

"Oh! There is, I forgot." She rummaged in the kitchen. Flour flew as she poured a handful of white-dusted bullets in his hand. "I took these, when you first came . . . well, I thought it was better to play it safe."

He shook them in his hand and flour drifted through his fingers. "You stole my ammunition?"

"Well . . . yes," she admitted. "It seemed prudent to make certain you were unable to shoot me."

He couldn't help it, he laughed. It was so like her—to take in a stranger, to relieve him of his bullets, and believe herself safe. Even though he was much larger and stronger and could hurt her in a hundred other ways, ways she'd probably never even heard of. And only the bullets; not the entire gun, of course. No, Maggie would be so scrupulous as to take only the minimum she thought absolutely necessary for her protection.

The laughter eased the tension between them. Margaret was grateful; she didn't want this painfully awkward morning to be the last memory she had of him.

For a second she debated what she was about to do before surrendering to the inevitable. "I have something else for you, before you go." She'd nearly decided not to give it to him. She didn't want him to read the gesture as . . . well, *gratitude* from an affection-starved spinster. And she was afraid he'd think it silly, so obviously inexpensive and homemade.

But if he caught a chill this morning, she'd never forgive herself.

A battered trunk in the corner of the sitting area served as storage. She opened the creaky lid, set aside two knitted throws, and pushed aside a bag of fabric scraps. Ah, there they were.

"Here." She went to him and looped the length of nubby wool around his neck. The scarf's color was as she'd remembered, a medium blue of unusual vibrancy, only a shade darker than his eyes. "Mittens, too," she said, handing them to him.

"I . . ." Fumbling for words, he cleared his throat. Very little surprised him anymore. Even less caught him off guard. But she'd given him a present. A present. Fancy that. "I don't know what to say."

"'Thank you' usually works."

"Thank you." Bending swiftly, he stamped a kiss right on the corner of her mouth.

"Oh, well . . ." She fixed him with a severe look. "You must promise to wear them. I will not hear of you bumbling frozen to some other poor woman's door."

"Yes, ma'am," he said, and grinned.

Reaching up, she adjusted the scarf around his neck.

"Are you going to be staying in Redemption long, do you think?" *And will you come to see me if you do?* Though the words weren't said aloud, they both heard it as clearly as if it had been spoken.

"I don't know." When was the last time he'd been so tempted to make promises he couldn't keep? "I doubt it."

"Oh." Her hand tapped the air, as if she'd intended to touch his chest and then thought better of it, before dropping her arm to her side.

So many quicksilver changes of mood between them; he couldn't keep up with them. Sometimes the closeness, the easy humor that they'd gained over the last two days. Then glimmers of the passion that they now fought so hard to keep submerged. The excruciating awkwardness he thought they'd left behind. And, most disturbing of all, something that felt very much like anger. Disturbing because there shouldn't be enough between them to spawn such a powerful emotion as anger.

His fist closed around the money he'd removed
from his bag while she'd fussed in the kitchen.
Pride was a fragile and unpredictable emotion, and
he hadn't had enough experience with hers to be
able to tell how she'd react to this. But then he
looked at the edge of her collar, where the badly
frayed fabric trailed cobwebs of thread along her
neck, and at her shoes, where the leather had worn
pale over her toes, and he thrust the bills at her.

"Here."

Color suffused her immediately, not the fine
pink he'd grown so fond of but a harsh red that
obviously marked her ire.

"Don't you dare offer me money."

"It's not like that," he rushed to explain. "It's for
the food, and the shelter, and the nursing. You've
earned this." And please let me give it to you, he
thought. It's the only thing I can.

"I don't need it." Even as she said it, she realized
they both knew better. "I don't *want* it."

"Maggie, please, I—"

"No." She spun away from him and wrapped her
arms around her middle. Though she didn't have
much, she'd given to him freely, first out of concern
and, later, out of . . . what? Friendship, affection,
desire? She had no word for it, but that he would
taint it with money made her stomach go hollow,
made her throat, already tight with his leaving,
ache even more.

"Maggie," he tried again.

"Just go, now. *Please.*"

Her eyes stung. She wouldn't look at him,
wouldn't let him see how much he'd hurt her. For

she knew that he would ride away and forget, and she would stay right there and remember.

"All right," he said at last. She heard the scuffle of his boots across the floor, the creak of the door, the muffled sound as he closed it behind him. Later, the rapid thud of hoofbeats.

I won't look, she told herself. I won't watch as he rides away.

Only a couple of days, out of an entire lifetime. Somehow they seemed to take up more room than that, in her heart and mind. It seemed impossible to her that she would never know what would happen to him, whether he lived or died, married or had children. Nothing.

Wearily she turned to clean up the remains of their breakfast.

There, carefully laid on one clear corner of the table, he'd left her something after all—his book.

And too many memories.

6

⚜

For the next two weeks, Margaret waited for the ground to thaw. Then there'd be dirt and work and the promise of growing things. Her muscles would tire and her hands darken with good earth. With any luck, perhaps her mind would even still.

But this interlude between the winter's struggle and the frantic burst of spring activity held nothing but the monotony of waiting.

She tried not to read the book he'd left her. It reminded her too strongly of him, of people who challenged death, risked life, and knew nothing of hard-won and vigilantly guarded security.

Three days after he left, after she'd scrubbed every bare surface in the place and knitted so furiously she tore open a scabbed-over cut and bled on the yarn, she gave in. She allowed herself only a chapter a day, but when she finished the last page, she simply turned back to the beginning and started all over again.

She slept badly. A dozen times a night, she awoke shaken and sweaty and almost brutally aroused. Though she reminded herself a hundred times that she'd functioned quite adequately without sex for decades, it made no difference.

It seemed as if, up until that night with Kieran, her body had been dormant, comfortably ignorant if not entirely content. Now that she'd awakened it, it quite emphatically wanted more.

Thinking perhaps that the bedclothes carried some of his scent, or the two of them together, and that was what invaded her dreams, she stripped the bed for washing. She stood over the boiling kettle, heavily salted with strong soap, with the wad of tumbled sheets in her arms. She closed her eyes, buried her nose in the old fabric, and inhaled deeply before she realized what she was doing and shoved the entire bundle in the scalding water.

Since it was still too cold to hang laundry outside to dry, she sentenced herself to an uncomfortable afternoon with the room swathed in white linens, a too obvious reminder, making it hard for her to move or work or even think.

The clean sheets didn't help. If anything, her dreams that night were all the more powerfully disturbing.

Today, she simply couldn't stay in her house anymore. She bundled up and braved a chilly spring wind to stake out her garden.

Chunks of hard earth showed between a few remaining smears of dirty gray snow. Another week of warm weather, at least, before she could start seeding, which made today's task little more than busywork. But the sky, a cool pale blue, was immense enough to dwarf even the golden yellow disk of the sun, and she could hear the faint trickle of water beneath the melting snow. Margaret imagined the bright green rows of her plants pushing up through the damp earth and felt more at peace than she had in weeks.

Since before he came.

And left.

She measured the northwestern corner of the bean patch and forced a splinter of wood through the icy dirt. The tight webs of string and stakes marked off precise squares—potatoes there, peas to the right, a bigger patch of squash, a pattern she'd planned with much thought and hadn't varied for years. It was as much as she could manage comfortably herself, and yielded crops that ripened at predictable intervals all summer long.

Impulsively, she yanked out the stick she'd just planted, took two giant steps back, and jammed the wood back into the ground.

Perhaps this year she'd try a slightly larger garden. It'd be a bit more work, but with good weather she might have enough crop left over to sell. With a little luck, and the money she'd get for all the handwork she'd done during the winter, she'd have enough to order a few books before the next winter set in.

Maybe, if she were very frugal and very fortunate, she'd even eke out enough to take a small trip. The river that powered Lessing's Mill ran into the Missouri, providing transportation for raw materials and finished products and for passengers as well. She'd always thought it might be interesting to ride one of the steamships.

She was mentally counting how much she might get for the calf that Daisy would be dropping any day when a faint "yoo-hoo" drifted over the plains to her. She shaded her eyes, just able to make out the old spring wagon that jounced over the cleared space between fields that served as a road.

She waved, and Martha Ann Perkins jumped to her feet, flapping at the air as if she would kick up a breeze of her own. The wagon hit a rut, nearly sending her tumbling over the side, but her husband Lucius caught her—he always did—and settled her back into her seat before any damage was done. Margaret counted the heads bobbing in the back of the wagon, trying to figure out how many of their children the Perkinses had brought with them this time. Four, Margaret thought. Maybe five.

Martha Ann waited—just barely—until the wagon clattered to a stop before launching herself from her seat. Though time had added a few lines to her face, and eight children more than a few pounds to her always-lush figure, it was still easy to see why she'd once been considered the prettiest girl in Redemption.

"Margaret! We missed your birthday again. I'm so sorry, I don't know how you'll ever forgive me," she said, enfolding Margaret into a muffling hug. "I wanted to come."

"There's nothing to forgive," Margaret said as

soon as she could speak again, and meant it. Nearly all the girls she'd known had drifted away years ago. When they got caught up in the thrill of courting and marriage and new motherhood, she'd been bound by the demands of her parents. Now, though they'd remained friendly, she couldn't call them friends.

Except for Martha Ann. And if the demands of her own family and farm, three miles out on the other side of Redemption, meant they managed to see each other only rarely, it only made Margaret cherish their friendship all the more. "If the weather's good enough to travel, you're needed in the fields. I know that."

"Yes, but this birthday was a big one." Her arm still around Margaret's shoulder, she leaned back, appraising. "And just look at you!"

"What?" Warily, Margaret glanced down. Was there some sign she'd been completely unaware of? Something that would hint to Martha Ann that, only two weeks ago, she'd let a stranger into her bed and her body?

"You're a mess!"

"Oh, that." An inch-thick layer of sticky black mud clung to the bottom of her old boots. Dirt streaked her skirt and forearms and probably her face, if she were fool enough to check.

"Yes, that." Martha Ann clucked. "I wish you'd let me send one of the boys over to at least turn over the ground for you this spring."

It was an old discussion, one Margaret had no intention of changing her mind about. "You just want to get one of them off your hands for an entire day."

"True." Her perfect nose wrinkled as she plucked at Margaret's dingy sleeve. "What are you waiting for? Go clean up. We're taking you to town for a birthday dinner."

"You don't have to—"

Martha Ann scowled. "You're not going to argue with me about this now, are you, Margaret?"

"No," she said, having long since learned better, and headed for the house to clean up.

Jamison's Hotel contained the only restaurant in town. But it was a good one, a pleasant room at the back of the inn, with plate windows overlooking the curve of the river. After a long winter alone, in a house where every splinter was so familiar she no longer noticed her surroundings at all, to be in a place so filled with color and new scents and people seemed almost overwhelming, battering at senses unaccustomed to so much to feed on.

"I can't eat another bite." Margaret pushed away her plate and leaned back in her chair with a groan. "And I thought that chicken was stuffed full to the gizzards when they brought it to us! It was no more full than I am."

"Sure you don't want to order some cake?"

"I already had a whole slice of dried apple pie."

"So?"

"I had two," Lucius added. "Not as good as Martha Ann's, of course, but I didn't have to battle John and Oliver for it, either."

"Oh, I understand now," Margaret said. "You said this was for my birthday, but the real reason we came is you just wanted to use me as an excuse to leave the children at their grandmother's for an evening so you could eat in peace."

"Uh-oh. She's on to us now, Lucius."

"Quick, bribe her with that present before she's tempted to tell on us. If the children find out, we'll never get away again."

Margaret started to protest, but neither of them paid her any mind. Martha Ann fumbled in her bulging handbag while Lucius pushed his chair back.

"Ben Lessing's over at his usual table, with his wife and that young assistant of his, waving at us. I'd better go over and see what he wants. If you'll excuse me a moment?"

Her hand still groping around in the bottom of her bag, Martha Ann looked up at her husband. "I suppose we should come, too."

"You stay here. You don't get much chance to chat, just the two of you. I'll tell him you're . . . contagious or something."

"Lucius Perkins, someday you're going to get what you deserve."

His eyes softened, and he gently brushed a finger down his wife's cheek. "Yeah," he said quietly, and made his way across the room.

"That's why I married him, you know," she said.

"Because of how he looks from behind when he walks across the room?" Margaret said, shocking them both.

Martha Ann grinned. "Well, that too," she agreed. "That was a good one, by the way. Perhaps I'm finally rubbing off on you."

Or it took much more than mere words to scandalize her now, Margaret thought.

"I married him because he'd laugh with me," Martha Ann went on. "All my other beaus, I'd say something I meant to be funny, and they'd stare at me like I'd just spoken in tongues, and then they'd start yammering about my violet eyes. But Lucius would always laugh."

For a moment Margaret pictured Kieran, sprawled comfortably on her bed, his eyes dancing with amusement as he flipped over a truly pitiful hand of cards.

They'd laughed, hadn't they? And a few other things, too. Lovely things. Sinful things, ones any respectable woman would regret and forget as quickly as possible.

It's done, Margaret reminded herself. There's nothing of it you can change now, even if you wanted to.

"Oh, here it is!" Martha Ann unearthed a small, newsprint-wrapped box and set it on the table in front of Margaret. "Open it."

"You didn't have to."

"I know," she said cheerfully. "But now you owe me one. One of those lacy scarves you do so well would be perfect. Green, do you think? It goes so well with my hair. Now hurry up!"

"All right." Despite her protests, she eagerly ripped at the paper, no longer able to pretend she wasn't delighted with the gift. Shredded paper spilled out of the open box, nesting a tiny glass vial. "Oh!"

"It's attar of roses. Take a good whiff, now, I can't wait to see if you like it."

Late sunlight through the windows glinted on the curve of glass and the clear amber liquid within. The gift was frivolous and feminine and totally useless to her.

She didn't know when she'd ever been so touched.

She removed the stopper and brought the bottle beneath her nose, filling the air with the heady scent of summer-ripe roses.

Carefully she closed the bottle and snuggled it back into the safety of the box. "Thank you, Martha Ann, it's wonder—"

Martha Ann's breath came out on a hiss, and her hand clamped around Margaret's wrist. "Lordie, Margaret, would you look at that!"

Alarmed, her gaze followed Martha Ann's.

Kieran.

Her first thought was, *He's still here, so why hasn't he come to see me?* Her second, *My Lord, what if he comes to see me?*

She'd assumed he must be long gone. Had even, maybe, convinced herself that she was glad of it. She'd certainly never expected to set eyes on him again.

He was speaking with Mrs. Jamison, gesturing to a small, candlelit table near the window. He smiled at the innkeeper's wife, and part of Margaret protested. *Oh, no, he's not supposed to smile at her like that. He's only supposed to smile at me.*

Stupid, of course. And so obviously wrong. But there'd been only the two of them, and the little world they'd carved from the storm, and in some way she'd almost believed he didn't exist anywhere else.

She'd forgotten that only *they* didn't exist anywhere else.

Martha Ann let out a low whistle. "Forget that silly perfume, Margaret. This is a *much* better birthday present. When he comes by, I'll trip him, and you can just throw yourself on top of him. He doesn't look like the type to protest too much."

"Martha Ann!"

"Hmm? You don't want him? Really? How generous of you, since you do owe me a gift. This would probably be at least five or six holidays' worth. All right, you trip him, and I'll throw myself—"

"We *can't*," Margaret said, aghast. She knew full well Martha Ann had no intention of tripping Kieran, but she certainly didn't put it past her to drag him right over to their table for introductions. All she really wanted to do was slink out before he saw her.

Making a mistake was one thing. Quite another to be confronted with living, breathing evidence of it right in the middle of a roomful of Redemption's leading, and decidedly proper, citizens.

Worse yet, despite that horribly painful morning, and all the agonizing second-guessing since, despite all evidence to the contrary, she couldn't seem to entirely convince herself that it had been such a terrible mistake.

"Of course we can," Martha Ann said. "All right, perhaps I wouldn't really trip the poor man. Wouldn't want to risk damaging those lovely bones, anyway. What good would he be to you then? But this is no time for maidenly vapors,

Margaret. How often do you think a man like that walks into Redemption?"

She probably would have been much better off if he never had.

"I don't think he's really all that attractive."

"Are you mad? Or ill? When was the last time you had your eyesight checked? There's no other explanation for it. He could set old Mrs. Gilliam's heart a-knocking."

"Mrs. Gilliam died six months ago."

"Exactly."

Kieran saw her.

He'd been scanning the room, and she knew the instant his gaze rested on her, those too-well remembered blue eyes. His expression didn't change, the polite mask of vague interest in Mrs. Jamison's recitation of the evening's menu. Then his gaze flicked on to the next table, as if Margaret was worth only a moment's interest.

She should have been relieved to know that he'd obviously do nothing to give her away. That he hadn't let slip the slightest hint that there'd been anything between them. Darn it, she *was* relieved, and that painful little catch in her chest was only worry that he might change his mind.

"If he ever kisses you, you must promise to tell me every single detail."

Margaret focused on the table, on the shredded wrappings from her gift, and on the dirty fork and knife she'd precisely balanced on the edge of her plate. If she didn't have to look at him, perhaps she could start breathing normally again.

"I don't know how Lucius puts up with you."

"Lucius has been a very happy man for eighteen years because of this particular part of my disposition, I'll have you know. The only worrisome part is that our daughters take after me. Thank the Lord, Carrie got herself married off good and early."

Martha Ann bent to peer more closely into her face, and Margaret ducked her head, afraid she'd see far too much there.

"There you go again. Your cheeks are almost as pink as my peonies. I can't believe you still blush like that, after knowing me for all these years."

Thank goodness, Martha Ann had attributed her heated color to the less-than-demure conversation, instead of the sheer mortification and raw shame that were the truth. "Perhaps I wouldn't, if you didn't work so hard at making me."

"I can't help it. It's simply too easy, and you do it so very well."

How did you look at someone, when you were trying so hard to seem like you weren't? Her head lowered, she peeked through her lashes. He'd taken his seat, a small table across the room.

So alone. And so . . . different. Oh, it was the same silver-shot hair, the same pared-down, elegant face. Even the same simple, well-worn clothes over his subtly powerful body.

But here, surrounded by people she knew, it was so obvious how little she knew him. How far out of her experience he was, as beyond her reach as the king of England. Someone whom, if she'd had any sense, she'd have admired from a distance and counted herself lucky to have met him once but had always known was not for the likes of her.

Lucius returned, slipping into his chair next to his wife.

"What did he want?" Martha Ann asked.

"Wanted to let me know that, if we wanted to put off the spring mortgage payment a bit—after the cold winter, and paying for Carrie's wedding and all—that it was fine with him." Lucius shrugged, as if it was of no importance. "I told him not to worry about it, we'd be right on time like always."

"That was kind of him," Martha Ann said, her tone discreetly neutral.

The residents of Redemption all knew how lucky they were to have a businessman like Ben Lessing in town, one with a heart and patience as well as a seemingly endless bankroll. One who'd be willing to wait on a loan payment, if need be. But Margaret thought it might have been even nicer to have a banker who didn't remind a man in a public restaurant that he *owed* a mortgage in the first place.

"Margaret!"

The brimming excitement in Martha Ann's voice should have warned her. "What?"

"He's coming over here!"

"No!" she whispered. Sure enough, Kieran was wending his way through the tables that cluttered the dining room, heading straight for her.

What was he planning to do? It shocked her that in some ways she knew him so well, knew what his mouth tasted like and how the breath shuddered from his chest when she touched her lips to it, and yet she couldn't guess what he'd do now. Whether he'd introduce himself like a polite stranger or simply announce to everyone that he'd been her lover.

Only the suspicion that bolting from the room like a scalded cat would be a great deal more noticeable kept her rooted in place. But, dear Lord, whatever could she say to him?

"I know him," Lucius said. "Met him over to Chaney's Store last week. Irish name, doesn't give much of himself away. Good listener; let Oliver Chaney ramble on for the better part of an hour before he excused himself."

"Hello," Kieran said, extending his hand. "Kieran McDermott. We met last week."

"Of course." Lucius pumped his hand and turned to the women, making quick introductions.

"Delighted to meet you, Mrs. Perkins," he said, bowing over her hand while she beamed at him. He turned to Margaret. "And Miss Thayer—"

"Very nice to meet you," she put in quickly, unwilling to take any chances on what he might say. She'd never kept a secret from Martha Ann, never lied to her, and wasn't at all certain she could pull it off now. But what had happened in those few days, the good and the painful and the astonishing, belonged to her alone. She didn't want it examined and dissected and commented on.

She doubted Martha Ann would be too condemning. Even though, despite her bold speech, she'd made darn sure Lucius took vows before she indulged the more passionate parts of her nature.

But Margaret was terribly afraid that Martha Ann would never understand why she'd let Kieran walk out her door.

"So, Mr. McDermott," Martha Ann said brightly, "will you be staying in Redemption long?"

"I haven't decided," he answered automatically. So, that was how she wanted it, was it? Didn't even want to admit she knew him?

He supposed it was no better than he deserved. At the very least, he should have warned her that he was still in town. She must think that, having spent himself in her, he had no further use for her.

He must have aimed Charlie in the direction of her house a dozen times. But he couldn't quite figure out what he could say to her.

Oh, hello, there, remember me? The man who took your virginity and left? I decided to stay around for a while after all. And, by the way, while I'm here, maybe I could bed you now and then?

Though that sounded right appealing to him, he doubted he'd escape with his skin intact, and he wouldn't have blamed her a bit.

"Really?" Mrs. Perkins leaned toward him and turned up the brilliance in her smile.

Did it bother her husband to have her smiling at other men like that? Kieran suspected that, if his senses hadn't been so fully occupied with the woman sitting quietly by Martha Ann's side, she might have dazzled even him. But Lucius only grinned with amused tolerance and picked at the remains of a slice of pie.

"Your family be joining you soon, I imagine? Your wife, your children?"

"I have little family, I'm afraid."

"Really? That's too bad," she said, but her voice held elation rather than sympathy.

Margaret wondered if anyone would notice if she simply slid under the table. As Martha Ann chatted brightly with Kieran, Margaret leaned over to whisper to Lucius, "Why don't you stop her?"

"Do you really think I could?" Unconcerned, he snitched the curve of crust left on her plate and popped it into his mouth.

"If you're staying awhile, maybe you'd appreciate getting to know a few of our citizens," Martha Ann suggested.

Margaret could see it coming; much longer, and Martha Ann would have her and Kieran halfway to the altar before either of them got in a word of protest. Desperate, she gave Martha Ann a swift kick under the table.

Unfortunately, there was one thing she'd forgotten about Martha Ann Perkins.

She always kicked back.

"Next Saturday night, there'll be a party in the town hall. Last chance for us all to kick up our heels before we get too busy with the fieldwork."

"Oh?"

"Music, too. Dancing even. Everyone brings a covered dish for supper, but you don't have to worry about that. Margaret can make a bit extra for your share."

"Thank you for the invitation. I wouldn't want to impose, though."

"Oh, it's no imposition at all. We'll be devastated if you don't come. Won't we, Margaret?"

If Maggie hunched down in her chair any farther, her eyebrows were going to be level with the tabletop. If he had any decency at all, Kieran thought, he'd let her off the hook and refuse.

But, in nearly two weeks of steady investigation, he'd gotten exactly nowhere. He'd forced himself to go slowly and carefully. Although his first priority was the missing girl, he also sought the man she'd run off with, the man who'd spent months posing as William Dalrymple's employee. If the Uncatchable Man ever suspected that Melissa Dalrymple was Kieran's only link to him, Kieran had little doubt he'd rid himself of Melissa in the most expedient way.

So he'd been uncharacteristically cautious, ingratiating himself with the residents of Redemption as inconspicuously as he could. Unfortunately, the townspeople were both close and closemouthed.

He'd even—on a tip from the friendly bartender at Red Fred's Saloon—hunted up the town's lone fancy woman. He'd bought an hour of her Tuesday afternoon, and she'd happily spent the time answering his questions, but he learned nothing of any use.

He needed a chance to get to know more of Redemption. He needed an insider, someone who would introduce him around and who had lived here long enough to be respected and well informed.

He needed Maggie.

"I'll be there."

7

Margaret truly intended to stay home Saturday night.

It would not be unusual, certainly nothing that would be remarked upon. All those years of her mother's illness, she'd never felt able to leave Eleanor home alone for something as frivolous as entertainment. Since then, it wasn't often that there was both little enough work and good enough weather for her to attend the community's events.

But Martha Ann wouldn't hear of it.

Her entire family in tow, she showed up at four o'clock. She seemed completely unperturbed by Margaret's rather desperate protest that, after not having seen Martha Ann twice in three months, Margaret couldn't handle seeing her twice in one week. She waved off Margaret's insistence that she simply couldn't go because she didn't have a dish to contribute—how fortunate that Martha Ann's hens had begun laying so well she'd simply been forced to make up an extra baked custard so as not to waste the eggs.

Martha Ann had not spent years dealing with eight recalcitrant children for nothing. She coerced Margaret into what passed for her best clothes—a tight-sleeved blouse of cotton sateen, its pink printed carnations only slightly faded, and a seal-brown cheviot skirt, its worn hem crease hidden by the vine of bright green leaves she'd embroidered over it. After dousing her in attar of roses, Martha Ann bundled Margaret in the back of the big wagon between her two largest sons and informed Lucius that now they could head for town—and he best be quick about it, too, for she had a hankering to dance.

Due to Benjamin Lessing's generosity, Redemption's town hall was an unusually fine one. Monday through Friday the big, whitewashed frame building on the edge of town was used as a school; on Sundays, the desks went out and the pews came in. But on an occasional Saturday evening, it fulfilled a far more festive function. And if, long ago, some people had thought it inappropriate that the same building that served the Lord on Sunday morning served as a dance floor on Saturday night, those objections had long since bowed to practicality.

Tonight, the hall had been mostly cleared out, leaving only a bank of tables on one side already laden with food, facing a row of chairs across the sanded space that would serve as a dance floor. A battered piano that, it was rumored, had once

stood in the corner of the saloon until Fred decided
that he required a newer model, occupied the far
corner. Beside it, Mortimer Grandin was already
tuning up his fiddle.

At any other time, Margaret would have been
delighted by the wide variety of food that she never
bothered to prepare only for herself. But she was
too worried about looking up from a plate of dev-
iled eggs to find herself staring right at Kieran to
give the spread the attention it deserved.

It was most unfair, she decided. A woman who'd
given in to a fling, to a night of passion with a mysterious stranger, should never have to lay eyes on
that stranger again.

It was simply too humiliating otherwise.

Her plate filled with whatever she'd been able to
grab quickly, Margaret hid herself in a clutch of
women, carefully placing Martha Ann between her
and the door. She scooted her chair over a little
until she found just the right angle, affording her a
clear if limited view of the entrance without, she
hoped, revealing herself.

She picked at her food, an eye on the door and
an ear to the conversation that buzzed around her.
The topics seldom varied: husbands and children,
upcoming weddings and babies.

Margaret couldn't blame them. Family women
all, they took full advantage of an infrequent
opportunity to talk over their homes and work with
other women just like them. But it left little room
for anyone who didn't share their concerns to join
the conversation.

The women were, for the most part, near her

own age. She'd known many of them for years, had attended school and church with most of them. And yet, in their midst, she felt as far out of place as she would have in the laughing cluster of young men who grouped near the front door, watching the young women arrive.

There was a widow or two in the group, and a couple of women who'd never borne children. But Margaret was the only one who'd never married, never had a child, never even had a steady sweetheart, because for so many years, no man had been willing to take Eleanor along with his bride.

There'd been a few suitors, after her mother's death. Margaret held no illusions about them. They were widowers, men who needed a hardworking wife, particularly one who came with a full quarter section, and so didn't much care if she might be past childbearing age.

Eleanor's ghost would surely have come back to haunt her had she given up a home and land of her own and become some man's unpaid housekeeper merely to assuage her own loneliness. It hadn't taken long before the callers stopped, and Margaret hadn't let herself regret the decision.

But at least she was no longer the lone woman who'd never taken a man to her bed. For all the lurking shame and embarrassment and stubborn guilt that had come from that night, an unruly and prideful corner of her was glad for that, at least.

Having little to contribute to the discussion, she huddled in her hidden corner, watching the pickled beets she didn't even like bleed into her creamed potatoes. But as each minute that Kieran didn't show up passed, she felt the knot of strain in her stomach ease a little more.

Chores came before church, ensuring Sunday morning came early in Redemption, so the musicians eased into their first number while the late afternoon light still streamed, clear and spring gold, through the windows. The loud hum of conversation dimmed to a low murmur beneath the music, and several men slipped out the front door for a smoke before their wives could come looking to dance. A half-dozen couples braved the empty dance floor. Several of them even managed to bob in time to the music—no easy feat, when the rhythm kept changing to suit Mortimer's whims.

Margaret let out a deep sigh of relief. Surely, if Kieran planned to show up, he'd have arrived by now.

Intending to go scrape off her plate and pack it away, she rose, shaking down her rumpled skirts.

And plopped right back down again.

Kieran was here after all. He stood near the front door, coolly scanning the room as if he knew precisely whom he was searching for, oblivious to the wary glances and whispered comments directed his way.

He'd been in town long enough that, by now, everyone there had surely heard of the man staying at Jamison's Hotel. But by Redemption's standards, he was still a stranger, and strangers did not simply wander into community events as if they belonged.

Martha Ann leaned over to her, whispering excitedly into her ear, "He's here!"

"I noticed."

"Aren't you going to go over and welcome him?"

"No."

"Well, I think you should. Poor man is probably lonesome, here in town all by himself, and no family of his own. Come on, I'll go with you—"

"No," Margaret repeated firmly. "Leave it alone, Martha Ann."

"But I surely hate to see a man so lonely—"

"He doesn't look terribly lonely to me," she observed dryly.

Sure enough, Kieran was already leading pretty, blond, and all-of-eighteen Isabinda Salisbury out to dance.

Now what? she thought. Her instincts urged her to play it safe, to stay as far out of Kieran's path as possible. Was she really going to hide in the corner all evening?

Suddenly disgusted with herself, she jumped to her feet.

She was wasting entirely too much time worrying what Kieran McDermott thought of her.

True, she'd made lustful—and quite enthusiastic—advances to a man she'd known scarcely more than two days. She'd given her virginity to a stranger without a hint of promise or vows.

At best, he must think her sinfully wanton; at worst, pathetically desperate.

It occurred to her that her inability to pin the same labels on him, simply because he'd been born male, was grossly unjust.

Determined, she headed across the room, toward Martha Ann's hamper. She'd no intention of carrying around a dirty plate all night long just to avoid Kieran.

Kieran and Isabinda whirled by. For an instant, his gaze met hers directly, and she stopped in her tracks. His eyes were too blue, and they'd seen too much of her, for them to have as little effect on her as she might have wished.

Then he simply bowed his head, murmured something to Isabinda, and danced on past.

"Well," Martha Ann said, disgruntled, "you sure were right about him."

Her back to the dance floor—not on purpose, she told herself—Margaret packed away the remains of supper. "Who?"

"That McDermott." Her youngest child, two-year-old Katie, squirmed on Martha Ann's hip. She broke off a corner of a spice bar and popped it in Katie's mouth. "Do you know, he hasn't danced with anyone over the age of twenty all night long?"

"I hadn't noticed," Margaret said coolly, hoping that would be enough to end the subject. She really did not want to talk about Kieran any longer.

Bad enough that he invaded her dreams. She did not appreciate him invading her Saturday evening, as well, and right now all she wanted to do was go home. If she could pry John Perkins away from his new sweetheart, maybe they could finally get out of here.

"Well, he hasn't. I never would have thought it of him. He seemed like a man who would have better taste than that." Katie squirmed. "Oh, you want down, sweetie? Here you go." As soon as Katie's feet hit the floor, she took off, lurching right into the middle of the dancers. Martha Ann chased after her. "Come back here!"

Fitting an empty pan snugly into the corner of the basket, Margaret surveyed the remains of the evening's meal, trying to recall if any of the other dishes belonged to Martha Ann.

"Hello," Kieran said, no more than a foot from her left elbow.

Margaret was rather pleased with her reaction. She didn't jump, didn't stutter, didn't even glance his way. "Hello." She reached for the red-checked napkin that had held a dozen of Martha Ann's special potato rolls.

"Would you like to dance?"

"Not particularly."

Irritated, Kieran gave serious consideration to simply turning on his heels and walking out of that damned town hall. The evening had been nothing but one frustration after another.

With most of Redemption at the hall, he'd figured it was a good opportunity to do a little poking around. Although he didn't really expect to get lucky enough just to stumble upon Melissa, he'd thought he might find . . . something. He'd peeked in most of the nicer houses in town, into barns and stables and sheds, looking for furniture or horseflesh that seemed beyond the owners' means. Perhaps a large safe in the house of someone who shouldn't have any need of one.

All he'd gotten was several scratches from the bushes that ringed Benjamin Lessing's property, a turned ankle from a gopher hole in the yard behind Chaney's Store, and an empty belly.

He'd arrived here to find most of the food long since eaten. He'd spent the better part of an hour shuffling around the dance floor with any young woman who even remotely fit the description William Dalrymple had given of his missing daughter. Except every girl he spoke to turned out to have lived in Redemption for years, and all their yammering and giggling had spawned one hell of a headache.

He'd actually been looking forward to dancing with Maggie. At least she, he was quite certain, wouldn't titter like an overexcited finch. And he knew damned well he liked the feel of her in his arms.

Except now she looked bound and determined to ignore him completely.

"Oh? Can't dance, huh?" A comment that was probably most unsporting of him, but he'd had a long day.

She folded the napkin into a precise square. For some reason that annoyed him immensely. The thing had crumbs all over it. Couldn't she just wad it up and put it away? Who folded up a used napkin like a piece of fine silk?

"I can dance."

"Sure you can."

She snapped the napkin into the basket with an angry jerk and turned to him. "All right."

They stepped out on the dance floor, and she took a position as far apart from him as she could without looking too obvious. They moved stiffly together, as out of tune with each other as the piano and fiddle that clashed at the other end of the room.

Every bit of the tentative friendship they developed in those few days had obviously been destroyed by what had followed. To her surprise, Margaret found she missed it. Silly to regret something so fleeting, but she couldn't deny it.

"Why don't you tell me about some of our fellow dancers?" he suggested.

"Why?"

"Why not? Better than my dragging you around the floor while you try to ignore me."

Her mouth thinned, and he had a perverse and near irresistible urge to kiss her and soften it up. "I would have thought all those *girls* you danced with would have made you feel quite welcome."

So, she'd noticed, had she? He was unaccountably and quite wickedly pleased. "Thought it only sociable to give the girls a thrill."

That did it. She glared at him, and he grinned, satisfied to make her finally look at him directly.

"If there's something else you'd rather talk about," he said, pitching his voice low and suggestive, "I'm willing."

"Who have you met so far?" she asked quickly.

"Not too many people, actually. This isn't the friendliest town I've ever been to."

"We've learned to be that way. Because of the river, this area homesteaded early. Indians surrounded us for years, so everybody depended on each other. And then, when the mill came in—well, let's just say that some people paid pretty dearly for being friendly to outsiders. We're all pretty cautious now, and the townspeople don't mix with mill employees at all."

She pointed out Benjamin Lessing, a nondescript man in his early forties. A clutch of townspeople gathered around him, and his only remarkable feature was an expansive smile. His assistant, Walter Cowdry—hired four years ago, Maggie told him— hovered at his elbow, a thin young man very much in his employer's shade.

Despite what he told her, Kieran had met several of the men already. He listened carefully to her descriptions just the same, hoping she knew something more about the men, something that would allow him to eliminate some possibilities. Those of unusual height he discarded immediately; the man he sought was of average size.

Other than that, he had little to go on. William Dalrymple had described the employee who absconded with most of Dalrymple's money, Melissa in tow, as balding, mustachioed, of medium brown hair. Other victims of the Uncatchable Man had given vastly different accounts of his appearance, but Dalrymple had received a note two weeks after his daughter disappeared, thanking him for his "generous contributions" and telling him that "oh, by the way, your daughter is quite . . . healthy."

So unless another thief had begun to appropriate his methods, the Uncatchable Man was who'd victimized William. And Melissa.

Despite his best intentions to listen to every word she said, however, Kieran found himself a good deal more interested in the way Maggie relaxed as she talked. The way she grew softer and closer and her movements fell in rhythm with his.

Margaret realized he'd stopped making

encouraging comments some time ago. "I guess that was more than you probably wanted to know." With a self-conscious laugh, she looked up to find him studying her, as if marking each feature.

"You can dance," he admitted.

"One of my father's few talents." And one of her very few good memories, when she was all of six or seven, her nose no higher than her father's belt buckle as he guided her through the steps. "He taught me years ago."

"He did a good job," he said, his tone intimate and far too familiar.

"Don't look at me like that."

"Like what?"

"Carefully. The light's still fairly bright in here, and you'll find every wrinkle."

"Wrinkles?" Where had that come from? He'd always been good at observing the things that mattered and ignoring everything else but, now that she'd brought it up, he supposed that worry and work had left their imprint on her face. It would have been surprising if they hadn't. "Yes, I guess you do have a few."

A frown flickered through her eyes. Oops, he thought, wrong answer.

He brought his hand up to cup her cheek, resting his thumb right on the crease that bracketed her mouth, the one that deepened when she smiled. "You know what I like about your skin?"

"What?" she asked, wary.

"How it turns pink when I even think of kissing you."

The color bloomed immediately, right on cue.

"See? There it goes now."

"Don't you dare," she warned.

"Don't I dare what?"

"Kiss me right now."

"Why not?"

"We're in public! Everyone would see. I'd be terribly embarrassed."

"Would I do that to you?" he asked, amused and tempted in equal measure.

"Yes," she said darkly. "You would."

"Name me one person who would care what we did."

"They'd all care. This might not be as small a town as it once was, Kieran, but they'd still all talk about it for weeks."

"Really? Well, hell, if they need excitement that badly, I'd be willing to give them some."

"Kieran!"

Maggie was beginning to look distinctly worried. He supposed he really should let her off the hook, except he couldn't remember when he'd enjoyed something so much.

Not counting one particular night in her bed, of course.

"All right, then, name me someone here that you really care what they think about you."

"Martha Ann."

"If I kissed you right now, in front of everyone, I bet she'd applaud."

An unwilling grin tipped her mouth. "You're probably right."

The music slowed. He tugged her closer, her hair brushing against his cheek. "You smell different."

"It's attar of roses." Darn it, Margaret thought, she shouldn't be flattered that he remembered what she'd smelled like. "Martha Ann made me wear it. You don't like it?"

"Yeah, I do. But I liked how you smelled before, too."

"How was that?"

"Just woman, and nothing else."

Danger. It seethed in every word he said, in each small brush of his leg against hers as they danced.

Once could be forgiven. One small sin, a lapse, an experiment. But anything more . . . she was terrified that this man could make of her something she wouldn't even recognize. Could lure out parts of herself that were far better left buried.

She jerked away, as if she could no longer bear his touch. "You shouldn't say things like that."

"What did I do wrong this time?"

He'd done nothing. It was her, her inability to put what had simply been a night of exploration and sport in its proper place. That, and her lack of experience with situations like this, and the way she kept wanting to make more of it than it was. "I have to go." She turned away.

His hand encircled her wrist gently, keeping her close. "I don't know how to treat you. Like a stranger, or an acquaintance, or a distant friend? Am I supposed to pretend I don't even know you?" he asked harshly. "For God's sake, Maggie, *I know what you taste like.*"

The memory was instantly alive, as if it had hovered very near the surface, waiting for a chance to seize her—his mouth hot between her thighs, his tongue urgent and seeking deep.

"I have to go!" she said, appalled to find tears threatening, stinging behind her lids.

"Maggie—"

She'd always believed that discretion was frequently the wisest choice.

Margaret fled.

8

❦

A copse of cottonwood, hard on the banks of the river, sheltered the small stone cottage. Despite its modest size, it was exquisitely furnished. The fluffy drift of a feather bed nearly hid the mattress of the big, carved rosewood bed. The small black stove in the far corner was the latest and most efficient model. And the lushly upholstered chaise exactly duplicated the one she'd once seen a very famous actress swoon dramatically onto, at the theater in Chicago her father had taken her to.

Her lover had insisted that nothing less would do for Melissa Dalrymple.

But now, as she paced the close confines, it pleased her not at all. For her lover was, once again, late.

There was a time that she thought that this would surely be enough for her. Though the cottage was nothing compared to her father's house, having someplace of her own, a place that she could retreat to whenever she wished, was something she had desperately wanted.

It had not taken her long, however, to discover that, though he gave her free rein here, it was not hers. No more than anything else she had now was.

They all belonged to him. Including herself.

She glanced out a front window. Moonlight brushed silver ripples on the wind-ruffled surface of the river. Lamplight from inside the cottage flowed out, illuminating two squares of tangled grass and underbrush. All else was shadows and darkness.

It would serve him right, she thought, to find her gone when he finally arrived. But if she didn't wait, then she'd be alone the entire night, as she had been most of the day, and she didn't want that, either.

The front door swung open abruptly, and Melissa jumped, her heart stuttering unevenly until she saw the familiar figure that slipped in.

"Oh, there you are. I didn't see you come up."

"I should hope not," he said smoothly, shrugging off his heavy wool coat and hanging it on a hook beside the door. "If you didn't see me, then I doubt anyone else did, either."

"You're late."

"Am I?" The petulance in her voice bothered him not a whit. He understood well which one of them held the power in this relationship. And she was learning. "I have responsibilities to attend to."

"And did you have a good time?" Melissa moved into the lamplight, knowing the thin silk dressing robe he'd bought her showed off her figure to good advantage. It was a seductress's garment, and pleased her much more than the childish frills her father had dressed her in.

"Not particularly." He came toward her, fingers already working on the buttons of his collar. It struck her once more how different he looked now than when she'd first met him, when he'd posed as her father's helpful and competent employee. No one who knew him then would have believed this the same man.

That was what had attracted her, for he was not at all handsome, not in either guise. But that ability to change himself completely, to merge into someone new—it fascinated her, drew her, frustrated her.

For that was what she craved for herself. To make of herself another woman, one new and clean and happy.

No, she reminded herself. It wasn't only what she *wanted*, it was what she was *doing*, right now. And soon the Melissa Dalrymple that had existed before would be no more than a distant memory.

To every person but one. Who she hoped remembered, and suffered for it, every day.

She folded her arms beneath her breasts, pushing them together to good advantage. Predictably his gaze fell there, his lips parting on a heavy breath.

"I had nothing to do," she complained. "Waiting puts me out of the mood."

"Not happy, are you, my sweet?" He smiled slowly, wondering if she had any idea how transparent her efforts to manipulate him were. "I could always take you home, I suppose."

She blanched, visibly struggling for control.

He reached out, brushed her arms away, untied the silken rope belt, and swept the cloth aside, baring her. She made no move, standing frozen as a terrified prey confronted with her doom.

He'd not intended to take her with him, those months he'd worked for her father and plotted to steal as much of Dalrymple's fortune as he could. But she'd been so pathetically easy to control, so desperate to escape, and all that luscious young flesh so very, very sweet. And she was far better off with him, anyway. "I thought you liked it here."

"I do," she murmured automatically. Whether she liked it or not had so little to do with it. But she'd expected something so different. Instead, her life was much the same as it had always been: long stretches of monotony and isolation, underlain by a thin, persistent thread of fear. "I just . . . I thought it would be different. More exciting."

"Bored, are you?" He drew a fingertip over her collarbone, between those firm white breasts, and circled beneath. "Perhaps we can find something to entertain you."

She remained compliant, utterly still.

"Would you like to come along on my next job?"

"Could I?" Now *that* would be better, she thought. Much more like she'd imagined. Danger and excitement and thrill enough so that there was no necessity to think. "Have you planned it already? Will we be leaving soon? Tell me about it."

"Not too soon." His hand drifted lower. "I have

responsibilities, as I said before. And my absences mustn't be too noticeable."

"Oh." She pouted prettily.

"But it will give you something to look forward to. And, in the meantime . . ." He drew her toward the bed. "This is much better than living with your father, isn't it?"

It's too much like living with my father, she thought, and let her mind go blank.

It had taken Kieran two days to make up his mind to do this, and now he couldn't find Margaret.

He had tried every way he could think of to talk himself out of it. He'd always worked alone, and truly doubted his capability to do anything else.

But he'd also never had so much difficulty narrowing in on his prey before, either. It occurred to him he'd been unforgivably arrogant about completing his task. After all, in the past he'd chased puzzles and solved riddles that no one else much bothered with, because the victims were usually helpless and destitute.

The man he sought this time, however, had had a decade of practice, maybe more, at eluding even the best investigators. Kieran detested the caution forced upon him, chafed under its constraints. But the Uncatchable Man must expect that someone had been set after him, and Kieran could not risk Melissa's life by making an impulsive misstep.

Kieran had no doubts he would still catch the man, though perhaps unusual circumstances called for unusual tactics.

At just after noon, he'd been certain he would find her at home—probably still at her dinner. But she wasn't in her house. Or in her garden, or out back by the well. He left Charlie munching on the new grass near the front door and went to check in that wreck of a shed she used for a barn, to see if her horse was there.

He found her there, on her knees in a pile of straw.

"Maggie," he said, leaning against the wall, "you have your hand up a cow's butt."

"I'd noticed that." She didn't glance his way, concentrating completely on the brown-and-white cow that lay, sides heaving, before her. "However, it's not precisely her butt."

"What, exactly, are you doing?"

"I'm—" She winced, and her arm disappeared farther into the cow. "I'm greasing the neck of her womb, with Vaseline and a little belladona, to soften it up. She's having a bit of a rough time with this one, aren't you, Daisy girl?"

He would never have imagined her like this. She was a small and slender woman who blushed at the slightest provocation. To hear her discussing the private parts of a cow without the slightest hint of embarrassment as she confidently and competently assisted a cow in giving birth— the contrast was surprising. And surprisingly fascinating.

"Do you . . . would you like me to help?"

"I don't think Daisy would appreciate that." She looked up long enough to flash him a grin. "I've got smaller hands."

"All right." *Thank God.* "If you're sure."

"There. That should do it for now." She removed her arm, shiny with grease and streaked with a dark substance that Kieran mercifully couldn't identify.

"She going to be okay?"

"She should be fine." Margaret got up and reached for an old rag to clean up. "Just having a big ol' bull calf."

"How do you know?"

"She usually pops a calf in less than an hour, so I'm guessing it's big. Bull?" She shrugged. "She carried this one almost ten months. That usually means it's male. Stubborn half of the species."

The glint in her eye told him she wasn't just referring to cattle. Teasing from her was so unexpected, it left him slightly off-balance, jumbling up the speech he'd rehearsed on the way over.

"Too bad, really," she went on.

"Too bad?"

"Bull calf's not worth as much. A male, well, you might get a breeding out of him now and then, if he's a good one, and some meat at the end. But a heifer—you'll get milk almost every day, and a calf every year. A lot more valuable and productive, a female."

If someone had told her that Kieran might catch her like this, wearing her dirty old clothes and her hair straggling out of its braid, in a smelly shed with her arm inside a cow—especially when he looked so clean and handsome—she would have thought she'd darn near die of the humiliation.

But he'd caught her by surprise, and she'd been too anxious about Daisy to worry about what she

looked like and what he thought of her. She'd
started bantering with him before she even realized
the words were coming out of her mouth. And she
was enjoying his surprise, the way he didn't seem
to know quite what to say to her. She was much
more used to feeling at a disadvantage when with
him.

"I didn't expect to see you."

"I really need to talk to you."

So he needed to talk to her, did he? It had been
three weeks since they'd . . . she tried to find a
label for it, couldn't come up with one that suited
her; since they'd done *that*, and he certainly hadn't
had much to say to her in all that time.

Having gotten the worst of the mess off her
hands, she flipped the soiled rag over the boards
that boxed in the mare's stall. "It'll have to wait.
I've got to take care of Daisy now."

"Will she take long?"

"Hard to say. An hour or so, I'd guess."

"I'll wait."

In the next hour, Kieran began to suspect that
Daisy did not require nearly as much attention as
Maggie gave her, but Maggie was having far too
much fun turning him into her assistant to give up
the game. He fetched water and string and every
other damn thing she told him to. He fed her sorry
excuse for a mare. He brewed coffee. He made
friends with the batch of kittens he found behind a
pile of hay.

He did not stick his hand up a laboring cow's
ass.

They hardly spoke; Kieran did not want to

impose—he'd be imposing soon enough—and Margaret didn't know what to say. But once he interrupted her to ask, "I don't see any, uh, other cows around here. Just exactly how did she get in this condition, anyway?"

That made her smile. "Sorenson, who plants most of my land, gives me use of his bull as part of his rent each year."

Three-quarters of an hour later, Margaret decided it had taken long enough. "I'm going to pull the calf some, see if we can get it out of there before she gets too tired."

"I might be able to do it, if you tell me how."

Margaret shook her head. Loose strands of hair clung to her temples and neck. She reached up to brush them away, remembered the condition of her hands, and checked herself. "No, I'll do it."

She'd turned down his offer of assistance. Kieran vacillated between insult and gratitude. "Come now, what have I been doing all afternoon but proving I can follow your orders? And you must admit I am stronger."

"It's better not to pull too hard, though. Could hurt Daisy inside, or the calf, if it's not done carefully." She huffed at the annoying wisps of hair. "If it's really stuck, though, I promise I'll let you have a go at it. I can tell you can hardly wait."

"All right," he said, almost sorry that it would soon be over. He'd enjoyed watching her, seeing her deliberate movements and confident manner, listening to the low, comforting murmur of her voice. "Just a moment."

He reached up and brushed the disobedient

strands of hair away, tucking them behind her ears, his fingers light and warm. "There."

He'd touched her before, much more fully, and in far more intimate places. But Margaret could have sworn her heart trembled.

"Oh." Behind her, Daisy lowed, and Margaret blinked. "I'd . . ." She gestured toward the laboring cow. "I'd better get to it, I guess."

"Yes." Much better, he thought. For if she didn't, he was likely to do something that would make them both forget about cows and missing girls and the fact that they knew nothing of each other but that they fit together in bed.

Because they fit together so extremely well.

Kneeling down in the straw, she again took up the position he'd found her in.

"That's the weakest excuse for pulling I've ever seen," he commented.

She smiled fleetingly. "I'm waiting for Daisy. It's much better if I pull when she's pushing."

"Oh."

Apparently a little extra help was all Daisy needed. It didn't take long before the calf came sliding out, nose pressed firmly between his folded knees. While Daisy set herself to licking him clean, Margaret quickly tied a few light weights to the tissue that still trailed inside the cow. To help expel the afterbirth, she explained.

"There. That should do it."

Margaret had half expected Kieran to give up and leave rather than wait around while she put birthing a calf ahead of talking to him. What could he possibly have to say to her that was so important?

But she had to admit that he didn't look particularly impatient, not nearly as out of place as she would have expected. He'd found the milking stool and perched his long body rather uncertainly on it. And he must have been petting one of the kittens, for a pretty charcoal-gray one had climbed up his arm onto his shoulder.

After being in a crouched position for so long, her legs had stiffened. When she awkwardly clambered up, he was there to assist her and hand her a clean length of cloth.

"I've never watched that before. It was interesting." The kitten wantonly nuzzled his neck, persisting even when Kieran tried to nudge it gently away. Not that Margaret blamed the kitten—it was an awfully nice neck. "Messy, but interesting."

"City boy."

"That's me." The kitten batted at his earlobe. "Ouch!" He scooped it off his shoulder, tucking it away in the curve of his arm. "What's this one's name?"

"Doesn't have one. What's the use of naming something that's going to die on you in a few years, anyway?"

"Hell, you could say that about almost everything. If you were going to eat it, maybe I could see your point." He frowned. "Where'd you come up with that, anyway?"

Her mother's words—they'd popped right out of her, an automatic response. She'd mouthed them without even thinking about them. How many other things had she repeated, or even done, without taking the time to examine whether she believed them or not, only because she'd heard them so many times?

"You're right." She scooped up the kitten and flipped it over to check its sex. "His name's Arne." Still holding Arne, she headed for the door. "Any more of that coffee left?"

"Sure."

She threw him a glance over her shoulder. "Thought you had something you wanted to say."

"I did."

"Come on, then."

She'd put him off all afternoon, and he'd only been amused by it. Now that she was ready to listen, Kieran found it hard to begin.

A small box padded with old clothes proved a perfectly satisfactory bed for the kitten. After Margaret had cleaned up, they sat at the table with two cups of coffee and silence between them.

"I . . . don't know where to start." He smiled weakly. "I've never done this before."

"I find that rather hard to believe."

"I'm not even sure I should be telling you this. But it doesn't seem I have much of a choice any longer."

He stared glumly into his cup, trepidation and concern written clearly on his handsome features. She'd never thought to see him so uncomfortable. What could he possibly have to tell her that could be so terrible?

"Just tell me."

"Back when we met, during the storm, I didn't lie, exactly, but . . ." He shrugged, wincing. "I didn't tell you the complete truth, either."

The gulp of coffee she'd just taken hit her stom-ach with a thud. Surely not . . . frantically, she tried to remember exactly what he'd said when Martha Ann had asked him about a wife.

I don't have much family . . . that wasn't exactly a *no*, was it, even though they'd all taken it to mean that at the time.

"Kieran, if you're trying say you neglected to mention that you have a wife stashed back east, and she's decided to come and join you in Redemption, you do understand I'll have to hurt you very badly, don't you?"

"No, of course not!" Sighing, he braced his fore-arms on the table and leaned forward, looking directly into her eyes. "I've mangled this badly. I'm just much more used to trying to keep my secrets close, rather than spilling them to someone else."

If he'd seen any other alternative to telling her, he would still be keeping his secrets now. Letting someone else in always opened the door to mis-takes, to actions and words he couldn't control.

But this was Maggie, he reminded himself. And he believed without a doubt that she could be trusted, or he wouldn't be there.

"Remember, I told you that I sometimes do favors for people?"

"Yes," she said. "I'd nearly decided you were an outlaw."

"Really?" He was charmed by the idea. "I'm sur-prised you didn't go ahead and tie me to the bed, then."

Mistake. He saw it immediately, in the way she withdrew from him, in the way the conspiratorial light died in her eyes. She obviously didn't care to be reminded of him in her bed.

He ignored the prick of that and went on. "It's not usually terribly complicated. Someone's partner runs off with their joint funds. A father wants to track down the man who seduced and abandoned his daughter. Or maybe someone just trusted the wrong person."

"And you . . . help?" she asked, trying to fit this into the bits and pieces she knew of him.

"I try."

"Why?"

"If they're poor, or powerless—which is usually the same thing—it's hard to get anybody to help. Someone's got to do it."

Something about the intensity and empathy in his voice made her think that he'd once been poor and powerless himself, though that was hard to reconcile with the confident and controlled man sitting across from her.

"It sounds dangerous."

He flicked his hand, a gesture that clearly said that danger was of no importance. "It gives me something to do."

"But—"

"I've never told anyone that before, right out like that." He blew out a relieved breath. There was obviously much more to it than he'd told her, so much more she wanted to know, but he'd just shut down the topic as clearly as closing a door.

"How do they find you, then?"

"The first few were almost by accident—I just happened to be there when someone was in trouble, and no one else was willing to do anything. After that—I guess a friend hears from a friend who hears from a friend . . . I really haven't given it much thought how they find me. They just do. Anyway," he set aside his cup, as if clearing the table for business, "I need your help."

"There's someone you're looking for . . . in Redemption?" She found it hard to believe. Redemption was a simple working town, not the sort of place for intrigue, villains, and good deeds.

"Yes." He laid the story out quickly and without embellishment, and that very plainness of the tale only made it seem all the more outlandish.

"And you think that they are *here?*" she asked incredulously. Impossible that an infamous thief and his young paramour could hide themselves in Redemption.

But Kieran seemed very sure.

"I know they're here," he said quietly. "I just can't find them—yet."

"But the girl—surely you know what she looks like."

"Only a description. She destroyed all her father's photographs of her before she left."

How odd, Margaret thought. "She must be very determined not to be found."

"She was probably just doing what she was told to do by the thief." His hands fisted, as if he were wishing the one he'd called the Uncatchable Man was there to use those fists on. "Think of it, Maggie. She was only fifteen when she met him . . . to be in the power of a man like that! God knows what he's doing to her . . . or making her do."

Anger shadowed his voice; pain welled deep in his eyes. It seemed to her that there was more, much more, to this than mere concern for a stranger and a difficult task he'd taken as his own. But he'd not met Melissa; he'd said he couldn't recognize her from more than her description. "There's some connection between you?"

"What?" His brows snapped together. "No, of course not. Nothing beyond what I've told you."

"Oh." How silly and shallow she'd been, she thought, when he'd first come to her door. She'd been caught up in his beauty and his body and his smile. She'd given little thought to what lay beneath that attractive, mysterious surface; she hadn't really even cared.

There was so much *more* in Kieran than she'd ever suspected. Even now, she knew she saw only the shadows and reflections of it; the substance, the real heart and depths of it, eluded her.

"I need your help," he said.

"Me?" It was too ridiculous even to laugh at.

"Yes."

"You're not serious."

But he looked serious.

"What could I possibly do?" she wondered.

"I need someone who can tell me about the town and its people, all the silly little details that might give me the hint I'm looking for. And I need to be accepted; if everyone sees you with me, all the time, and that you're comfortable with me and trust me, I'm hoping that they'll start treating me the same way. I can't get anywhere while they're all so much on their guard."

Margaret shook her head. "I have to tell you, Kieran, that I'm not nearly so much a part of the town as you seem to think. My mother was ill for years, and that kept me bound to the farm much of the time."

"It doesn't matter. You're still part of Redemption, as far as they're concerned."

"That's probably true." Maggie thought of the gun that she'd found in his pack, and newspaper accounts she'd read about the Uncatchable Man. And his victims. "Is it . . . dangerous?"

"Not for you." Didn't she know that, although his own safety didn't matter, he would never risk anyone else's? But he supposed she had no way of knowing anything of the sort about him.

"I guess—"

"I'll pay you five hundred dollars," he broke in before she had a chance to agree. He knew she'd say yes. She'd taken him in from the storm; she wouldn't refuse to help an innocent, endangered girl. But he wanted her to have the money. To, once he was gone, leave something behind him that would make her life better.

Because he suspected he'd done the opposite so far.

Her mouth fell open. "The lost-cause business must pay much better than I'd guessed."

"It does this time."

"How would we do it, exactly?" she asked.

"Well." He cleared his throat. "I think the easiest would be—" another pause, "if we pretended to be courting."

"I see." She couldn't deny that the idea appealed to her. All those people who'd assumed Margaret

Thayer would never have a real suitor would see her stroll down the middle of Redemption with Kieran on her arm.

But the excitement that budded within her had to do with more than just surprising the town that had labeled her a spinster years ago, and that frightened her.

"It would have to be strictly business," she said firmly.

"Fine," Kieran said. What else could he do but agree? He had no right to be insulted or disappointed or any other damn thing at her insistence on precise boundaries.

"All right then," she decided, ignoring the persistent nagging that told her to be careful, be safe. Be as far away from Kieran McDermott as you can be. "I'll do it."

9

On Friday night, the dining room at Jamison's Hotel brimmed with bachelors looking for a decent meal, several of Redemption's leading couples, and young men who hoped that springing for the cost of a restaurant meal would put them in good enough favor with their sweethearts to earn them a good-night kiss.

Margaret and Kieran occupied a table conspicuously in the middle of the crowd.

The indulgent, amused smiles occasionally turned their way told Kieran that his fellow diners put him squarely in the last category. Over the past several days, he'd grown rather accustomed to it; it seemed that Redemption was highly entertained by the spectacle of Margaret Thayer having unexpectedly, and quite publicly, found herself a beau.

He and Margaret had been seen strolling down Front Street. They'd picnicked beside the river, and twice he'd taken her to Jamison's for dinner.

Tomorrow morning, he'd every intention of escorting her to church.

His plan was working beautifully. His inquiries were now more likely to be met with a wink than suspicion, and even without Margaret at his side, men heartily welcomed him in the saloon and Chaney's Store—as long as he was willing to put up with a few interested questions of their own.

There were only two problems.

He'd yet to catch a whiff of either the man he sought or Melissa Dalrymple.

And if he and Margaret got any more damn *businesslike* about the whole blasted thing he was going to have to hit something.

Low conversation hummed around them, punctuated by the clatter of dishes and an occasional burst of laughter. Their table, however, was silent.

They'd run out of inconsequential small talk two days ago.

There was only so much people could talk about that didn't skate along the edges of being a little too friendly and, potentially, too personal. Even in Dakota, the weather only stretched so far as a topic.

Not that there wasn't some pleasure, Margaret thought, in simply sitting across a table from him. Dusk shadowed the room, the lanterns too few to beat the night back completely. The dim light made his face look leaner, sharper, even more harshly beautiful.

His hands were sinewy and sure. Light winked off the knife blade as he sliced his meat. He tucked a bite into his mouth, chewed, and shook his head. "Still cooked it too much."

In spite of herself, and her scrupulously drawn boundaries, Margaret had learned a few things about Kieran in the last few days. He liked his meat rare, his coffee strong, and his vegetables not at all.

"Maybe you should just tell them not to bother killing it next time."

He smiled. "My mum always said the same thing."

"Your . . . mum?"

"You didn't think I had one?"

"Well . . ." She tried to imagine him with a homey, gray-haired lady fussing over him, calling him "dear" and reminding him to wear his gloves.

She failed completely. "You said you never knew your father. I just assumed they were both . . . gone."

"I've got one."

Businesslike limits bowed to curiosity. "So how is it you never knew your father, then?"

He paused, fork in hand. Probably debating whether he would answer her, for she doubted he'd discussed this with anyone before. Then he set the fork on the edge of his plate and leaned back in his chair, crossed one leg at the knee, and settled in for the telling.

"My mum was an O'Leary, from outside Dublin," he said. "Took herself off to London to work in a fine house. Met my father there."

"That would be Mr. McDermott."

"So she said." A smile flickered in eyes and quickly died. "Mr. McDermott was the senior footman and was, I'm told, both virile and unlucky. He caught a fever not three days after he married mum, and it killed him in less than a day. But not"—he lifted his hands, palms up, as if displaying himself for her inspection—"before she conceived me."

"Ah."

"London was too sad for her after his death, of course, filled with too many memories, so she boarded a ship for America. I was born two weeks before they pulled into New York, she always told me."

"She told you." An interesting way of putting it. "You don't believe her?"

"I believe I was born on the ship to New York." He shrugged carelessly. "As for the rest . . . she needs me to believe that's the way it happened, and so I do."

She studied him carefully, trying to discern some hurt, some regret, finding none. The circumstances of his birth either bothered him not at all, or he'd buried them so long ago that no hint of turbulence showed on his surface.

"I have no idea how she paid for her passage, and I don't think I want to know."

"And then?" she prompted. This was probably very foolish of her, probing beneath his admittedly very lovely surface. Far safer to see him only as a compelling stranger; much harder to forget him, once she knew him as a man. But the urge to find out what had formed him, what drove him, what made Kieran McDermott, was stronger than the part of her that wanted to retreat to her dreary and comfortable safety.

"I grew up in New York." He grinned. "Fancy houses again. She was just a maid at first, then

Mum worked herself up to housekeeper. Even with a growing son who didn't always stay tucked away in the servants' quarters where he belonged."

"How interesting it must have been. All the things and people you'd have the chance to see, growing up in a place like that," she said. "I've never lived in a house with more than one room."

"It's not so good," he said, shaking his head slightly. "To be young and angry and wanting, and to see all these wonderful things and know they're not yours, and there's no way they ever will be."

And there was the emotion she'd searched for before. Pain, regret, and loss so clear and fresh it seemed brand new. It called to her, too much, too strongly, an instinct for comfort that said *take this man in your arms and help him forget.*

As if a lonely old spinster could give Kieran McDermott anything he needed.

If she prodded now, even a little, and he was willing, he'd reveal something that mattered. Some clue that would allow her to glimpse inside this fascinating puzzle that was Kieran McDermott.

Except that the comfortable barrier between them, which they'd cautiously opened a crack, just might shatter. And surely that was most imprudent.

She needed to think more, before she allowed so much to change between them. To be certain it was safe to take such a big step.

"And is your mother still there? In New York?" Better to talk about his mother than to talk about him.

"Hmm?" He blinked at the change of topic, then looked relieved. "Oh, my mother. No, when I left

New York and started spending so much time traveling, she came west, so we could see each other more often. Got a job in Chicago, looking after a widowed judge. Retired two years ago."

On familiar ground now, he relaxed. "She has a small cottage, near Lake Michigan. The judge has been trying to get her to marry him for at least ten years, but she insists it's simply not proper for him to marry his housekeeper. Though why it's any more proper for them to live two weeks at his house, then two weeks at hers, I'll never understand."

Margaret's perception of Kieran's mother as a little white-haired lady with a starched apron and an Irish lilt collapsed immediately.

"Are you shocked?" he asked, smiling as if he rather hoped she was.

"I haven't decided yet." He'd revealed a bit of himself to her. Whether it was sensible or not, it seemed only fair that she return the favor. "My father had a lover, too."

He tilted his head, suddenly alert, listening. A good listener, Lucius had called him. Perhaps that was why it didn't seem so hard to say this, though she'd never formed the words out loud before.

"He was a terrible farmer. When they struck gold in Deadwood, I guess he thought it was his chance at last." The truly sad part of it was, she supposed, that it had been such a relief to see him leave. Easier to have him gone than having to tiptoe around all the time, trying to keep peace between him and her mother and him away from the liquor.

"He wasn't any better at finding gold, as it turned out, but he found another woman almost right away." And had wasted no time in writing Eleanor to tell her. Had he really cared for that other woman, she wondered now, or had his new lover simply been such a terribly effective way of hurting Eleanor that her father couldn't resist?

"Well," she went on, shaking off the musings because there'd never be an answer for them, "he got caught in a mining accident a year or so later. He was still with her when he died, because she sent us his effects. Never could figure out why she did that. Maybe she just didn't want to bother with them."

Sympathy was rich in his eyes, all the more devastating because it held not a trace of pity. "We have something in common, then."

No, she thought, for although his experiences had made him reckless and greedy for life, they'd made her scared and willing to settle.

Except settling, she was discovering, had been so much easier when she hadn't known, had only vaguely suspected, what her life lacked.

She was very much afraid that *life* was what her life lacked.

"Well," she said, wanting to move back to less unsettling topics, "I suppose we should try and figure out what to do next."

Kieran sat back in his chair with a sound of disgust. "I've made so little progress—"

"Excuse me for interrupting, but I wanted to introduce myself before we had to leave."

Kieran looked up to find Benjamin Lessing

standing beside their table, his thumbs tucked into the pockets of his gray vest.

He should have been pleased for the interruption. If there was one person in Redemption who knew everyone, and their financial situation, it was Benjamin Lessing. And, too, Kieran had skimmed far too close to revealing things that were far better left buried. Things like Cynthia and the reasons he'd left New York.

He was accustomed to giving nothing of himself away. But the simple act of telling Maggie his real reasons for being in Redemption somehow threatened to break wide open years of constraint, making it all the easier to imagine telling her everything.

So he should have welcomed Benjamin's arrival.

But his first thought was that he would have preferred being alone with Maggie.

"Miss Thayer." Lessing acknowledged Maggie briefly and just as quickly dismissed her. "I'm Benjamin Lessing," he said, extending his hand.

"Kieran McDermott." Lessing's handshake was firm, brief, and completely without nuance—a businessman's handshake, one used a thousand times without there being any sort of genuine welcome behind it.

"Oh, I know." Lessing chortled. "Most of what happens in Redemption gets back to me sooner or later."

Kieran had seen Lessing several times over the past few weeks but only at a distance, behind his desk in the bank or across a room. This was the first opportunity he'd had to study Benjamin up close.

There was nothing unusual about Benjamin, save his impeccable dress and grooming. He judged Lessing's age to be perhaps a bit more than his own. Light brown hair, sleek and cropped short. Clean shaven—ruthlessly so, without a hint of whisker-shadow darkening his cheeks. Weakly colored blue eyes, remarkable only for the way they held Kieran's gaze, boring into his own.

"And this is my assistant, Walter Cowdry." He gestured vaguely over his shoulder.

Cowdry. Kieran had heard little of the man. Late twenties, maybe, very much the sort who faded into the background—or who was paid well to create that illusion. He had striking green eyes, though—pity that William Dalrymple had been unable to remember his larcenous employee's eye color. That would have been nearly impossible to disguise—which was why, of course, the thief had worn thick, heavy-rimmed spectacles.

"Pleased to meet you," Kieran said automatically, all the while weighing the possibilities. Could either of these two be the Uncatchable Man? The assistant certainly appeared younger than the thief was supposed to be, but age could be faked to a certain extent. And Lessing—that rounded pot of a belly would have been harder to hide, but not impossible. Still, with a prosperous bank and mill, he hardly seemed to need the money.

"Is Ruth here?" Maggie asked. "I'd like to say hello."

"Oh, no. Walter and I had business to discuss, and that just bores her to tears. She stayed home tonight." Benjamin chuckled, a big, rolling, friendly sound that embraced his listeners, making it almost unnoticeable that he didn't even bother to glance Maggie's way.

And that didn't make Lessing dishonest, Kieran thought, much as he would have liked to believe it. Just the kind of man who didn't think most women were worth a whole lot of effort—foolish, yes, but not unusual.

"I just wanted to welcome you to Redemption, let you know that, if you need anything while you're here, I'd be more than happy to help." Lessing tapped his fingers against his belly. "Are you thinking to stay in town long?"

"I hadn't decided."

"Oh, course not, course not." Benjamin beamed at Maggie this time. "I can see that you found something here to catch your interest."

Maggie shot Kieran an abashed look before dropping her gaze to the tabletop. Color stained her cheeks, creating an unmistakable impression of a smitten, hopeful woman. Kieran found himself wondering how much of it was the role she'd taken on and how much of it was real, and wasn't at all sure what he wanted the answer to be.

"Yes," he agreed. "I'm getting to like it here very much."

Lessing's eyes narrowed almost imperceptibly. "So, what brought you here in the first place? I love this town, God knows, but it's not exactly on the way to anywhere, and we're not what you might call a destination all on our own."

And it's your town, isn't it? Kieran mused. *And you intend to make darn sure it stays that way.*

"Maybe I just like the sound of Redemption," he said slowly.

After a long moment Lessing nodded, apparently accepting Kieran's explanation. "I can understand that." He rocked back on his heels. "Well, I won't keep you any longer from your . . . meal. And I have things to attend to. If you'll excuse me." He nodded to them each in turn.

"Of course," Maggie said politely. "And please give my regards to your wife."

"I will."

He strolled away, Walter falling in step behind.

"What was that?" Maggie asked.

"What?"

"That 'I can stare longer without blinking or looking away than you can' thing. Was that one of those male contests, like seeing who can spit the farthest? Martha Ann told me about those."

Caught, Kieran grinned. "Yes."

"Really?" Maggie craned her neck to peer after Benjamin's departing figure. "Who won?"

He gave her a long, cool look. "Who do you think?"

"Oh, forgive me." She waved a hand, as if excusing her foolishness. "I don't know what I was thinking."

She—Kieran tried to find the right word for it, settled for *delighted*—Maggie delighted him. And, though it made the time they had to spend together a good deal more enjoyable than it could have been, it also distracted him from the job at hand.

"Now," he said, "before I try and figure out what to do next, would you like a piece of pie?"

"I already had one!"

"I know, but you didn't finish the crust. If you

only eat the filling, you have to eat two to make it equal one whole piece."

"I only ate the filling because I'm already stuffed." She puffed out her cheeks. "I'm beginning to think that this whole thing was simply a ruse, and you take some kind of perverse pleasure in trying to fatten me up."

"Aw, you figured it out." And wouldn't she be surprised, Kieran thought, to know how close that was to the truth? He remembered the limited supplies in her kitchen, and the thin, tensile strength of her body under his. He enjoyed watching her eat, the deep pleasure she took in having a full and delicious plate of food set before her. Enjoyed, too, seeing her face already growing slightly rounder, softening the clear angles of her cheekbones, fading the blue-tinged shadows beneath her eyes.

"Does that mean you don't want any more?"

"No more!" She crossed her arms on the table and leaned forward to smile at him. "So what are you going to do next?"

"Hell if I know. I've checked out every damn house in town."

He hated this, she thought. Didn't deal at all well with frustration and failure. A week ago she might not have recognized the signs, he hid them so well. A bare tightening of his jaw, the way his hand curled into a fist and clenched. And, always, that hint of old pain in his eyes.

He'd told her he took on these jobs over the years because he simply had nothing else to do, and he was well suited to the task. She wondered if he realized how much he claimed them as his own, and if he recognized the hurt they caused him or if he had it too efficiently boxed away.

"Are you certain they're here?" she asked.

"Yes. I . . . no." His knuckles whitened. "Every bit of evidence I found—it wasn't much, but it all pointed to Redemption."

"Have you ever been wrong before?"

He tilted his head, giving it some thought. "No."

"Then they must be here."

His mouth softened, almost easing into a smile, an acknowledgment of her faith in him.

"I'd assumed they were together," he said, thinking it through as he spoke. "And that who they were would be fairly obvious. It must be a man leaves town regularly without anybody thinking anything odd about it. But of the half-dozen men who fit that description, none of them have any young women under their roof. Or anywhere nearby, far as I can tell."

"If he wasn't living right in town, though, maybe no one would notice if he had a girl stashed at his place. At least, not for quite some time."

"No," he agreed. "But most farmers can't leave their places for stretches of time. Unless he has a partner, of course, but he didn't seem the kind to be willing to share. Even when he used a gang for a holdup, he recruited them right beforehand and cut them loose after. I talked to a couple of them who got caught after a bank robbery in Milwaukee. They were pissed as hell that he left them holding the bag, but even so, they couldn't tell me much of any use."

Her head bent, lost in thought, Maggie fingered

the handle of her knife. She'd taken to wearing her hair differently since he started squiring her about town, dressed high in front but with a loose swath looping down her back. It shone quietly in the lamplight, not a bright eye-popping gleam but something softer, subtler, like brushed gold. Even through his frustration, he couldn't help but notice how nice it looked.

"Maggie?"

"Hmm?"

"What are you thinking about? You seem very far away."

Her hazy expression cleared. "What about Stephen Dodge?"

"Stephen Dodge," he repeated, trying to place the name. "I don't think I've come across him."

"No reason you should. He's not around much." Alert now, she ticked off everything she knew. "He showed up here, oh, maybe seven or eight years ago. Nobody knows from where; he's not the social type. Got himself a quarter section about four miles north of town. Kind of a strange choice, actually. It hasn't got good water, so he's got to lug it in when the weather's dry."

"Know anything else about him?"

"Very little. He comes into town every now and then for supplies, and then no one will see him for months."

"Neighbors?"

"Hardly any. As I said, there's not good water up that way, and you're running hard against Indian country. Be foolish to take land around there when there's plenty closer to the river."

It wasn't much, Kieran thought. But it was more than he'd had before. "All right," he said, coming to his feet. "You give me directions, I'll drop you off at home, and then I'll head on out there, see what I can find."

"I don't think so."

"What do you mean?" He counted out a few bills and dropped them on the table. "Is there something else I should know?"

"It's just not that easy to find," Margaret said, "and you're still not all that familiar with this area. I doubt you'll be able to find it by yourself. Especially not in the dark."

"I'll manage."

"I think I'd better come with you."

Without even thinking about it, she turned so he could help her shrug into her coat. Amazing how easily, automatically, they'd fallen into these habits, like a couple who'd been performing these small services for each other for years.

"I'm not sure what I'm going to find, Maggie. It would be safer if you didn't come along."

She knew that. Could still hardly believe she'd made the offer, and, more, had every intention of being most insistent about it.

A little quiver of fear already curled in her stomach. But it was getting harder and harder to leave him at the end of each evening, to go back to her empty house. Even with Arne there, though she'd never had a pet before and quickly grew to love his fuzzy warmth and throaty purr, that barren room was still much less appealing than spending a little more time with Kieran.

There was the lure of watching him work, too, of seeing him focus all that formidable drive and will without the necessity of disguising it because there were others around who might begin to wonder.

Most of all, she hoped that if she went with him, he was much less likely to go charging in, putting himself in danger. For, if the Uncatchable Man had eluded Kieran, not to mention all the others sent after him, for this long, he must be a clever and brutal man. And the thought of Kieran racing blindly, albeit heroically, into danger made her sick to her stomach.

She could all too easily imagine Kieran risking himself in order to rescue Melissa Dalrymple. Although she worried about the girl, too, she had every intention of making sure Kieran protected himself in the process.

She slipped a hand beneath her hair, tugging it from beneath her coat collar, and turned to him. "I'm going with you."

His expression was hard, almost angry. Once, that might have frightened her. Now, though there were other things about his presence in her life that scared her, his anger did not.

"When we began this, I promised you would be safe," he said.

She smiled, hoping she looked less worried than she felt. For, although she had every faith he would protect her, the habits and concerns of a lifetime were very hard to ignore.

"I will be," she said.

10

"There it is," Margaret said.

Light bled down from the big white disk of the moon, clearly revealing the small tarpapered shack that squatted on the empty land. A good moon for searching out a lone shack on the prairie; a bad one for sneaking up on someone without being seen.

"Not much of a place, is it?"

"No."

The shack was no more substantial than an oversized crate. Flattened tin cans had been hammered, overlapping, to cover half the outside walls, gleaming like giant fish scales. Kieran would have been willing to bet that every meal added another can or two. By next winter, perhaps, the place would be better insulated against the cold. It looked like it needed it.

"You said the Dalrymples were wealthy, didn't you?" Maggie asked doubtfully.

"Yes."

"Hard to imagine her in a place like this."

"It is." The bright moonlight did nothing to soften or pretty the place up. Only compared to the rickety, windowless shed that tilted several feet behind it did the shack look like it might offer reasonable shelter.

Old barrels and rusty cans had been placed all over the ground, open mouths upturned, waiting for rain; Kieran could catch distant glints of tin. Quiet thickly blanketed the earth. Even what small sounds there were, the screech of a night bird, the steady whisper of the wind through the grass, the thudding of the horse's hooves, were quickly absorbed into the hush, serving more to emphasize the quiet than dispel it.

"What now?" Margaret asked. "It doesn't look like there's anyone around."

"I'm going to take a look." He laid down the reins. He'd rented the buggy from the livery earlier in the week, along with an uninterested gray gelding—a man couldn't be expected to "court" properly on horseback, and Charlie didn't much take to being in harness. "You stay here. If anything happens, I want you to get out of here as fast as you can."

"If anything happens?" she repeated, her voice going high and thin. "Like what?"

He shrugged negligently. "Just something unexpected. Nothing to worry about."

A strip of bare land separated the place where he'd stopped the buggy from the shack. The ground had been turned at some point; near the rig, chunks of dirt were just visible, threaded with

dead stalks. It looked like it had once been cultivated, maybe for flax, by a farmer who'd long since
lost interest in his crop. To their left sprawled
untouched prairie, new grass pushing up between
the tangle left from last summer. Too bad it hadn't
had a few weeks more of growth; the grass might
have been long enough to provide some decent
cover.

"Actually," he decided, "it would be better if you
got down in the buggy and hid. That way if someone comes along, it'll look empty."

"You want me to hunch down and hide in the
bottom of the buggy, but there's nothing to worry
about," she said flatly.

She had him there, and he grinned at her. He
pulled back the side of his duster, revealing the pistol tucked at his waist. "There really isn't."

Only a man would be foolish enough to think a
gun would be reassuring.

Her hand lay on the seat between them. He covered it with his palm, chilled from the spring air,
and she caught her breath. Though, occasionally, as
he'd guided her down the street or helped her into
the buggy, he'd touched her, those had been
respectful, casual, and completely impersonal con-
tacts. This was the first time, since that night in her
bed, that he'd touched her deliberately and with
promise.

She hadn't realized how much she wanted it.

"Maggie," he said softly, "this is what I do."

Precisely what worried her.

He stood and hopped down, making the wagon
tremble, and walked toward the shack. Upright,

boldly, making no attempt to hide himself from the harsh illumination of that huge, early summer moon.

Margaret cast a longing glance at the snug space at her feet, the curve of wood in front and the seat behind, surely high and dark enough to shield her from the sight of anyone who wasn't right on top of her. Sighing in regret, she clambered down and hurried to catch up with Kieran.

He stopped walking. "Get back in the wagon."

"If there's really nothing to be concerned about, what difference does it make if I come along with you?"

"Who's in charge of this investigation, anyway?"

"I didn't know anyone was *in charge*," she said, attempting a light tone even though her pulse pounded in her throat.

"Good point." An unsettling gleam in his eyes, he crossed his arms before his chest and studied her, as if trying to make up his mind about something.

"If you're thinking about throwing me over your shoulder and carrying me back to the buggy, let me just say two things," she said quickly. "First, if I make a lot of noise—not that I'd be foolish enough to purposely give you away, mind, but who can tell what I might do when I'm surprised?—whoever's in that shack, if there is someone there, is going to know you're coming real quick-like. Two, as near as I can tell, there's nothing in that buggy to tie me up with."

He felt the smile well up inside him and just managed to hide it. She obviously had no idea that he knew a dozen—maybe two dozen—ways to keep her restrained, quiet, and out of sight.

But he wasn't going to. She was a grown woman, and if she'd decided she was ready to take a few chances, to take a step or two beyond that safety she'd so carefully built on that pitiful little farm, wasn't that her choice?

He remembered when he'd first started on this path, all those years he'd sought vengeance and little else. His mother, and those few people he called friends, had all tried to stop him. Had spent days yelling, pleading, threatening, trying to make him change his mind.

It had made no difference to him. He'd done what he had to do despite their protests. In turn, he'd give Maggie the respect denied him—he'd trust her to know her own mind and follow her own instincts. Even more so, because back then his judgment had been clouded by rage and grief, while there was no reason hers should be anything but completely clear.

Also, he'd absolutely no intention of letting one single hair on her head be harmed.

"All right. We'll go around to the left over there, where there's at least some grass for cover. I want to come up on the side of the shack. With any luck, there's a window, and I can get a look at what's inside. Stay behind me, and if anything happens, the first thing you do is *drop*."

"Drop," she repeated, knowing her answering smile was a mite wobbly. Hard to tell if that thrumming in her veins was excitement or fear, though she suspected it was a little of both. "Got it."

He glided sideways, his eyes always turned to the shack, his footsteps barely whispering through the few inches of new grass. Although she tried to copy him, her own motions seemed outrageously loud to her, punctuated by the distinct crunch and crackle of last year's dried stalks.

She was not a large woman. It seemed most unreasonable that she made so much more noise than he did.

The sudden thud of wood on wood—a door whipped open and resounding off a wall?—stopped her in her tracks.

The sharp crack of a rifle froze her completely.

She was on the ground before she even knew Kieran had moved. The impact drove the air from her lungs, the taste of dirt and fear strong in her mouth as he sheltered her body with his own.

"Guess there was someone in there after all," he whispered. "I thought I told you to drop."

More shots, and slight thuds of the bullets peppering the dirt all around them, the two sounds so close together they were almost indistinguishable.

She tried to ask "What now?" but all that came out was a harsh little croak.

"Okay," he said, his voice still low, mouth so near to her that, as he spoke, his breath swirled over her ear, "I'm going to roll over that way a little. When I stand up, you start making your way back to the wagon—stay down!—and head for town right away as fast as you can get that gray to go."

"But—" *But* was all she could manage. She'd spent a lifetime avoiding fear and had little experience with it. Somehow she'd gotten the impression that terror caused energy to surge, made you stronger and faster and wild, so you could escape, like a rabbit cornered by a coyote. Instead, she felt like every muscle and bone in her body had locked into place and refused to move. Her heart, her lungs, her brain, all paralyzed in that single instant when she'd heard the first shot.

"But nothing. Don't worry about me, I've been in a hundred spots worse than this. But it'll be a lot easier if I don't have to worry about you. Got it?"

She tried to nod in assent, to whisper yes, but achieved only a grunt.

"Here we go," he said.

With the sudden release of his weight, air rushed into her lungs. Her head down, surrounded by the thick grass, she couldn't see anything. But she could hear Kieran, the rustle of grass as he rolled, the tiny plops of his weight hitting the earth, all still underscored with the horrid report of shots, slower now, evenly spaced, as if intended to be more cautionary than lethal.

Unless, of course, Kieran rolled right into their path.

He'd gotten perhaps twenty yards away from her, Kieran figured. It should be enough.

Bits of dirt sprayed no more than two feet to his left, and he flinched.

"Stop!" he shouted and jumped to his feet. *"Stop!"*

He heard the ratchet of a bullet being chambered, then nothing more for a long moment while he waited, muscles loose and senses attentive.

"Give me one good reason why I shouldn't kill you right now." Dodge—if that really was who'd shot at them—had a smooth voice, colored with just a touch of the South. He wasn't angry, Kieran judged, or driven by any other emotion he could detect.

Off to his right, Maggie was making little squeaks of fear, though they were soft enough and far enough away that he doubted Dodge could hear them. Poor scared Maggie; she simply wasn't used to being shot at.

And she didn't know what Kieran knew: that, although Dodge himself was invisible in the darkness that cloaked the cabin's interior, the dull gleam of the crushed tin cans clearly outlined the doorway he must be standing in. Kieran, clothed in black and dark gray against the dark shadowed flatness of the land, would be far more difficult to discern.

Nor did she knew that his left pocket had a hole carefully slit into it, and that his hand hovered at the butt of his gun. If Dodge fired again, so would he.

And he was a better and faster shot.

"Well," Kieran said thoughtfully, as if he'd been mulling it over, "it'd really be an awful lot of work to bury me out here. Ground's mighty hard. But you couldn't just leave me lying there bleeding—it'd draw coyotes for sure."

Dodge gave a bark of laughter. "Ain't heard that one before." He must have taken a step out of the door; Kieran caught a brief flash of moonlight on the rifle barrel. "And you sure is a bold one, I'll give you that. You lost?"

"Only if you're not Stephen Dodge."

"Who are you?" he asked, voice emptied of all amusement. There was emotion there now, something harsh, fright or anger or simply the vigilance of hard experience. Without the cues of Dodge's stance or eyes, Kieran couldn't tell for sure.

"Kieran McDermott," he said. His knees flexed, preparing. If this was the man he sought, he might well try to gun him down right now.

The man stepped farther away from his shack. Kieran began to pick out the contours of his form; a leg here, the curve of his shoulder there. "I heard o' you," he said flatly.

What now? Kieran had no answer for that. He was not unknown in certain circles, but Redemption was far from his usual haunts. It would have been better for now if no one in Redemption knew of how Kieran often spent his time. It would make them curious and careful; both would complicate his task.

"Step out here's so I can see you."

"Only if you'll do the same."

They approached each other warily, like two predators who recognized their own kind but had yet to decide whether the other constituted a threat—this time.

Dodge looked to be in far better shape than his shack, Kieran noted immediately. Sturdy build under a simple knit shirt, flapping untucked over canvas pants as if he'd been interrupted in the act of dressing. Uneven but not unattractive features. Dodge carried the rifle across his body, not an immediate danger but a clear and quickly employable warning.

"You said you'd heard of me."

"Got a cousin, down in St. Paul. Daughter got herself all twisted up about a rich pretty boy whose daddy owned a big store down there. Made her all sorts of promises, but when she told him he was gonna be a daddy, too, he gave her ten dollars and told her to go away and not bother him again. And if she ever tried, he'd make sure my cousin lost his job in the flour mill. Made a couple other threats, too, I heard."

Kieran ran through his mental gallery of remembered faces, some young, some old, all desperately troubled, and clicked on a frightened girl with pretty blue eyes. "Mary Dodge."

"Guess it's really you, then, if you know her name."

"Yes. How is she?"

"Okay." But Kieran noted that Stephen didn't relax his stance, keeping his rifle ready. "Got married last year, neighbor's boy, who didn't seem to mind claiming the baby as his own, not when Mary come with such a big dowry. How'd you manage that, anyway?"

Kieran shrugged, as if it had required no more effort than slapping a mosquito. "Mary's . . . friend . . . had a few other things that he'd rather his parents not know about. He was willing to pay rather handsomely to make certain they never found out." Kieran smiled, remembering. He'd enjoyed that one. "He would have married her, even, but by then Mary no longer wanted him. Smart girl, that niece of yours."

"You here on another job?"

"Yes."

Suddenly Dodge's tension increased palpably. His shoulders lowered, the barrel of the rifle swung just a fraction Kieran's way. "What kinda job?" he asked, voice menacing despite its strictly even tone.

How interesting, Kieran thought. There was something here, but was it what he sought?

"I'm not all that comfortable standing around with a rifle on me. Mind if we go inside to talk?" Though he didn't dare glance Maggie's way, he'd been listening for the sound of the wagon heading out. Nothing. Maybe she was too scared to reveal her position that obviously; if he got Dodge into the shack, she could escape.

"I mind."

"All right," Kieran agreed easily, pretending the refusal didn't disturb him at all. He didn't want Dodge speculating on why Kieran might be anxious to get him inside.

"So what you doin' here?" The rifle bore edged another inch forward.

How to play it? The simplest, Kieran decided, closing his hand around the butt of his pistol, just in case Dodge was the thief after all and decided that the best response to Kieran's explanation was a bullet. "Got a missing girl, some missing money, and a real unhappy father."

"Oh." Dodge's defensive stance eased immediately, and he loosened his grip on his gun, letting the butt end rest on the ground. "Why you out here, then?"

"Just checking everything out." He gestured to

the shack. "Seemed like a good place to hide someone. You're pretty isolated."

"Sorry I can't help you—in consideration of
what you done for my cousin's girl, and all—but I
don't know anythin' about it." Now that he'd
apparently decided Kieran wasn't a threat, Dodge
clearly wanted him to be gone. He edged back
toward his shack.

"Are you sure? Maybe something you've seen,
though you didn't mark it at the time. A man traveling with a younger woman who didn't look to be
related to him. Maybe even something . . ." Kieran
chose his next words carefully, probing for a reaction, "*sick* about their relationship. A grown man
lusting after a young girl."

"Nope."

Not a flicker of anger. Dodge was either not
involved or very, very good at hiding it—which, of
course, the man he searched for would be.

"You're sure."

"I'm sure. Now I'm gonna have to ask you to
leave. Not to be unsociable, but mornin' comes
pretty early, and I got work to do."

"Of course." Kieran pointedly looked around
him, at the land that couldn't even be called a
neglected farm because it had never gotten worked
enough to earn the title of farm in the first place.
"But answer me this—why are you out here, in the
middle of nowhere, on this sorry piece of land?
People in town say you disappear, sometimes for
weeks at a time. Where do you go?"

"Why do you care?"

"Call it curiosity."

The sound Dodge made might have been laughter, though Kieran wasn't optimistic enough to label it that.

"I ain't gonna answer your question because you're damned curious."

"I answered your question, told you who I was and why I was here. Call it a fair trade."

A distant scream pierced the night, a small animal falling prey to its hunter. The wind picked up, a single cold gust that rippled his coat and fell quiet again.

"Maybe I got a lover," Dodge said at last. "And maybe she's married. And when she tells me it's clear, I go. Don't suppose you'd know much about somethin' like that."

"No." Kieran knew more, far more, about it than Stephen Dodge would ever suspect. Or anyone else would ever know. "I'll be leaving now." There'd be nothing else to learn here tonight.

Kieran never turned his back on another man—particularly one with a gun—if he could help it, so he backed slowly away. He wanted to run and search for Maggie, but, so far, Dodge had given no indication that he even knew of Maggie's presence, and Kieran would rather keep it that way if he could.

Perhaps ten more yards, and Dodge's silhouette melded completely with the dark rectangle of his doorway. Kieran heard a muffled whump, as if Dodge had closed the door behind him, but that could be easily faked.

Kieran gained the place where he thought he'd left her, near where the grass met the churned earth of the abandoned field. Hard to be certain, but there seemed to be a shallow depression in the thick prairie grass. No Maggie, though. Perhaps she'd made her way back to the buggy after all.

"Maggie," he whispered, loud as he dared.

He zigzagged toward his rig, making bigger and bigger sweeps through the tall grass.

Not once when Dodge had held a gun on him had Kieran felt even a stirring of fear. He'd been in similar situations too often and was too adept at escaping them. Though, he admitted to himself, a good part of his skill at survival could be chalked up to the fact that he rarely cared all that much about the outcome. His opponents always protected themselves first and never believed that Kieran would really risk his own life so easily. So they'd rarely been able to predict his next move, an advantage he'd relied upon for years.

It would catch up with him someday, and he'd accepted that fact long ago.

But now, as he called louder and still received no answer, something unfamiliar and ugly chilled his belly. He'd been certain Maggie was not hurt by Dodge's random shots. Could he have been that wrong?

He found her already on the front seat of the buggy. She was hunched over, curled in on herself like a frightened kitten. In her deep brown coat and dark bonnet, she'd been nearly invisible until he was almost upon her.

"Maggie? Are you hurt?"

No answer.

He climbed up to take his seat beside her; she didn't even acknowledge his presence.

"Maggie?" he repeated again gently, concerned the shock of being fired upon had been too much for her. "Why didn't you answer when I called your name? I was worried about you, Maggie."

She whipped her head around then. The moonlight struck her face fully, and the look she gave him should have sliced right through his chest as easily as Dodge's bullets could have, her mouth set, eyes sparking.

Margaret Thayer was killing mad.

11

After that, Maggie didn't again acknowledge his existence. Didn't answer him, didn't look at him, didn't so much as blink at him. Considering the way she'd glared at him, Kieran counted himself lucky. Finally, he dragged a woolen blanket from beneath the seats, draped it around her shoulders, and started for home.

They'd traveled nearly a mile when the first hit came, the thud of her closed fist against his shoulder. A minute later, a slap against his chest. He pulled the gelding to a stop. The soft blows came faster now. Thud. Whap. Whump. Another thud.

He made no attempt to stop her, just let her pound him around the shoulders and chest. She had to get it out somehow. If she really wanted to hurt him, he figured, she'd be hitting higher—or lower. And a whole lot harder.

He couldn't have said how long it lasted before she slumped on the seat beside him, finally spent, her head sagging and her breathing ragged. Cautiously, uncertain whether it was the right thing to do but knowing of nothing else, he gathered her in his arms and pulled her close.

"Shh," he said. "It'll be all right."

"I . . ." Her words came out as small explosions, muffled against his chest. "Oh, I *hated* that."

"I know. You'll never have to do it again." He knew the motions and words of comfort. He'd used them often enough. For sometimes when he'd set out on a particular task, the answers he found were not the ones he'd hoped for. And so he'd have to go back to the person who'd contacted him in the first place—that desperate, hopeful person—and tell them that, this time, he'd been too late to fix it.

But this was different—he wanted more than to go through the motions of consolation. He needed to soothe her so much he could scarcely breathe with it and felt echoes of her pain as his own.

"You just—you just stood *up*, you idiot man! While he was *shooting*, and you popped right up so he could kill you!" she said, incredulous.

"I told him to stop."

That earned him another slap, a loud flat one on the left side of his chest. He'd thought it was terror that propelled her anger; instead, it seemed more as if she'd . . . been worried about him. He was unexpectedly and quite deeply touched.

"They usually do, you know," he told her.

"You're not serious."

"Yup. People are curious. They want to know who's after them, and why, and how much they know. They want to find out answers, before the only person they can get answers from is dead. It almost always works."

"Almost! What if it doesn't?"

He'd no intention of answering that one. If he did, she'd go scurrying away to the other side of the buggy seat so fast he'd be left hugging nothing but air and probably topple right over on his nose.

"I don't know how you do this," she said. "I thought I was going to be sick to my stomach. Come to think of it, I might yet."

"Warn me if you are, okay?"

"You don't deserve fair warning."

"Probably not." She started to settle in; Kieran could feel her relaxing against him, her body softening, her head shifting slightly until it fit just right in the curve of his neck.

"But it has its moments, you know," he said.

"Facing death? And here I thought you were a reasonably intelligent man. I haven't the faintest idea what those benefits could possibly be."

"Don't you feel it?" He couldn't help it; his hand stroked her back, eased up over her shoulder and down again of its own accord. Not such a terrible thing to do, when there were so many layers between his hand and her skin. Damn it! There were way too many layers between his hand and her skin. "Your heart beats harder. The blood fairly rushes through your veins, the air churns in your lungs. Everything is clearer, sharper. It tastes more, smells stronger, *is* more. Don't you feel it?"

And suddenly it was there, strong, tempting, shredding the rest of her fear. Feeling remarkably like passion.

"You're not even breathing hard."

"Perhaps I'm just too used to it; it doesn't have the same effect on me anymore." But a strain had entered his voice, deepening and enriching the tone.

She really should move away, she thought. But she'd had a hard night; didn't she deserve a little scrap of comfort? He had such lovely strong arms.

She compromised by changing the subject but staying put. "Did you really do that?" she asked softly. "Help Mr. Dodge's niece?"

"You heard that?"

"Mmm," she said.

Her sound of agreement was much too similar to a hum of pleasure for Kieran's peace of mind. And body.

"The wind was just right," she continued. "I caught most of your conversation. Did you?"

"Yeah."

"That was very nice of you."

He wasn't unfamiliar with this, that shadow of admiration and hero worship in her voice. When he was successful at a job, the people he'd helped were usually grateful, sometimes embarrassingly so. If he was the slightest bit worthy of Maggie's esteem, he'd tell her the truth right now—that he was no kind of hero, only a man attempting to use what time he had left in the world to make up, just a little, for all that he'd done so wrong. Hell, it wasn't as if he had anything else to do with his life.

He should tell her. But he'd fought so hard, every moment he spent with her these last few days, not to touch her. And now here she was in his arms, and she felt so good, and he didn't want to let her go. Not yet. Didn't want her to greet him with that slight reticence, that tiny shading of fear and revulsion that he knew she would, had she known the truth about him and all the things he'd done. About the dark side that went along with whatever good he managed to do. A necessary side, but far from a pretty one.

And so he did what he rarely did—he indulged himself. He kept his mouth shut, and he kept her close.

"And what about the rest?" she asked. "Do you think he told you the truth?"

"Maybe. It could be Dodge. He has the opportunity, certainly. And he was definitely hiding something." Reluctantly, he pulled back a little, torn between wanting to feel her in his arms and the desire to see her face in shadows and moonlight. He kept one hand lightly on her shoulder, a slight compensation. "He definitely didn't want us inside his house."

"There could be any number of reasons for that."

"True." Though he knew it was too far away to see it, he glanced in the direction of that pitiful shack. "It's hard to reconcile the Uncatchable Man with that place. He wants recognition, wants people to acknowledge what he's done. I can't put what I know of him together with this, being entirely alone out in the middle of nowhere."

"And with all that money, why would he live in a place like that, anyway?"

"Because no one would ever suspect. He might

not spend all that much time there, just a stopping point between thefts. And we don't know what it's like inside, remember?"

"It can't possibly be good enough to make up for the outside," Maggie said. "But you're just talking through it, aren't you? You believe him. About the lover."

He tried to sort through the tangle of knowledge and emotion, wondering if Dodge's words about his married lover had cut too close to home for Kieran to judge them properly. "Yeah, I believe him."

"Me too," she agreed. Her laugh surprised him, an unexpected bright bubble of sound in the night. "Your mother. My father. Melissa Dalrymple. And now even Stephen Dodge and his mysterious woman. Do you suppose I am the last person in the entire country to take a lover?"

That's it, Kieran thought, and gave in without a struggle. What more could a man be expected to take?

He brought his hands up, cradling her face, and she stilled. "We could fix that," he murmured.

Her pulse stuttered and picked up speed. How easily he did that, Margaret marveled. It took nothing more than a word, a look, the slightest of touches. As if her body responded more readily to his thoughts than her own.

Worse, she wasn't entirely certain she minded if it did.

"Are you blushing? There's not enough light to pick up colors," he said. "Hard to believe that you're not pinking up a little."

"I'm not."

His fingers moved against her cheek, her jaw-line. "Your skin is awfully warm, though. Like it's heating up."

"Getting shot at tends to put things in perspective," she insisted. "Maybe it cured me and I'll never blush again."

"What a waste that would be. We'd better experiment a little and test it out."

And then he kissed her. Openmouthed, all lips and breath and emotion and nothing else, a tentative exploration. Sweetness, restraint, tenderness, that somehow seemed so much more powerful than mere passion, because it involved the heart and soul as well as the body.

"What was that?" she whispered, dazed, when he finally lifted his head.

"I think," he said, as softly as the stroke of his thumbs along her cheek, "that was our first kiss."

"Our first kiss?"

"Mmm-hmm. We had a second kiss, and even a twenty-second." She sensed his smile as much as saw it. "But I'm not sure we ever had a first one. About time, don't you think?"

"Oh." It was all too confusing, and neither her brain nor her heart seemed willing to sort it all out. "Kieran, what are we?"

"I like you." His fingers slipped down, rested against her neck. "I want you," he said, a statement, a plea, an invitation.

But, try as they might, neither one of them could envision a time and place where there could be anything more between them than this. For, in the end, he would go and she would stay and that would be that.

"It isn't enough, is it?" he asked.

As the *want* beat hard and tempting in her, oh, how she longed for it to be. "No."

In the end, Kieran was the one who made the wise choice and pulled back, surprising them both. One last brush of his fingertips along her jaw, and he slid over on the seat and took up the reins. "We'd better go."

He clicked to his horse, the buggy jolted, and they rolled toward town.

Though Stephen Dodge lived north of Redemption and Margaret east, they had to go back through the center of town to reach Margaret's house, turning and following the river, because no roads ran directly across the unsettled countryside.

It wasn't a quick trip under the best of conditions. At night, it took twice the time, for the road—which, where Kieran came from, wouldn't be called a road at all—was pocked and rutted, and they had to drive slowly.

Margaret slept at night. She worked hard during the day, and the few times she stayed awake long past sunset, it was usually to nurse a sick parent or animal, turning the hours around midnight into a blur of fatigue and endless worry.

Now, she found herself unwillingly fascinated by the night.

Perhaps it had something to do with the man who rode beside her. After that unsettling talk—

and kiss—they didn't speak again, but his presence overwhelmed her. It sharpened her senses, heightened the sounds, sweetened the smells, much as he'd claimed danger could.

He wanted her. The memory of his words seemed as essential to her as breath, and every bit as sustaining.

But the night also drew her. A softening flowed just under the crisp coolness of the spring air, the promise of approaching summer. The sky shimmered with stars, so big, so bright. The steady, soothing clop of the horse's hooves beat beneath the murmur of the wind. And duties and chores and boundaries seemed very far away.

Redemption looked unfamiliar so late at night, the houses taking on personalities of their own; solid, staid, cheerful, depressed. Here and there a light flared in a window, and Margaret speculated on the stories behind them. That one, on the second floor of a sturdy brick house—perhaps a nightmare had awakened a little boy, and his mother had lit the lantern to banish the dark's terrors. And there, a weak light shone in one of the rooms over Chaney's Store. Probably Oliver's daughter Anna had a new beau and couldn't sleep for the excitement, and instead had turned to the latest *Harper's Bazaar* for distraction.

Heavens, Margaret thought, smiling at herself. When had she gotten so fanciful?

They reached the river and turned east on Front Street. They passed Red Fred's Saloon, still in full swing. Light and music spilled out onto the street, quickly followed by a reeling drunk. The commotion and liveliness of the saloon contrasted sharply with the quiet restraint of the rest of the town. She'd no idea Red Fred's did such a lively business.

Kieran and she hadn't said a word to each other since he started them toward town again. There might be something between them, but they couldn't go backward and dared not go forward, so there didn't seem much to say. But when they passed the saloon, Maggie spoke without thinking. "Is it always like that?"

Surprised that she'd breached the silence, Kieran glanced at her. The light from the saloon's windows allowed him to see her clearly for the first time since they'd left for Dodge's. She looked a little worse for the wear. Dirt streaked her left temple and her hair straggled down her shoulders. A stalk of grass poked right out of what remained of her topknot like a bizarre hair ornament. He decided not to mention it.

He really hadn't been sure she'd ever speak to him again. First he'd gotten her scared practically out of her drawers at Dodge's. Then he'd kissed her like he meant it—which he did—but he'd been completely unable to give her any promises at all.

Hell, he wouldn't talk to him either.

"What did you say?"

"Is Red Fred's always like that at night?"

"Pretty much."

"Where do all those men come from? Don't they have families to get home to?"

"The cattle spreads west of here, a few of them. But some of the rest have families, I guess."

She made a *hmph* of disapproval. "I suppose

you spend all the time you're not with me in there, too."

"Some," he admitted.

She frowned.

"But I'm working when I'm there," he put in quickly. "Investigating. Asking questions."

"Uh-uh." She sniffed primly, but mischief sparked in her eyes.

Thank God, Kieran thought. What he'd told her earlier was the truth—he did like her. It bothered him that the *wanting* seemed to be getting in the way of the *liking*. Though he couldn't seem to do anything about the wanting part, neither act on it nor get rid of it, he still didn't want to give up the liking.

But it seemed she'd decided to forgive him. He was so damn relieved he almost kissed her in gratitude—but then, kissing was what had gotten him in trouble in the first place.

If he couldn't kiss her, he'd have to do the next best thing.

"You forgot to answer me," he said. "Back there, when I kissed you, I asked if you blushed. Did you?"

"I am now," she admitted.

He grinned, and the silence that fell between them this time was a good deal more comfortable than the last.

They left the east end of Redemption, nearing the mill grounds. The mill itself was new, built only four years before when Lessing had declared the old one inadequate and expanded the operation. It stood three stories high, built of the brick Benjamin had shipped up from St. Louis. Moonlight gleamed dully on the rows of windows. Kieran could barely make out the wooden towers on each corner of the building—stairwells in front, toilet towers in back, jutting out over the river.

Cottages and small outbuildings scattered the grounds around the mill, holding offices, storage facilities, and living quarters for the workers. At the far end, hugging the river, the mill laid claim to an unusually large grove of cottonwoods, supposedly the biggest stand of trees along the Missouri or its tributaries anywhere in the territories.

Kieran stopped the buggy and studied the place. All the buildings, including the boardinghouses and cottages, were dark; morning came early and reluctantly for the mill's workers.

"Maggie, do you know how many people work there?"

"Hmm." She'd read something about that in a recent edition of the *Redemption Journal*, in an interview with Benjamin Lessing about the difficulty of getting enough quality wool and his plans to start grazing sheep on a thousand acres north of town. "A hundred and fifty or so, I believe."

"How many women?"

"More than half, certainly."

Kieran slapped the reins against his palm. "She's got to be there."

"In the mill?" It was hardly the kind of life a pampered young woman would be drawn to.

"I've looked everyplace else." Kieran shook his head. "I should have seen it sooner, but I kept assuming I'd find them together. She left with him, and they were seen together as far west as Yankton."

"If something happened to separate them, wouldn't she just go home?"

"Maybe she's too ashamed. She helped the man steal a good chunk of her father's money, after all." There'd been something wrong about this whole search, right from the start. Even now, though he felt closer, something still felt . . . off. He kept trying to pull in all the threads and tie them together, and they kept slipping out of his hands. He couldn't put his finger on what exactly bothered him so much, and that angered him. "Hell, if I could just get to her to tell her . . . I talked to William Dalrymple for hours. He wants his daughter back more than anything in the world."

Maggie looked at the dark hulk of the mill. In the darkness, it loomed large and solid over everything around it, taking on a distinct air of menace. She should be happy that Kieran would soon rescue a young girl from that place and bring her home to the safety and love of her father. But all she could think of was, *He won't need my help anymore. And when he finds her, then he'll go.*

She tried to imagine her life when this was all over. No longer waking up knowing that, later in the day, he'd come to take her "courting." Not spending each moment with him breathless and shaky because maybe, just maybe, he'd take it in his head to kiss her . . . and she'd let him. Never again having him tease her, his eyes lighting up when her cheeks went hot with color.

He'd been in her life for only a few, brief weeks.

And she was very much afraid, and almost as certain, that he'd be in it for the rest of it. That missing him would take it over in the way that knowing him did now.

"What are you going to do?" she asked.

He snapped the reins over the gelding's head, signaling him to start walking again.

"It looks like," he said, "that it's time for me to get a job."

12

~~~~~~~~~~~~~~

Spit-shined and polished, his hair still
damp from a fresh combing, Kieran presented himself at the offices of the Lessing Mill first thing the
next morning.

A small brick building perhaps a hundred yards
from the mill housed the offices—just far enough
away that the clamor of machinery and work was a
pleasant, industrious hum instead of an annoyance.
He gave what he hoped was a hesitant knock on
the door.

A pretty, fair-haired young woman let him in.
Right age, right size, right color hair to be Melissa,
he noted immediately. Neat, if simple, clothes.

"Can I help you?" she asked in a pleasant voice.
But he had the impression she didn't appreciate the
interruption. Heels clicking on the wood-planked
floor, she hurried back to her desk after giving him
only the briefest glance and buried her nose in a
pile of papers.

"Uh"—he scratched the bridge of his nose—
"I'm here to see the superintendent."

"He's not here." She picked up a pen, scribbled
a few words on one of the papers. "We're a little
shorthanded here; he went on down to St. Louis,
looking to see if he could pick up some more mill
girls."

Kieran wondered if the superintendent took a
lot of "hiring trips." That was one possibility for his
having made so little progress, if the man he'd been
searching for was safely out of town.

"That's what I come about," he said. "I'm
lookin' for work."

That got her attention; she looked up from her
papers, gaze sweeping him from head to toe before
inclining her head toward a door at the rear of the
room. "Walter—Mr. Lessing's assistant—is here
today, looking over some orders. I suppose you
could talk to him."

"Thank you." Kieran bobbed his head.

This was a stroke of unexpected luck; if nothing
else, he'd get an opportunity to get a better look at
Walter Cowdry without Lessing's muffling presence.

"What are you waiting for?" the girl asked
sharply, clearly impatient to get him out of her way.

"Should I just go on in?"

"You might try knocking," she said, shaking her
head at his ill manners as she bent to a thick ledger
book, obviously dismissing him.

He wasn't used to women—even such a young
one—being in such a hurry to get rid of him. He
hadn't realized what a high opinion he had of his

effect on women, he thought, rather bemused at his conceit.

He rapped on the inner door, fashioned of unvarnished, unpainted wood with only minimal sanding. Apparently Walter Lessing didn't waste his wealth on fine trappings for the help.

"Come in."

Kieran shuffled in, head bowed. The role of supplicant had never come naturally to him, though he'd improved at it the more he became removed from the reality of it. This had the added complication of playing out his charade before a man he'd met before. He had to give the appearance of humility and a touch of desperation without changing his demeanor so drastically that Cowdry noticed.

Walter bent over a simple pine desk neatly stacked with books and ledgers and correspondence. Thin-lensed spectacles shielded his eyes; he hadn't worn them at the hotel. He'd removed his jacket, but his sleeves still closed properly at his narrow wrists, and his shirt was buttoned all the way up to his throat.

"Mr. Cowdry?" he asked with just a slight hesitation.

"Just a moment." Cowdry held up one finger as he quickly scanned the letter he held in his other hand. He folded the paper, tucked it away in a drawer, and finally looked up. "Ah, Mr. McDermott, isn't it? We met at Jamison's the other night."

"Yes."

Cowdry leaned back in his chair, tucking his thumbs under his braces. Away from his employer, his head was higher, his gestures freer. Even his clothing was a bit more fashionable, presenting the image of a bright, ambitious businessman. "What can I do for you?"

"I'm looking for work."

"Really?" Surprised, Walter straightened. "You've been staying at Jamison's, I understand."

"Yes."

"And you've rented a rig from the livery. And are dining out regularly."

"That, too," Kieran admitted. Cowdry appeared to have been checking up on him, if he knew that much about Kieran's movements in Redemption. The only question now was, why?

"In other words, Mr. McDermott, you've given every impression of having, well, less-than-strait circumstances, shall we say? Given that, why would you want to work at the mill? It is not easy work."

Kieran ducked his head, giving every appearance of being abashed. "Guess the room and the buggy and the food are why I'm needing a job now."

"Hmm." Cowdry picked up a pen and ran his fingers down the length of it. "Not terribly wise of you."

"Courtin' takes money."

That brought an indulgent smile. "Yes, I suppose it does."

"How about it? I'm willing to do most anything."

Walter studied him while he fiddled with the pen. Kieran allowed himself to meet his gaze fully, letting a bit of pride show through.

"I'm sorry," Cowdry said. "But I can't help you."

How best to play this? Anger, perhaps; see how deep Walter's veneer of confidence and command went. "Mr. Lessing said, if I needed anything while I was in town, that I should come to him," Kieran challenged.

Walter gripped the pen tighter and his mouth thinned. "I'm aware of that, but we simply have nothing available right now."

How interesting; the implicit threat to go over Walter's head to Lessing might have angered Walter a bit, but it didn't disturb him. He seemed quite confident Benjamin would back him up.

"Will you let me know if something comes up?" Kieran asked. No use pushing a lost cause any more today. Cowdry had his mind made up.

"Of course," Walter said smoothly, and they both knew he really meant *not a chance*.

Kieran turned and left.

Walter heard voices murmur in the outer office, McDermott's deep tones and then the sweet tinkle of Lucy's laughter, though he couldn't make out the words. The front door thudded shut behind McDermott—thank heavens he hadn't slammed it. Walter had been sure the man would; he'd seemed quite angry about being turned down for a job. Shortly after, she came in.

"Lucy," he said, as she leaned against the door-jamb, crossing her arms under those lovely breasts. For a moment he wondered if she did it specifically to lure his attention there. But surely Lucy wouldn't be that calculating, especially here in the office.

"You turned him down."

"You heard."

"Mmm-hmm." Slowly she tilted her head, revealing the delicate curve of her throat. Lucy always moved languidly; it was part of her appeal, making him wonder what it would take to make her move faster. "And he stopped and told me on the way out."

"He did? What else did he say?"

"Nothing much. Just wondered if I've worked here long, and what I did before."

Walter frowned. "What did you tell him?"

"Why, the truth, of course," she said lightly. "So why didn't you hire him? We can always use day labor, if nothing else." She sighed longingly. "It might be . . . nice to have him around."

Walter's frown turned into an all-out scowl. "Maybe that's why I didn't hire him. The women don't need the distraction."

Lucy smiled; Walter was so beautifully easy to provoke. She liked the days he worked in the office best, enjoyed practicing her wiles on him, seeing how little it took to get the desired response. Her desirability was the only power that a woman had in the world. Thank heavens she'd finally learned to use hers to her own advantage.

"I suppose I could . . . rough him up a little. So he wouldn't be such a distraction." As if she cared what the man looked like. But Walter didn't know that.

"That won't be necessary," Walter snapped. "The truth is, Benjamin told me not to hire him if he came in."

"Really?" Now there was a little tidbit Lucy hadn't expected. "Do you know why?"

"How should I know why Benjamin does anything?" Walter said, clearly disgruntled.

"You *are* his assistant."

"For all the good it does." Walter jabbed his glasses back up on his nose, leaning forward eagerly. Only one thing that could distract Walter from her feminine charms, and that was business. "When Mr. Lessing hired me, he told me he did so for my intelligence and my education, but he proceeds to ignore every word of advice I give him. All he wants me to do is follow orders."

"He seems to be doing all right the way things are."

"But he could be doing so much better!" Walter's eyes—his best feature, she'd always thought, those bright green eyes—lit up.

Here we go again, Lucy thought, losing interest. Walter's when-I'm-in-charge spiel.

"Someday, Lucy, I'm gong to have a mill of my own—sooner than you think, too—and then I'll . . ."

Nodding politely, Lucy didn't bother to listen anymore.

She'd heard it all before.

"They really wouldn't give you a job?" Margaret slid a plate of fried ham and potatoes in front of Kieran and took her own seat. "I thought they were always shorthanded."

"That's what I'd heard." Kieran plucked at the

front of his shirt and sniffed at the cloth. "So, what do you think? I stink and nobody told me?"

"Oh, I didn't mention that? I'm sorry." He mock-scowled at her, and Margaret hid her smile behind the rim of her coffee cup.

She couldn't be terribly sorry that Kieran wouldn't be working at the mill. If he had been, he wouldn't have nearly as much time to see her, and, well . . .

Margaret stopped her thoughts just short of *I'll miss him*. There was too much pain lurking behind that eventuality, and no reason to deal with it until she had no choice.

But, she admitted to herself, she was getting rather accustomed to not having to eat alone. Even today, when there was no one to impress with their "courting."

Kieran had decided they didn't need to be seen together in town as often. It had served his purpose— he'd been introduced to most everyone, they were accustomed to his presence, and they accepted his reasons for staying in Redemption.

The prospect of no longer having to publicly spoon with Kieran so often relieved her. She'd liked it at first, the surprised and speculative looks sent her way by people who'd long ago written her off as an old maid. She'd been amused by the young women who tried and failed to capture Kieran's attention before, bewildered, they turned to studying Margaret with an expression that clearly said, *How has she managed to fix his attention? What has she got that I haven't got?*

But after a while, it began to feel . . . intrusive.

Both a reminder that it was all for show, and a spur to force them into the illusion of intimacy, an illusion that Margaret found herself much too easily drawn into.

"What are you going to do next, then?" She enjoyed trying to predict Kieran's next move, even though she almost always guessed wrong. But she was getting much better at it with practice.

Kieran gave his attention to slicing his meat into little cubes before answering, delaying. He knew Maggie wasn't going to like this.

"There are a number of possibilities," he hedged. In the guise of peppering his potatoes, he peeked at her. She was almost smiling, that little half dimple in the corner of her mouth flirting with him. He figured he might as well enjoy it while he could, because in a minute she was probably going to start yelling at him.

He sighed, wondering why he was putting it off. He was getting soft, he thought, and it was entirely Maggie's fault.

Just like this supper. How had he fallen into the habit of eating with her almost all the time, even when, like tonight, he couldn't even come up with the flimsiest of excuses?

Because he liked it, that's why. He wasn't here because it was necessary to the investigation. He was here because he wanted to see her, and no point in pretending anything else.

After so many years of working entirely alone, watching every word he said to every person he met, he'd succumbed without even a struggle to the luxury of having someone to talk it all over with. Someone to sift through the pieces of the puzzle with, who'd listen to his ideas and his theories and turn them back on him.

And he hadn't even fought against it, even though he was pretty damn certain it was a really bad idea. He'd done all right all those years all by himself. But this time was different, and he was different.

The one thing he had fought—hard—was to keep his hands off Maggie. Now only a few feet away across the table, she bent her head. A piece of hair fell down, twined against that tender little spot beneath her neck, and he knew that if he kissed her right there, she'd moan with pleasure, and he was having a real hard time remembering why the hell he wasn't supposed to touch her.

Oh, yeah—he had a vague notion it had something to do with his honor, and not seducing a virtuous woman when he wasn't able to offer her more. And Maggie was still a virtuous woman— one lonely and passion-filled night didn't change that.

However, that inconvenient code of honor didn't say anything about that virtuous woman seducing him, did it? If he set his mind to getting Maggie to put her hands on *him*, instead of the other way around . . .

"Kieran?" she prompted.

But it wasn't going to work when Maggie was really, really mad at him, he thought glumly. He sighed and plunged in.

"I'm going out in the open. Quiet investigation isn't getting me anywhere, so I'm going to let everyone know why I'm in Redemption and see where that gets me."

"You want everyone to know—including him—that you're hunting the Uncatchable Man," she said coolly, her face perfectly composed. When had she learned to do that? he wondered. Her expressions used to be so easy to read. He didn't want to think he'd forced her into that, into curbing her honesty and emotions.

"Yes."

"Like flushing game."

"Like hunting a big ol' fat pheasant," he said.

"Kieran," she said quietly, steel edging her voice. "Pheasants don't shoot back."

"Maggie—"

"You're trying to get him to come after you, aren't you?"

"Not exactly, I—"

"You want him to try and kill you."

"I wouldn't put it that way, no, but—"

"What other way is there to put it, Kieran? You're making yourself an easy target. You want the man to come and try and kill you so you can try and get him first, isn't that right?"

Maggie sawed her meat as if attacking a piece of hide—preferably his. She didn't have to put it so baldly, did she? It sounded bad, just laid out there like that.

Even though she was right.

"I'm going to take precautions," he said.

"Really?" She eyed him skeptically. "Like what?"

"Well . . ." He searched for inspiration. "Ah—I'll let out that I have associates back in Chicago, and that I've been wiring them everything I've learned so far. So, if I'm killed, my colleagues will know just where to look. My death would be the only sure evidence that the Uncatchable Man is here, don't you see? He won't want that."

"Wires," she said flatly. "I don't suppose he'll think to check if you've actually been sending them, will he?"

"I've thought of that," he said, pleased to be able to block this argument. "I've been sending cables all along. They're in code."

He didn't like the way Maggie gripped her knife, and he wasn't at all fond of that gleam in her eye. "What are they, really, those cables to your associates?"

"Well . . ." He considered making something up, but he'd gotten out of the habit of lying to Maggie and didn't much feel like starting again. "I have to let my mother know I'm okay."

"They're to your *mother?*" Maggie huffed, the sound halfway between exasperation and amusement. It occurred to Kieran that his mother often made that same sound when she talked to him.

"Look." Briefly, he thought about reaching across the table and taking her hand in reassurance, but it would probably violate that don't-touch-Maggie rule. And this time, he wouldn't be able to pull away after just a kiss.

He'd never really believed the theory that it was easier if you didn't know what you were missing.

He did now. "It'll be all right, I promise."

"Of course it will," she said briskly. "Because you're not going to have to do it."

"Maggie?"

"Because I already got a job at the mill."

"What!"

"Mmm-hmm." She tucked a potato into her mouth, chewed as if they were having a pleasant mealtime conversation of no consequence whatsoever. "They're always in need of matrons for the boardinghouses, women of 'good character and housekeeping skills.' I start in two days."

"What are you talking about?" he said, surprised when Maggie didn't flinch. He'd sounded dangerous, even to himself.

"Oh, well." She speared a chunk of ham, waved it around. "Martha Ann came over for just a little while today, around noon; she had to go into Redemption for supplies. One of her nephews—Lucius's brother's boy—was delivering a load of wool to the mill and saw you leaving the office. He told his mother, and she told Martha Ann. Martha Ann thought I'd like to know that you'd applied for a job, so you must be planning on staying in Redemption for a while." She beamed at him, entirely too pleased with herself.

"You guessed what I was going to do, didn't you?"

Her eyes downright twinkled at him. "Perhaps I had a hint. All I had to do was think of the most dangerous, most risky, most get-right-out-there possibility, and that was the one you were most likely to choose."

"You can't do it."

"I don't see why not. I'm of good character—at

least, as far as they know—and I've good housekeeping skills, don't you think?"

He knew enough not to answer that. "It's dangerous." Because if you do, he thought, I'm going
to lock you up right here in this room and never let
you out.

Oh, interesting idea.

A flicker of alarm showed her in eyes, quickly
extinguished. "I don't think it will be terribly dangerous. I'm not going to do anything, except talk to
a few of the girls, find out where they came from
and how long they've been at the mill. I don't see
how anyone can take exception to that."

"I won't let you," he growled.

"Really?" A bit of temper showed now in her
eyes and the set of her shoulders.

"What about your animals? Your planting?"

"You met John, Martha Ann's oldest boy? He's
always looking to make a little extra money—he's
taken a shine to Isabinda Salisbury. I hired him this
afternoon."

He felt himself scrambling, trying to catch up
with a woman who was a step ahead of him all the
way. Was this really the same stuttering Margaret
Thayer who'd barely been able to look at him without blushing?

"Not to mention," she went on smoothly, "that, of
course, you can't tell everyone in town why you're
here now. They know we've been . . . friendly, and,
well, it really wouldn't be safe for me, would it? If
I'm working at the mill and everything?"

"Really."

His voice went low and soft, warning Margaret

that maybe she'd gone too far, too fast. He set aside his plate, his cup, as if clearing the space before him. He looked at her across the table, his mouth and eyes determined, unreadable.

Uh-oh, she thought, *I'm not going to like this.*

"I guess I'm just gonna have to break your heart," Kieran said.

13

Light shimmered softly in the old cottage, flickering over the two naked bodies on the bed. Candles; Melissa had decided she liked candles better than kerosene. They were more romantic, and they smelled better.

Beside her, her lover lay relaxed, half-asleep, satisfied with sex. Almost bloated with it. She'd given him a good one tonight.

Now he'd have to listen to her.

"I want to talk."

"Hmm?" he mumbled, flopped over so he faced her, eyes still closed. Hoping she'd leave him alone so he could drift off to sleep, she figured. Men always wanted to go to sleep after, it seemed.

"I want you to talk to me."

He opened one eye. "About what?"

"It doesn't matter." Hardly anyone ever took the time to talk to her. Or listened to her. Her father had certainly never bothered. Once she got old enough that people could no longer dismiss her as a child, she'd thought it would change. But then, men had been interested in other things but talk from her, and women—well, she'd never figured out other women.

Not that it mattered, when men were the ones with all the power. "When we first met, you used to talk to me all the time."

He sighed and consigned himself to his fate. He'd have to listen to the little twit. She used to be so delightfully obedient. Lately she kept trying to get . . . more from him. More time, more attention, more of everything he couldn't afford to spare. Didn't she realize he was a busy man?

It might be best to simply get rid of her. But she lay fully naked on the bed next to him, gloriously uninhibited—what came, he supposed, from training them so young, before all the old biddies got a chance to plant "virtuous and modest" thoughts in their heads—and he thought he'd keep her around awhile longer. Redemption had so few real entertainments to offer.

He let his fingers trail idly over her breasts. "What do you want to talk about?"

"How about your next job?" she suggested eagerly. "Will we be leaving soon? Have you picked another target?"

"No, not yet." An instinct had been prodding him for some time, telling him to lie low. He never ignored his instincts. "But perhaps we make our little trysts more exciting for you in the meantime."

"Exciting?" she said doubtfully.

"A little more danger." His thumb teased her

nipple, and he frowned when it didn't respond to his stimulation. "A slightly less . . . private setting, perhaps?"

He felt his breath coming harder; the idea might not be having the desired effect on her, but it was exciting him. He moved closer, intending to pull her beneath him, but she shifted away.

"That sounds nice," she said. "But what am I supposed to do the rest of the time?"

I don't care—he would never be stupid enough to say it to her. He liked his pleasures far too well. But he often thought it.

"You have a job, Melissa."

"A job! A boring, stupid job. How long do I have to do it, anyway?"

"Until I say so," he said sharply, losing patience.

Melissa batted his hand away from her breast. As if he thought she would allow him such liberties when he spoke to her like that! "Why?"

"Because your presence would be too obvious otherwise. I've told you that."

"I don't like it."

"You have a new boardinghouse matron, I heard," he murmured, looking to distract her. She'd do what he wanted in any case, but he'd rather make it easy. "Do you like her?"

"I don't know. She's only been there five days." She shrugged indifferently. "She makes good cakes. And she bought a lot of books—now all anybody does is sit around and read . . . not that I'm interested in talking to them, anyway."

"Poor dear. No wonder you're bored." The distraction worked; this time, when his hand came searching, she forgot to pull away. "I heard she's no longer seeing that McDermott."

"No. I heard her talking to her friend about it, how he'd broken her heart." Melissa felt only disdain for a woman who'd allow a man to do that to her. When she'd overheard them talking, the little catch that had pinched up in her throat was only pity. What else could it be?

"I want you to stay away from her."

"What?"

"Prim little old maid. I'm afraid she'll rub off on you, and we can't have that," he said, injecting a teasing note into his voice. He wasn't entirely convinced that everything between McDermott and the woman was as it seemed, and he wasn't taking any chances.

"But she's just—"

"Haven't we talked enough?"

He was forever trying to tell her what to do, Melissa thought. At first, she'd been happy to go along with his wishes, because she knew he could help her get away. And she'd had a lot of practice at doing what she was told.

She was getting very tired of it now.

"Yes," she agreed, pasting on a bright, false smile.

But they'd see about that.

The twelfth cottonwood in, along the river. Counting them off, Margaret touched each trunk as she passed, her hands brushing the dew-dampened bark.

The night was far too dark to see the trees. Low clouds blotted out the moon, leaving only a faint, tarnished gloss on the river and full darkness every-where else. The covered sky held in the day's heat, making the night unusually warm and sweet as only almost-summer can be, the air just tinged with the scent of budding wild roses and water and damp loam. The river whispered softly, calling her along.

She stumbled over a tangle of wild grapevines and cursed; she'd tripped over what was probably the same one two nights before, but how in the world could she avoid it when she couldn't see a dad-gummed thing?

This clandestine meeting stuff was really getting ridiculous.

Moving into the boardinghouse had complicated things a great deal more than she'd anticipated. Kieran couldn't simply slip in to see her, for she was supposed to be suffering from his cruel jilting; she'd not been able to talk him out of that plan.

Nor could she try to meet him during the day. She had work to do, and people who'd want to know where she was heading off to if she left the mill grounds during the workday. She had a few free hours in the afternoon sometimes, when she got ahead on the evening meal, and had suggested simply rendezvousing at her house, but Kieran hadn't wanted to take the chance.

They'd settled on meeting every other night, at midnight in the cottonwood grove, next to a differ-ent tree each time. She thought it was probably going to extremes in the name of safety. Who would ever have expected that Kieran would be more cautious about something than she? But she suspected Kieran had arranged the meetings like this not only for safety's sake but because he rather enjoyed this cloak-and-dagger routine.

She, however, did not. Tonight was only the third time she'd dragged herself from bed, swaddled up in dark clothing, tiptoed out of the house, and trekked across the grounds and into the trees.

She was already really, really tired of it.

Occupied with fussing about Kieran's forcing her to wander around in the dark, Margaret almost missed the assigned tree. She stopped, debated whether to go back and count them again, and called it good enough.

"Kieran," she whispered, and then, more loudly, "Kieran!"

"I'm right here," he said, materializing right out of the gloom, only a foot or so away.

She jumped. "Must you do that?"

"Feeling a bit testy tonight, are we?"

"We aren't feeling anything." If he startled her one more darn time, she was going to swing first and ask questions later. It'd be no more than he deserved. "You're cheerful enough. Had a good day, did you? Somebody shoot at you or something?"

"No, not yet."

"You don't have to sound so disappointed about it."

"Oh, but I am." The sooner the Uncatchable Man decided to come after Kieran, the sooner he could make sure that he posed no danger at all to

Maggie. For, though he'd done everything he could to protect her by disassociating himself from her, it wasn't enough to satisfy him. He suspected nothing would be.

He knew she considered the elaborate precautions surrounding their meetings ridiculous. Under any other circumstances, he might have agreed. But just the thought of Maggie at any kind of risk they might have avoided through a bit more caution made his heart freeze up.

Not that he cared about her, beyond a certain friendly admiration, he told himself. And a distinct, but perfectly understandable, lust for her body. Thank God he'd been cured early in his life of the affliction of loving a woman; once had been more than enough, and he was never leaving himself open to that pain again. But he felt responsible for Maggie, as he would for anyone who got caught up in one of his jobs.

And, too, meeting her like this allowed him to indulge a sneaky little hope that, on a romantic night, all alone in the woods, she might just decide to throw herself in his arms and have her wicked way with him.

Please, God.

"Let's walk," he suggested, half-aroused and restless just from thinking about it.

"Walk?" she asked, incredulous. "Walk where? I can't see anything!"

"I can."

"Of course you can," Margaret grumbled. She'd yet to discover anything he couldn't do, and do very well. Especially . . . oh, she daren't let her

mind travel down that particular path. Hard
enough to be this close to him as it was.

"Come on. I've been out here awhile. My eyes
have adjusted. I won't let you run into anything,"
he said, and took her hand.

Such a small gesture, taking her hand. Still,
her heart skittered. Shameful that she should
respond to him so easily, to something that meant
so little.

Their two earlier meetings had been distinctly
unsatisfying. She hadn't been at her job long
enough to have much to tell him, and he avoided
the subject of what he did all day long—which
meant, she figured, that it was something ridiculously dangerous. And, in the darkness, she'd
been unable to see his face clearly, which frustrated her to no end. If she had to get up in the
middle of the night and haul herself out here, at
least she should have something nice to look at as
a reward.

But now she realized that something else had
disturbed her a great deal more.

She'd been waiting for him to touch her all
along.

"Are you coming?" he asked, gently tugging her
hand.

"Yes." *Anything you ask, anywhere you ask.
Just don't let go.*

Her world narrowed down to nothing but the
darkness, the sound of his voice, the firm warmth
of his grip on her palm. He didn't hurry, just
wound his way through the trees and bushes with
the unerring step of a night hunter.

Which, she supposed, he was.

"So, how was your day?"

His mundane question almost made her laugh. It sounded less like this was a clandestine meeting, two spies searching out a deadly thief, than the routine conversation of a long-married husband coming home to his comfortable wife. The budding laugh died, turned into a pang for what would never be.

"Fine," she said, determined not to get tangled up in wishful thinking, not to waste her time with regrets. "Martha Ann came over for tea, to console me over your heartless perfidy."

"Uh-oh. Is there going to be an attempt on my life after all?"

"Maybe." She considered, decided him to tell the truth. "I think she suspects that there's more going on than she knows. I'm not used to lying to her, Kieran, and she's known me a long time."

"Is it going to be a problem?"

"I don't think so." Margaret thought back. There'd been concern in Martha Ann's manner, certainly. But there'd also been interest, and perhaps a little satisfaction. "Even if she does suspect, she won't say anything unless I tell her it's okay."

"Fair enough."

He was willing to trust her judgment on something so important, that easily? Unaccountably, all out of proportion, pride warmed her. It shouldn't have surprised her; her feelings all seemed out of proportion where Kieran was concerned. More fear, more hope, more passion, more anger, more joy.

More everything. As much as it terrified her, it made her feel vibrantly, giddily alive.

"How about you?" she asked. "You told everyone in town who you were and why you were here, didn't you? What happened?"

"They all think I'm out of my mind."

"They're shocked and appalled at the suggestion that a ruthless outlaw could be one of them?"

"All right, so you told me so. You don't have to rub it in." He squeezed her hand in warning. "They think it's one big joke. Not that it matters—I'd learned pretty much all I could from them already, and this was worth the chance. I might add that a number of people are quite upset on your behalf, that I would lead you on merely to get information about the town."

"There's a good thing about it, though. The girls all feel terribly sorry for me, jilted by an unfeeling beast like you."

"Oops." He jerked her hard to one side, barely avoiding the tree that loomed in her path. It took her off-balance, sending her stumbling right into his chest.

She heard his quick intake of breath, and his arms came around her. For support, she told herself. Only for support. No reason to get carried away.

"Sorry," she said, wishing she didn't sound so breathless, hoping he'd attribute it to her near fall, and not to the truth—it had nothing to do with almost hitting the tree, and everything to do with being so close to him, and remembering too well what it was like when there was nothing between them but skin.

"Don't be sorry. You can fall into my arms any time you want."

Margaret flushed, grateful for the darkness for the first time, so he couldn't see it and make some comment about making her cheeks—or the rest of her—turn pink. He'd been saying things like that more and more often lately, light, seductive little remarks that set her head to spinning. She was working very hard to take them in the friendly, flirtatious vein they were meant.

Or almost certainly meant. For each time, she battled the suspicion, the *wish*, that perhaps he intended them exactly as they sounded. After all, he'd seemed to . . . welcome her advances once before.

And believing that was extremely dangerous indeed.

Only one night with him had sent her life into a tailspin, had drawn her into things and actions she'd never dreamed of. She knew her life, and she with it, would never be the same. She'd never again accept and welcome that comfortable complacency she'd found sufficient before.

If only one night with Kieran had caused that, what would she be like after a few more nights? A sensation seeker, a faithless wanton, forever in search of someone, anyone, who could make her feel like that again? Or, at least, who could distract her enough so she'd forget for a while.

She'd learned to take a chance or two over the

last few weeks, surprising herself. But she didn't think she had it in her to take this one.

Kieran loosened his arms.

"Ready to go on?" he asked. Not that he really wanted to let her go; not at all. However, if he held her any longer, she was bound to notice exactly what effect she had on him. If that happened, he wouldn't be responsible for what came next.

"I believe so."

Just her hand again now, and the sound of her shuffling along behind him in the dark. He suppressed a sigh of regret. He liked her hand well enough, but it wasn't as interesting as other parts of her. Unless it was doing something like . . .

Whoa, boy. Stop that line of thought right there. Otherwise he'd grab her and take her right there in the middle of the woods, among the old leaves and new grass and night sounds, and there were a hundred good reasons why he couldn't do that.

He just couldn't remember them right now.

"Tell me about the mill girls," he said. Work. Work was good. Work was distracting.

"Oh!" She sounded pleased with herself. "I've eliminated all but three of them from my boarding-house, I think."

"Three?"

"A lot of them have dark hair, thank goodness, which makes things much simpler. Though I suppose she could dye it, but I don't see how without my noticing, one way or the other. And several have been there too long to possibly be Melissa."

"So who are they?"

"There's Ida Goss. She's from Chicago, or so she said. An orphan. Beautiful manners."

"Can learn those in an orphanage, too, if there are enough nuns around." He pulled her to the left, wove her around another tree. "Who else?"

"There's Lily."

"Lily?" His words grew shorter, sharper; she could almost hear him mentally filing away all the information she gave him.

"I don't know much about her. She's . . . prickly. Keeps to herself."

"Last name?"

"I don't know. Just Lily, she says. Her eyes . . . she's got the saddest eyes, Kieran."

Regret crept into her voice, and rich empathy. He should have known that she'd be drawn into it, he thought, that she'd take those girls to heart and be hurt by it. He slowed his pace, squeezing her hand because he couldn't bear not to and it was the only comfort he could give her.

"I want you to quit, Maggie."

"We've been over this before, Kieran. I'm safe enough. And besides, I like it."

"What do you mean?"

"I do. They're so . . . grateful, everything I do for them. I don't think the matron before me could cook at all." It was so nice to see what she made appreciated, to see the girls gobble the food she'd made them and the weariness fade from their eyes just a shade, as if she'd given them a wonderful gift, one no one had ever bothered with before. It took such minor effort on her part to make the meals a little special for them.

"Not like you, anyway."

"They all adore Arne. He purrs from the time they get home until they leave the next morning."

"I'm losing my favored status, aren't I?"

"Without a doubt. I brought in a few books, some magazines for the parlor. You can't know how much they enjoy them, Kieran! They're all so tied to that place, I think they were beginning to forget that there was a whole world out there." And she'd learned a lesson that she should have been wise enough to know years ago—that the easing of loneliness lay in doing for others, not in having others around who could do for you.

"How much of the money I paid you are you spending on them, Maggie?"

"There's a household allowance, for food and supplies," she hedged.

"How much?"

Caught, she sighed. "Not much. They need it more than I do." She dragged on his hand, stopping him so she could lecture him properly. "And we're not going to discuss that anymore, Kieran, do you understand?"

"All right." If he'd learned one thing about Maggie, it was when a topic had been closed, and this one was. He began walking again, because every time they stopped he started thinking about kissing her. "How old are they, Ida and Lily?"

"Hard to say for sure. The mill ages the girls

fast." She paused and considered. "I'm guessing they're just about right, though."

"You mentioned a third?"

"That's Lucy. She's got a room of her own, because she works in the office instead of in the mill itself." The other girls crowded together, five or six to a room. "The rest resent her because of it, so she stays away. I don't know her as well—she doesn't come down to the parlor in the evening. She looks right, though."

"In the office? I think I met her. Pretty."

"Yes, she is. The others probably would be too, though, if they had enough rest and time to worry about such things."

"But at least they have you to cook for them now."

"Yes." She'd worried about enough money and enough food for most of her life. But she was learning there were worse things.

The mill girls knew where their next meal would come from. But their life was bound by bells—start at 5, breakfast at 6:30, lunch at 12:30, and, at last, closing time at 7 when they'd slump home to the boardinghouse, wearing exhaustion as tangible as the woolen fibers that clung to their clothing.

Yes, she'd had to worry about hunger. But she, at least, had some choices in her life, about when and how and what to do. And she owned something of her own: the land, the house.

They owned nothing but the clothes on their back and the few belongings they stuffed beneath their bunks. Most of what they earned went for their room and board—and they had no choices about that, either; they were required to stay at the boardinghouses at the mill.

All they had were their jobs. And, if that job were to be lost, then they'd have hunger to worry about, too, quick enough.

She felt a deep revulsion for every trace of boredom and impatience she'd felt with her own life. Now, it seemed shamefully like self-pity to her.

"Well, what do we have here?" Kieran halted abruptly in front of her, and she almost ran right into his back.

"What?" She squinted around him, saw nothing but more darkness.

"There." He drew their joined hands up, pointed to the right. "A cabin of some sort."

She looked harder, determined to see some of what he saw. Perhaps the darkness was a little thicker there, more densely even.

Or she could be imagining it because she wanted to because Kieran said it existed and she didn't want him to have such advantage over her. "Oh! I think I know what it is. There's a cottage around here somewhere, used to be where one of the overseers stayed. Mrs. Clinghorn—the matron in the house just north of mine—told me. He had to move back into one of the cottages closer to the mill, so he could keep a better eye on things, and he wasn't too happy about it."

"When, do you know?"

"A year or so ago, I believe she said."

"Interesting."

"I suppose we're going in."

"I am. You, on the other hand, could just plant yourself right behind this nice big tree here, safe and sound. It would make me very happy."

"I believe we've had this conversation before, Kieran."

"I was afraid of that."

14

The door rattled loudly, an unnatural sound in the stillness of the sleeping grove, when Kieran tried to open it.

"Locked." Kieran listened carefully, testing the air for any hint of other intruders. Maggie and he had disturbed a few small animals as they passed, but the scrabbling sounds had mostly settled down now. He heard nothing else suspicious.

"What now?" She leaned over his shoulder, tested the door herself. "Are we going to break a window?"

Lord, what have I done? he wondered. She sounded almost pleased with the prospect. "No, we're not going to break a window."

"Oh."

The warm weather had almost prodded him into leaving his duster home tonight, but all those big pockets were just so darn useful. Thank goodness he hadn't. He rummaged around in the bottom of the right one.

"Here. Hold these." He dumped a candle and a tin of matches into her hands and dug deep again. "Ah, there it is," he said, pulling out the tool he needed.

"What else do you have in your pockets?" she said, intrigued.

"Anything we could possibly need."

"Anything?" she purred, shocking them both with her seductive tone, enough to make them both pause for a moment and mull over tempting if decidedly impractical possibilities.

"Maggie—" He cleared his throat and tried again. "Maggie, I don't suppose I could talk you into standing over there behind the trees after all? I'm going to have to light the candle to see what I'm doing. It'll make us a clear target in this darkness."

"No."

"I didn't think so."

She lit the candle herself, edging over to shield the light and, in the process, Kieran. She wondered at this strange, irresistible, and certainly absurd compulsion to protect him.

She knew perfectly well he could protect himself. She just doubted whether he would.

The flame, though small, seared eyes accustomed to impenetrable blackness. Kieran bent, working at the lock with the sliver of metal he'd pulled from his pocket.

"Can you hold the candle a little further down?" he asked.

She moved closer, lowering the stub to a few inches from the doorknob. The light was too weak to really dispel the darkness; the night swallowed it within a foot. But it revealed Kieran. Not the whole man, different parts shifting into shadow and light as he worked. First a gleam of his hair, silver and black, night sky and moonlight mixed into one. Then one side of his face, a strong cheekbone and jaw and the deep hollow between them. His hands, strong fingers moving with spare delicacy.

"Ah, there she is." The lock clicked open.

"She?"

"It works so much better when you treat them like a woman."

Maggie prudently reserved comment.

This time the door gave easily with a gentle nudge, sliding open on well-oiled hinges.

Kieran ushered her inside where they both stopped, letting first impressions of the place wash over them before they began to search in earnest.

"Awfully nice furniture for an overseer," Kieran commented.

"No wonder he didn't want to leave."

"Most of it looks fairly new." The single flame Maggie held didn't provide much illumination, but a cluster of fat white candles stood on a sideboard. He took the candle from Maggie and went to light them, first prodding one of the tips with his finger to test the wax. There was a hint of softness there, he judged, more so than the fairly warm evening explained.

"Yes," she agreed. The extra light should have made the room more cheerful. It didn't. Instead, it revealed an odd mix of furniture, simple next to more expensive pieces. A fluffy comforter twisted awkwardly over the bed.

She ran a finger over the table. Not too dusty, but a dark stain streaked one corner, and a puddle of hard candle wax marred the center.

In all, she had the impression that, though someone had made an attempt to clean the place up, they either hadn't cared much or had no experience in the task. "What do you think?"

"I'd say we've stumbled across a love nest," he said flatly.

"Theirs?" Maggie asked, immensely grateful there'd been not a hint of seduction or playfulness in his tone. Perhaps the place repelled him as much as it did her, imagining one of *her* girls in that bed with that horrible man.

"Maybe." He rubbed her shoulder lightly, a supportive gesture, as if he knew it bothered her. "Might as well get to work."

"What are we looking for?"

"Hell if I know."

Maggie took the pine bureau pushed against the far wall, between two narrow windows. Kieran headed for the kitchen.

"Finding any food?" she asked, sliding open a drawer with a grating shriek.

"Nope. You hungry?"

"Of course not. I just thought it would tell whether anyone was living here or not."

"Think you're getting good at this investigating stuff, don't you?"

If there'd been anything heavier in the drawer

she opened than a froth of extravagent dressing gowns, she might have been tempted to throw it at him. "Found anything yet yourself, Mr. Expert?"

"All sorts of things."

"Like what?" she challenged.

"Said I found things. Didn't say they were *useful*." He moved on to the next cupboard and pulled out a half-empty bottle of wine. He uncorked it, tipped the neck against his finger, and tasted a drop. "Hasn't been open too long; it's not vinegary at all yet." He tilted the label toward the light. "Expensive stuff, too."

They searched the room for another ten minutes, by tacit agreement leaving the corner that held the bed for last. Maggie decided she didn't want to know what Kieran was doing when he jerked back the bedding and swept a candle closely over the sheets and pillows. She turned away.

The small bedside table held another brace of candles. She pulled open the small drawer beneath.

"Kieran, look at this."

He stepped to her side and she handed him the pocket watch that had lain in the drawer, next to a pile of handkerchiefs. He held the watch flat in his hand so they could both examine it and brought the candle close.

The etched gold shone expensively, light melting over the rounded sides.

"Heck of a thing to forget," she commented.

"Or he can't wear it in public, in case someone might notice he had something beyond his means."

Kieran flicked the catch open with his thumb.

"Not quite one fifteen," he said, closing the lid. "I'd better get you back."

"Yes."

"You'll be tired tomorrow." His attention shifted from the watch to her, and his businesslike expression softened with concern. "I'm sorry."

"Don't worry about it." She had the rest of her life to sleep. She didn't know how much time she had left with him, but it wasn't enough.

"Where exactly was the watch?"

"Here." She showed him, and he carefully set it back as she'd found it. "You're leaving it here?"

He nodded. "There's no monogramming or anything else that might lead me to him, and I'd rather he didn't suspect we were here. I want him coming back."

"You're sure they were here, then?"

"Somebody's obviously been here recently, and using the place fairly regularly, but not living here. Unless Redemption has yet another pair of lovers engaging in clandestine trysts, I'd say it's a good bet."

"And you're going to try and catch them next time they come back," she concluded. "Oh, I hope it works! I'm trying on my end, but there are two other boardinghouses. Mrs. Clinghorn is friendly, but I've not even met the other one, and trying to sort through so many girls . . . I'm not sure if I'll be able to find her."

He gave a noncommittal "Hmmm."

"Kieran, what aren't you telling me?"

"I'll keep an eye on this place."

"And?"

Glancing around the cottage, taking one last look for what they might have missed, he avoided her eye. "It looks like we're through here. Let's go."

He took her elbow to guide her, but she wasn't budging. "Kieran."

He shot her an unhappy look. "I've got a good idea who it is, anyway."

"Who?" she asked, aghast that he'd narrowed in on someone without letting her know—and without getting her opinion on his suspicions.

"I'm not telling you."

"Kieran."

"That's not working this time, Maggie, saying my name in that tone of voice."

Maybe not. But it didn't mean guilt wouldn't. "Why not?" she asked, injecting every bit of hurt and injured pride into her voice she could.

"You're a lousy liar, Maggie. If I tell you who it is, what do you think is going to show on your face the next time you see them?" His voice grew harsher, sharper. "And damn it, Maggie, if he ever for one moment suspected that you knew, then you really would be in danger." He traced her jaw—just one finger, just one touch that clearly conveyed what he didn't say: *If anything happens to you, I couldn't bear it.*

Well. She could hardly be too upset about that, could she? That he worried about her? But her curiosity wouldn't allow her to drop the subject that easily. "I'm getting better at it."

"You think so?"

"Yes."

"But you thought you had me fooled right then,

didn't you? That I believed you were really hurt that I didn't tell you who I believe it is?"

Her jaw dropped, and, grinning, he placed his forefinger beneath her chin and gently shut it.

He'd read her too easily. But, she suspected, she probably read him better than almost anyone, too. It warmed her, that he let his guard down with her the way he did with no one else.

It also frightened her, more than sneaking around in the middle of the night. Maybe even more than being shot at. Because, the more she knew him, the more she saw behind his reckless, careless facade, the more she cared.

And she already cared far too much as it was.

"Think of it, Maggie. You know who I suspect, and you know he's been using one of 'your girls.' You see him walking down the main street of Redemption, whistling, having a nice afternoon stroll, and he tips his hat to you. What would you do?"

"I . . . well . . . all right, so maybe I'd go for his throat, probably," she admitted reluctantly.

"Thought so."

"I still want to know. I think I could hide it, Kieran. He doesn't know me as well as you do."

"It won't be long now," he promised. "I'll watch this place. And this gives me all the more reason to believe that either the Uncatchable Man or Melissa— maybe both—are connected with the mill. I'll search the office next, see what I can find in there. With any luck, this'll be all over soon."

All over. The words echoed in her mind, empty, lonely.

There'd be another quest for him, another

person to save. There always was. And she . . . she'd be safe and secure. In control. With the money he'd paid her, surely better off than she was before. Maybe she'd even keep working at the mill; the girls needed her.

Except, no matter how many other people she and Kieran pulled around them, she was acutely afraid they'd both still be alone.

"So how long did you say you'd been at the Lessing Mill?" Margaret asked, nudging the plate of lemon snaps and sand tarts closer to Mrs. Clinghorn. She'd already discovered that Mrs. Clinghorn's tongue was considerably looser after it had been iced with sugar.

"Almost three years." She appraised the boarding-house parlor with a critical eye. "I must say, it looks ever so much better in here. The woman who held this position before you, Mrs. Lloyd," her mouth pursed, "though I'd be the last one to speak ill of another, and I was always rather suspicious of the *Mrs.* part, was not well suited for this job. I spotted it months before they finally discovered the truth."

"Hmm." Vaguely approving noises at regular intervals were apparently all that was required to keep Mrs. Clinghorn, a very proper widow on the far side of sixty, talking. Though Margaret had no interest whatsoever in her—as she'd heard it rumored drunkard predecessor, she didn't want to risk turning off the spigot by interrupting. Who knew when something useful would spill out?

"Now, the *other* matron—" Mrs. Clinghorn stopped, shook her head slightly.

"Miss Habelmore?"

"I don't expect she'll be here that long, either. Not many have what it takes to keep all these girls in line."

"They don't seem to stay long."

"No. No stamina, not a one of them." Mrs. Clinghorn tasted her coffee and dumped in another heaping teaspoon of sugar. Margaret wondered whether the substance in Mrs. Clinghorn's cup was still liquid or had thickened into a mud-colored slurry.

"The girls, too?"

"Those girls!"

"Mine seem like decent enough girls." Margaret longingly eyed the plateful of cookies. She really should start watching what she ate a bit more carefully; her skirt had gotten noticeably snug around the middle. But it was so very pleasant to have so much to choose from, and a reason to make more than the spare meals that were all it seemed necessary to prepare for herself.

Surrendering, she selected a sand tart, plucked the blanched almond off the top, and popped it in her mouth. If she didn't watch it, her sweet tooth would soon rival Mrs. Clinghorn's.

"You'll have your hands full keepin' 'em that way, I'll wager. I do." She sighed, long-suffering. "Now, I used to work for a doctor, back east—"

"Do you think so?" Margaret broke in, trying to steer Mrs. Clinghorn back on topic. Tales of the saintly eastern doctor would do her no good at all. "You've had trouble with your young ladies?"

"Oh, my, yes. Why, when I first came here, I even caught one or two of them sneaking out at night! Put a stop to that right quickly, I can tell you. If you wouldn't mind a word of advice—"

Maggie heard the thud of a door resounding against the wall, then a commotion in the front hallway.

"Miss Thayer!"

After a quick glance at the clock on the mantel—no one was expected back for hours yet—she jumped to her feet and hurried out of the room.

Just over the threshold Ida Goss and Lily, a heavy blanket wrapped around their shoulders, slumped together, as if they couldn't manage to go any farther on their own.

"Are you ill?" Lily's head was still down, but Ida looked up, her face pinched, and Margaret rushed to them. "Come on, let's get you to—"

"It's not me," Ida said. "Lily, she got her hand caught in the carding machine." She peeled back the blanket that covered them and Margaret gasped. Batting and strips of flannel wrapped Lily's right arm to the elbow, a thick padding already stained with bright, seeping red.

Ida blanched, swaying. Afraid both of them would go tumbling to the floor, Margaret quickly stepped to Lily's other side and grabbed her waist and shoulder, trying to find a way to support her that jostled her injured hand the least.

"Mrs. Clinghorn, you take Ida's place, all right? Let's take Lily right on into my room. I don't want to chance the stairs."

They made their way slowly down the hallway, Lily a hunched, silent figure between them, nearly all her weight on Mrs. Clinghorn's sturdy arm. Margaret glanced over her shoulder at Ida, who'd drooped against the wall. "When will the doctor be here?"

"No doctor coming."

"What?" Good thing she'd had a secure grip on Lily. "You mean no one's been sent? Well, go, then! Dr. Ballard's office is on Front Street."

"Can't." Ida straightened, her gaze firmly fixed on the floor, and shifted from foot to foot. "Got to get back to work. Meachum tol' me to bring her here and get right back."

"Meachum?"

"The overseer," Mrs. Clinghorn supplied tightly.

"Ida, we need a doctor. Follow the road to the river, you can't miss it—"

Ida slowly lifted her head, guilty eyes begging Margaret to understand. "I needs my job, Miss Thayer." She whirled and bolted.

"No doctor."

At first, Margaret didn't hear Lily's strained whisper.

"Don't talk now, Lily, let's just get you to bed first, all right?"

"No doctor!" she repeated, shuddering as if the effort to form the words had been too much for her.

Over Lily's bent head, Margaret and Mrs. Clinghorn shared a look that silently agreed to wait until they got Lily settled before taking up the subject again.

They eased her down on the bed, and Margaret got her first look at Lily's face. Though fatigue and the wear of her work had marked her, Lily must have once been a pretty girl. Now, every trace of that had vanished. Anguish distorted her ashen features; grime, tears, and a copper-colored splotch of blood streaked her face.

"I've done some nursing," Mrs. Clinghorn said gently. "Let me take a look at it, dear, and let's see what we can do."

"Lily," Margaret said. "I've got to go find someone to send for the doctor. I won't be gone long, I promise."

Lily's left hand shot out and gripped Margaret's wrist fiercely. "No doctor!"

"Lily, please—"

"Can't—" She gasped as Mrs. Clinghorn gently began unwrapping her wound. "Can't pay!"

"Surely the mill—"

"No. Say it's . . . my fault. Careless."

"Lily, I can't believe that—"

To her left, Mrs. Clinghorn touched her shoulder, gaining Margaret's attention, and shook her head. Mrs. Clinghorn had been there far longer than Margaret and knew the way of the place; she, too, obviously believed the mill wouldn't pay.

Lily moaned. Mrs. Clinghorn was halfway through the thick bandaging that covered Lily's hand, the fabric getting darker, glistening, as she went deeper.

"For God's sake, Lily, *I'll* pay!" For an instant, Lily's fingers tightened around Margaret's wrist. Then she let go, her body collapsing on the bed like a deflated balloon, and nodded wearily.

Margaret ran from the house. Who to send? She didn't want to leave Lily long enough to run all the way into town herself. She headed for the cottages that housed families, and grabbed the boy she found grubbing in the mud in front of a tiny brick box of a house. He said his name was McAuliffe, and the rest of his family was working. She promised him a dollar and sent him off to town as fast as his skinny legs could carry him.

When she returned to the boardinghouse, Mrs. Clinghorn was just removing the last of the bandaging. Margaret caught one sight of the mangled mess that had been Lily's hand and her stomach lurched.

Light-headed, she grabbed the back of the nearest chair to steady herself.

Margaret had butchered chickens and delivered calves and preserved pork. If asked, she would have said the sight of blood did not particularly bother her. But this was something else entirely, this blasphemy the machine had made of human flesh. Yet she found herself unable to look away.

Lily's fingers were crushed, unrecognizable, oozing fresh blood. Farther up the back of her hand and wrist, Margaret could see the small, densely packed rows where the sharp carding wires had bit deep, a mosaic of bright red dots.

"Did you find someone to send to town?" Mrs. Clinghorn dipped a cloth in water and dabbed lightly at Lily's hand. Lily groaned and twisted on the bed.

"Yes. Timmy McAuliffe. The doctor should be here soon."

"That's good." Mrs. Clinghorn paused, peered closer, and drew out a long, red-slicked wool fiber. "That's very good."

15

Dr. Ballard had three dingy gray tufts of hair on his head, and as he wound the last strip of linen bandage over Lily's hand, they all chose to point in different directions.

"There," he said, gently laying her wrapped hand on a clear square of linen, "all done. The bleeding has stopped for the most part, and I've splinted it with pasteboard, but you're to move this as little as possible, understand?"

Her eyes shut, as they'd been since Mrs. Clinghorn had unwrapped her hand and she'd gotten a glimpse of the mess, Lily nodded.

"Good."

Margaret had known Dr. Ballard for years. He'd treated her mother with skill, a genteelly confident manner, and what Margaret now suspected was a great deal more patience than her mother's various ailments had deserved. She'd never seen him so grave, so infinitely gentle, which told her better than any words the severity of Lily's wounds.

"May I see you in the hall for a moment, Margaret?"

"Of course."

He ushered her out, then closed the door behind him.

"We'll need some luck, Margaret, but I believe we might be able to save her hand after all."

"Oh, thank God."

"Yes, we should. He'll have more to do with it than I, if we manage to pull this off."

"What shall I do for her?"

"She needs a great deal of rest, mostly," he said. "She's lost a fair amount of blood. If you could get some nourishment down her, a good strong broth fairly regularly, it would help."

"Of course." Perhaps the McAuliffe boy would go back in to town for her, she thought, beginning to plan, and fetch her a nice big piece of beef. "Her hand, Doctor? Will she be able to use it?"

He rubbed his shiny temple as if it pained him. "We'll have to wait and see. She's young, but she's not terribly strong. I used plenty of padding, and the splint should support the bones, but if she begins to bleed again, or the hand swells too much, we'll have to take it back off. Call me right away if you see signs of either."

"Of course."

"My biggest concern right now is the pain. Her nerves are in shock right now, and much of her hand is probably somewhat numb. When it wears off, the pain might become a great deal worse."

Worse? How could Lily possibly endure it if the pain got any worse?"

"Is there anything we can give her?"

"I'll leave some powders with you. No more than four times a day, however; they are dangerous if overused. And you must make certain she stays in bed, rests for at least three full days. If she's well enough then, bring her on into town to my office and I'll check her out there. Otherwise, call me back if there are any problems, and I'll decide about further treatment."

"Thank you." She saw him out, then hurried back to her room. She met Mrs. Clinghorn in the doorway.

"She's resting," Mrs. Clinghorn said. "I'd better get back, I'll have hungry girls coming in soon."

"Thank you for all your help," she said, and meant it. She'd never have suspected that Mrs. Clinghorn would be so cool and compassionate in a crisis. "I don't know what I would have done if you hadn't been here."

"If you need anything later—it'll be a chore, taking care of an invalid and running this house, too. If I can help, let me know. It's not so much trouble to cook a little more while I'm at it."

"Thank you. Dr. Ballard said she needs a lot of rest, mostly, so I think we'll be fine."

"I'll see myself out." Mrs. Clinghorn took herself down the hall.

Margaret stood in the doorway and studied the still form on her bed. Lines of strain marked Lily's even features, and shadows bruised the skin beneath her eyes. Except for the big club of her bandaged hand lying on top of the quilts, she looked tiny beneath the bedclothes, a child aged long before her time.

"You can come in," Lily whispered. "I'm awake."

"You shouldn't be." Margaret crossed the room and took the chair beside the bed that Dr. Ballard had used while he worked. "Dr. Ballard said you need to rest. Three days, at least."

Lily swallowed. "My hand?"

Margaret took a deep breath, praying that what she said next would remain the truth. "You're not going to lose your hand."

Dampness lined Lily's closed lids, spiked her lashes, but not a tear escaped. "I'm going back to work tomorrow."

"You can't, Lily. It'll be all right."

"Have to." She opened eyes dark with shock, the blue purpling almost to the shade that stained the skin beneath. "Can't lose my job."

"You won't."

"Yes, I will," she whispered. "Happened before. Anne Markham."

"I'll talk to . . . someone. You're not to worry about it."

"Meachum, he'll . . ." The words came harder now, and Margaret tried to shush her, tried to insist she rest, but Lily wouldn't quiet.

Meachum again. Margaret was beginning to think she just might need to have a talk with this Mr. Meachum.

"My baby," Lily whispered brokenly.

"You have a . . . baby?"

"Yes," she said, voice hushed with exhaustion

and wonder. "Back . . . in St. Louis. My family . . . wouldn't talk to me anymore, after they found out. Couldn't . . . take care of him."

Lily has the saddest eyes I've ever seen, she'd told Kieran. No wonder.

"This was . . . only job I could get. Found a lady who'd take care of him for me . . . long as I keep sending the money." The tears broke free then, spilled over, pouring over her cheeks. "*Have* to."

"It'll be all right," Margaret promised. She had no right to, didn't have the least idea how she'd do it, but somehow she'd make this right. She'd ask Kieran for help, if it came to that; he had a lot of experience at fixing problems.

She stroked the dampened strands of hair off Lily's forehead, over and over until Lily's eyes fluttered shut, her breathing slowed, and she fell fitfully into sleep.

Then Margaret eased away and went in search of the obviously severely misguided Mr. Meachum.

Margaret stalked across the mill yard. With each step, the noise from the mill grew, and so did her anger. Still, the clamor that met her when she yanked open the door to the mill stunned her. The sound roared toward her with a force as palpable as a blow.

She stepped onto the mill floor and walked into hell. Aghast, she stopped and stared. Scouring vats poured out heat and steam, weighing down the heavy, lint-filled air. The grimy, broken windows allowed in only minimal light, and Margaret wondered how the workers could be expected to see what they were doing.

And always the noise, persistent, high-pitched, pulsing painfully right behind her temples. How in the world did they ever stand it? She'd been inside only a few minutes; her girls must endure hours and hours here.

She grabbed the nearest sweeper, a boy of perhaps eight, his broom a good six inches taller than he was, and mouthed "Mr. Meachum?" at him.

He pointed to the far end of the mill floor, at an open door, the rectangular window set into the rough wood smeared with steam. Margaret picked her way across the room, skirting the machines by as big a margin as possible, for she couldn't look at those big metal monsters without instantly recalling Lily's crushed hand.

She passed a few of her boarders, their worried gazes clearly expecting the worst, and she smiled reassuringly.

Lily would be all right. She would be even better after Margaret got her hands on that beastly overseer who'd demanded Ida return to work immediately and who'd led Lily to believe that she might lose her job.

She'd seen Mr. Meachum only from a distance across the mill yards. Her impression had been of an immensely intimidating man. He looked even more so here, hunched over a ridiculously undersized desk in this tiny cube of an office.

"Mr. Meachum." When he didn't look up, she reached behind and closed the office door, marginally blotting out the din of grinding gears. "Mr. Meachum!"

"Open the door." She found herself having to watch his mouth carefully, to match the movement of his lips to the few sounds she could catch to decipher his words.

"Excuse me?"

"Need to hear what's goin' on on the floor."

"Mr. Meachum, I'm here about Lily—"

"Can't hear you."

"I'm here about Lily!" she shouted, trying to remember the last time she'd shouted at anyone. She could easily have blamed it on the noise, but the truth was, it matched her mood.

"Lily? She gonna lose the hand?"

"No, she's not going to lose the hand."

"Good. Put her on light duty tomorrow. Maybe just feeding the roper—"

"Mr. Meachum!" she screamed at the top of her lungs and found it immensely satisfying. "She's not coming to work tomorrow!"

"She ain't?" He shook his head. "Gonna have to dock her pay, then."

"Lily seems to be under the misapprehension that she's in danger of losing her job—"

"She can't do the work, she ain't got a job," he said shortly.

"Lily received her injuries at *work*, Mr. Meachum. It is the mill's responsibility to—"

"No responsibility. Ain't our fault if the girls are careless."

"Mr. Meachum! This is intolerable!" Margaret squinted, envisioning Mr. Meachum's big round head being stuffed into the picker that stood right outside the office door. "You must take care of this girl! She must have full pay while she recovers and a job to come back to as well! Medical care, too!"

"I'm done talking to you." Rather than sliding back his chair, Meachum simply took hold with his meaty hands and shoved his desk aside. He grabbed her elbow and steered her out of his office, across the mill floor, and right out the front door.

"You cannot do this—"

"I damn well can." He gave her a little shove, which from such a huge man was enough to send her stumbling out into the yard. "You got a problem with how I run my workers, you take it up with my boss!"

And he slammed the door shut.

"Well!" Margaret stared at the closed door in disbelief. Of all the—

Take it up with my boss.

Margaret whipped around. Back across the mill yard she went, skirts flapping behind her like sails in full wind. She burst through the door of the small building that served as the main offices, where she'd applied for her job in the first place.

Her forehead creased in a frown, Lucy was ensconced behind a desk, leaning back in her chair, staring at the door that led to the back room. Her hair shone, her blouse was clean, her hands pink and unscarred.

Margaret thought of the mill floor she'd just left, the noise, dark heat, and overpowering smell of lanolin and machine grease. No wonder the other girls resented Lucy.

"Lucy, there you are. Who is that horrid Meachum's boss?"

"Hmm?" The chair creaked as she swung around. "Meachum?"

"The overseer. There's been an accident. Lily was hurt at the mill, and I need to speak with Mr. Meachum's superior." Though everyone is Meachum's superior, she thought with snide satisfaction.

"Oh." Lucy's brow cleared. "That would be the mill superintendent, I suppose."

"And where might I find him?"

"St. Louis."

Margaret suppressed a sigh, checking her frustration. It was not Lucy's fault. "St. Louis?" she prompted.

"He's on a business trip."

"Who's in charge here, Lucy?"

Lucy's gaze slid back to the door. Whatever did the girl find so fascinating there? "That would be Walter, I suppose."

"Good." Walter Cowdry had always impressed her as a reasonable and intelligent man. Margaret began to hope she might clear this all up quickly after all. "Where might I find him?"

"Right back there." Lucy pointed to the door.

"Excellent." Deciding the severity of this particular situation allowed her to dispense with politeness, a blasphemy that would have sent her mother to bed for a week, Margaret marched to the door and reached for the knob.

"Miss Thayer?"

Margaret paused and glanced back over her shoulder. "Yes, Lucy?"

"Lily . . . is she badly hurt?"

So, the girl was not as indifferent as she'd led

them all to believe. "I believe she's going to be all right."

Lucy smiled tentatively. "I'm glad."

The door swung open before Margaret had a chance to reach for the knob again. "Lucy, would you—Miss Thayer!" Walter stepped into the outer office. "What can I do for you, Miss Thayer? I do hope you're not quitting on us already."

"No," she said briskly. "But there is something you should be aware of."

Quickly she filled him in on the basic facts of Lily's accident. He winced as she described Lily's injury, and his expression grew grave upon hearing Dr. Ballard's prognosis.

"I'm glad it's no worse than it is," he said. He removed his spectacles and began polishing them against his crisp shirtfront.

For the first time since the accident had happened, Margaret's righteous anger began to ebb. Surely everything would be taken care of properly.

"Thank you for informing me," Walter said, nodding at her. What astonishing eyes he has, Margaret thought. Amazing she'd never noticed them before. "And now, if you'll excuse me, I must get back to—"

"You don't understand," Margaret broke in. "That poor girl is under the impression that the Lessing Mill will not be paying her doctor's bills."

"Ah . . ." Walter hooked his eyeglasses over his ears and shot a quick glance at Lucy, who'd sat up in her chair and was listening attentively. "Mill employees are responsible for their own medical care, this is true."

"But she was injured on the job!" Margaret protested.

"Regardless, all our workers pay their own medical bills. They know this when they come to work for us. And they receive fair wages, surely enough to cover the occasional doctor bill."

"Forget about Dr. Ballard's fees for now," Margaret said impatiently. There were much more important issues at hand. "Lily is under the impression that her job is in jeopardy if she does not return to work immediately. If we could set her mind to rest on this one issue, I am certain it would aid her recovery immensely."

"Well." Walter tucked his thumbs behind his braces and shot another pleading look at Lucy. So, that was where the wind blew, did it? However, she'd no time to ponder that development now. "We have great difficulty in keeping all our positions filled, as I'm sure you know. As long as Lily can perform the work satisfactorily, it's very unlikely that there wouldn't be a place for her when she's ready to return."

"So, though her evaluation of the situation was correct, as a practical matter she need not worry about it?" Margaret asked politely.

Walter grinned, relieved. "Yes."

"Let me see if I've gotten this straight." Margaret narrowed her eyes at Walter, who was quickly replacing that detestable Meachum as the villain of this piece. She held up her hand to tick off her points. "First, though Lily received her injuries on the job—solely due, I am quite certain, to those deplorable working conditions—there are no allowances for her medical care and she will not be paid at all during her recovery. Am I to assume, however, that, during that period, she still will be held accountable for her room and board?"

Walter looked distinctly uncomfortable. "Well, yes, Miss Thayer, but I assure you this is standard industry practice."

"Second, she must only *hope* that her position is held open for her while she's unable to work?" Margaret held up another finger. "Third, if she—"

"Miss Thayer, you simply do not—"

"Kindly do me the courtesy not to interrupt while I am speaking." Margaret fixed him with an expression she'd seen her mother use a hundred times, though she'd never tried it herself, and Walter shut up. Why hadn't she realized before just how useful that look could be? "Third, if Lily sustains any permanent disabilities from the accident, she is of no further use to the Lessing Mill?"

"You are painting this in the worst possible light, Miss Thayer—"

"And what, exactly, other light is there?"

"Miss Thayer," Walter said desperately, "surely you do not think that this would be how I would run things? If I—" He broke off, his shoulders slumping.

And well they should slump, for clearly Walter, as had Meachum, intended to pass the blame on up the line. "You can rest assured that I will be speaking to Mr. Lessing about this. I am certain that he would not approve of this hard-hearted shirking of the mill's responsibilities to his employees. Next time that I—"

"Here's your chance," Lucy put in.

"Excuse me?"

Face alight with interest, Lucy cocked her head toward the door behind Margaret. "Mr. Lessing's right here."

"Right here?" Calm, Margaret told herself. Businesslike. Benjamin Lessing surely understood the benefits of earning his employees' loyalty, as he had done with Redemption's residents. She smoothed her hands down the front of her skirt, brushing out any stray wrinkles, took a deep breath, and turned to face Benjamin. "Mr. Lessing, several things have happened today which I think you need to be made aware of. There's been an accident at the mill—"

Benjamin held up a hand, cutting her off. "I've been standing here for a while. I think I pretty much heard everything."

"Oh." Prepared to run through the entire story, Margaret paused to mentally flip forward a few pages, to all the arguments for why the Lessing Mill had to take much better care of Lily than it apparently intended to. "Then you understand my concerns."

"I understand." Benjamin strolled across the room, hitched his thigh up on the corner of the desk, and crossed his arms over his chest, clearly at ease. "I understand that—except for that ill-advised statement of his personal opinion at the end there, which he knows full well has no place in business—Walter has given you a pretty fair summary of our position."

"What?" Margaret burst out, too shocked and outraged to say anything else.

"I surely admire your coming to your boarder's defense like this," Benjamin continued. "It certainly tells me you are right for the job we hired you to do. But from now on you should concentrate on your work and leave the running of things to those of us who can do it better."

"Mr. Lessing, I cannot believe this is your final position on this matter. You've cultivated a reputation in town for kindness and generosity, and to find that it does not extend to your own employees truly shocks me."

Benjamin's eyes went cold. "As I said, I admire your dedication on that girl's . . . I believe you called her Lily?" At Margaret's nod, he continued, "Lily's behalf. But is this really an issue you want to risk your job on?"

Anger wasn't an emotion Margaret was particularly familiar with; she'd buried her own years ago. But now she found it had its uses. It allowed her— no, forced her—to do something that she never imagined she'd do: stand up to Benjamin Lessing.

"Mr. Lessing," she clipped out, "I have managed to survive for some years without your *job* and, if it comes to that, I believe I can struggle along again without your help. But these young women, they do not have that luxury. If you would only—"

"Would they be better off if there were no Lessing Mill at all?"

"Of course not. That's not the point—"

"You've been on the farm a long time," Benjamin said. "You don't understand business. The textile

industry is a competitive one, and I'm bidding for
every contract against mills on the east coast. I
chose to found this mill here, Miss Thayer, because
I believed the territories needed a mill of their own.
If I paid for every employee's little injury, and all the
days they don't feel up to working, I'd be out of
business in no time. No one would have a job, not
just this girl. And the town wouldn't have all the
money that this mill brings to it, either."

Or to you, Margaret thought. A well-reasoned
speech, designed to please. One that, if she didn't
know Lily, hadn't seen her crushed hand and
looked into her terrified, pain-shadowed eyes,
Margaret might even have believed.

"Surely there is a middle ground," Margaret said
crisply. "Between the demands of a competitive
business and out-and-out cruelty. I do not believe
that living up to your responsibilities to your
employees necessarily means financial ruin. On the
contrary—"

"As I said, Miss Thayer, you don't understand
business." Benjamin stood up and patted her on
the shoulder. Genial, paternal, and utterly dismis-
sive. "I, on the other hand, have no more time for
this nonsense. You trundle on back to your duties.
I've got some real work to do."

"Fine," she said. But she'd learned a lot these
past few weeks. "I guess I'll just have to go on into
town and see what kind of help I can drum up
there. The town can be very generous, you know.
I'm sure that many of them would jump at the
chance to assist a young woman who, through no
fault of her own, found herself helpless, injured,

and destitute. Particularly when I tell them that she has so few other options."

Gotcha, Margaret thought as Benjamin stopped in his tracks. He'd carefully cultivated his munificent image in Redemption, enjoying it to the fullest.

"Those people owe me."

"Yes," Margaret agreed. When it came down to siding with Margaret Thayer or Benjamin Lessing, Margaret had no doubt on which side of the fence most of her acquaintances would fall. Not that she blamed them one bit; they had families to support, too. "But they also respect you."

They both knew that once she'd told her story, Benjamin Lessing would never again inspire quite the same awe and admiration he'd always owned in Redemption.

He studied her carefully, as if trying to decide how easily intimidated she would be. Margaret thought that perhaps it was the first time he'd ever really noticed her. She lifted her chin, trying to convey her firm determination.

How had she ever gotten to this point? It amazed her, that would she take a chance like this against the most powerful man in Redemption.

But what good was all that independence and self-sufficiency if she couldn't use it on behalf of someone who needed her help? Perhaps she'd allowed herself to be consumed by worry about her own survival for far too long. She'd forgotten there were others in far worse circumstances than she.

Finally Benjamin broke out into his familiar, expansive smile. The cold hostility in his eyes ruined it. "All right, Miss Thayer. Now that I've had a chance to think about your points, I've decided they've got some merit. It's not like I don't feel badly about what happened. We'll make sure the poor thing is taken care of."

The poor thing. *Thing*. That summed it all up right there, didn't it?

But he'd said he agreed with her, promised to take care of Lily, and she couldn't chance antagonizing him further. "You'll hold her job for her? And pay her until she's well again?"

"I said I would." He spun on his heel, signaling for Walter to follow him.

How impolite of him, Margaret thought as the front door creaked shut behind the two men. He hadn't even bothered to say good-bye.

16

Margaret pressed a hand to her fluttering stomach as fear gave way to relief and exhilaration. She'd actually done it! Who would have thought?

"That was nice of you," Lucy mumbled.

"Hmm?"

Lucy's chin hovered around her chest, and her eyes stayed firmly focused on her desktop, as if what she said embarrassed her. "What you did for Lily, fighting for her like that."

Like no one ever does for you? Margaret wondered. Of all the girls living in the boardinghouse, Lucy had seemed the most self-contained, smugly satisfied with her office job and her private room. But there was a tremor underlying what she'd just said, a coloring of regret.

"You didn't have to do that," she went on.

"Yes, I did," Margaret said.

"Oh, well, I suppose so." Lucy's fingers trailed

over the edge of the desk. "No one else would have."

"That's not what I meant. I had to do it for me, too."

Lucy's head snapped up. "What?"

Feelings were things to be curbed, controlled, kept to oneself. Margaret had always accepted that advice unthinkingly. Why chance burdening others with your emotions? Most people wouldn't want to know them, and you risked having them turned back on you. But maybe Lucy needed to hear and see them as much as Margaret needed to feel them.

Maybe, instead, emotions were things to be shared.

"It's been a long time, Lucy, since I've cared for anyone like that. Since anyone needed me to fight for them."

"But . . . you have that friend. I saw you with her."

"Mrs. Perkins?"

"I think so."

"Martha Ann doesn't need anyone to fight for her. She does it quite nicely for herself already." Margaret smiled. "She's a wonderful friend, Lucy, but we've known each other for years. I'd forgotten how to *learn* to care about someone, to begin it."

Lucy picked at her thumbnail. But Margaret suspected Lucy was attending much more carefully than she seemed to be, and that what Margaret said next might be much more important than it appeared on the face of it.

"I forgot that you don't wait for someone to show they care about you, and that you don't choose to do it. You just . . . care."

Like she did about Kieran.

Margaret waited for the panic, for the rush of recriminations and dismay that surely would accompany such a realization. She found peace instead, the certainty that it wasn't the caring itself that hurt.

"Oh." If Lucy chewed on that thumbnail anymore, she was going to draw blood.

"Walter . . . I do believe he's sweet on you, Lucy."

"I know." She shrugged, as if it were of no consequence, but a flush tinted her cheeks. Jamming her hands in her pockets, she looked up, determinedly facing Margaret directly. "It'll be an awful lot of work for you, taking care of Lily, running up and down the stairs."

Subject closed, Margaret thought. Lucy obviously did not want to talk about Walter. "No, I put her in my room. It'll be all right."

"Your room? Where will you sleep?"

"In Lily's bed, I suppose." She hadn't given the matter any thought.

"Then you'll be running up and down the stairs all the time, anyway."

"The parlor, then. On the sofa."

"That'd be uncomfortable." Lucy rocked back on her heels. "You could take my room," she offered.

"Lucy, I know how much your privacy means to you, you don't have to—"

"Yes, I do," Lucy said, echoing Margaret's words back to her.

Margaret's head bumped against the wall, jerking her awake. She'd been sitting here for hours, huddled up against Mrs. Clinghorn's boardinghouse because it was nearest the office, watching for a telltale flare of light in the office window. Thankfully, no one had stumbled over her so far; she'd have one heck of a time explaining what she was doing there.

She squinted at the sky, trying to judge the time. Long, horizontal strips of clouds drifted across the half-full moon. Past one o'clock, certainly. Ida had offered to stay with Lily for a while, giving Margaret a chance to rest undisturbed. Instead, Margaret had slipped out here. Soon, though, she'd have to go back and relieve Ida.

The clouds shifted again. Oh, at last; a dark figure hunched over the doorknob to the office. "Kieran!" she whisper-shouted, climbing to her feet. Her legs had been crunched beneath her too long and they almost gave out beneath her.

"Kieran!" She hobbled across the small expanse of packed earth that separated the boardinghouses from the office.

"What the hell are you doing here?" His annoyance quickly turned to concern when he saw her limp. "What's the matter with you?"

"My foot fell asleep. I've been waiting for you for hours!"

"I mentioned to you I'd intended to search the offices tonight, didn't I?"

"Yes."

"That was remarkably stupid of me."

Regretfully, Margaret let his comment pass. Agreeing with him would have been just too easy, and they'd only end up squabbling about whether she should be here or not. "Let's get going, Kieran. I want to go home and get to sleep. Do you need me to light a candle so you can see what you're doing? I brought my own this time."

"How enterprising of you, but no." He pushed the door open. "There's enough light tonight."

She slid past him into the front offices. "Do you want to divide up? Which room do you want?"

"Let's do the back office first. Files of any importance are more likely to be in there."

That door was locked, too, and this time it took all of two minutes before the lock yielded to him.

"That's an interesting skill you have there, Kieran."

"It's occasionally useful."

"Sometime I'd like to hear how you learned something like that."

"No." He shut the door behind him, locking it once again from the inside. He moved swiftly around the room, pulling the shades down over the windows to prevent their lights from showing too obviously.

"Where do you want me to start?" she asked, after he'd lit two candles and handed her one.

"How about the desk? I'll take these files over here."

"Fine." At least she'd get to sit down, she thought, sinking into the big upholstered chair. The center drawer slid open easily, revealing a neat arrangement of papers, pens, and a ring of keys. "What exactly are we looking for?"

"Employment records, for one thing. Make note of any woman hired eight or nine months ago. Or anything else that looks interesting. If you find any travelogs, let me know right away."

"Interesting," she repeated. She picked up a stack of what looked like billing receipts and sighed. They did not look at all interesting, but she supposed she'd better look through them, all the same.

She worked her way slowly through the drawers, poking into folders, riffling through a clutch of letters. The promising tin box hidden far in the back of the middle drawer held only a stash of horehound candy; she surreptitiously slipped one into her mouth before returning it to its place.

"Kieran?" He was bent over the third drawer of the cabinet, the weak candlelight revealing a look of intense concentration as he flipped through the files with amazing speed.

She wished he'd look at her like that.

"You don't really read that fast, do you?"

"Yes," he clipped out.

"This bottom drawer of the desk is locked."

"Wait just a second, I'll—" His head whipped up.

"Kieran?"

He placed a finger against his lips to silence her.

"There's someone coming," he whispered.

"Do you always get caught in the act so often?" she asked. "First Dodge, now this?"

"Only when I'm with you." He angled toward the door, ready to place his body between whoever was out there and Maggie. "He's only unlocking the front door now. Here's the plan. I'm going to go on out there and see if I can catch him by surprise. You hide under the desk. You stay there, Maggie, until it's all over. Do you hear me, Maggie, I—"

He heard the grate of a window opening, turned and swore. Maggie was halfway out, one leg slung over the sill. She paused to glance back at him. "Aren't you coming?" she asked, and disappeared.

"Damn!" He headed for the window, but she was already gone. She raced across the yard, in and out of the bars of moonlight and shadow, heading for the mill. Why the hell had she aimed for the mill?

There was only one thing he could do.

He went after her.

He dashed across the mill yard—wide open, empty space, no cover at all, his shoulder blades twitching the whole way, expecting a bullet in his back. But at least if someone fired in this direction from the office, he was between the shooter and Maggie.

He caught up with her just before she reached the mill. The door to the stair tower wasn't locked, thank the Lord; there wasn't time for stopping to pick it open if it had been. He yanked open the door and stuffed her inside, slamming it shut behind him.

"Come on!" He heard the whoosh of her skirts, then the sound of her felt pelting on the stairway.

Up all three flights of stairs, right behind her. If their pursuer didn't hear them thundering up the steps it would be a miracle.

She finally stopped when she reached the top. It was too dark in the tower to allow him to see her, but he could hear her gasping for air, and that kept him from barreling right into her. He groped for the wall, darkness swirling dizzily around him.

Don't think about it, he ordered himself. Pretend you're still down on the nice safe ground.

"What the holy hell do you think you're doing?" The harsh whisper was wildly frustrating; he wanted to shout at her, damn it, so loud every timber in the place would shake with his words.

"Taking the high ground."

"Excuse me?"

"You know." Between trying to suck in air, she sounded pleased with her strategy. She wouldn't be nearly so pleased when he strangled her for scaring him half out of his wits. "Like in battle. The army who takes the high ground always has the advantage, don't they?"

"Jesus." The woman had gone out of her mind. She thought she was a strategist now. "And back there at the office? I was planning—"

"Sometimes there isn't any time for planning, Kieran. Sometimes you just have to take the chance and go."

"Dear God, what have I done?" he groaned.

Hampered by the darkness, he groped for her hand. She wasn't getting away from him again if he could help it.

"Kieran! Now is not the time—"

"Sorry. That wasn't what I was aiming for." He tried again, with better results. Her thin strong fingers linked tightly with his, and he felt better now that he knew exactly where she was.

"Kieran—" she whispered.

"Shh." Over the blood thundering in his ears, he strained for any whisper of sound that revealed their pursuer. From far below them came the creak of the door opening, the sound of furtive footsteps on the bottom of the stairs.

Kieran had guessed that if it was the Uncatchable Man who had followed them, he wouldn't risk a shot. There'd be little chance of hitting either of them, and it might draw unwanted spectators.

Kieran, however, had no such compunctions. And he had to keep whoever chased them from getting any closer. He aimed down the stair tower.

"Don't scream," he told Margaret.

And fired.

Damn it, she screamed, her voice echoing hollowly down the long shaft of the staircase along with the sound of the shot.

He heard the answering zing of a bullet, the thud of it hitting wood a fair distance below. But the stealthy footsteps stopped.

He gave Margaret's hand a tug, hoping she'd follow him without protest, and slipped out of the stairway and onto the third floor of the mill. His gun hand grazed the plaster wall, helping him fix their location.

"Where did that come from?" she whispered near his ear, barely audible. "The gun?"

Well, she'd lasted longer than he expected without comment. "Pocket."

"Oh." And then, after they'd crept farther along the wall, "Kieran? Do you know where we're going?"

"Yes."

"How? I can't see anything. You can't see in *this,* can you?"

He almost said yes, just to annoy her. "I'm touching the wall."

"So?"

"So you didn't think I'd have already checked this place out thoroughly?"

"Oh."

Almost there, Kieran judged. Now the only question was just how loudly Maggie was going to protest.

And whether he could really do it.

"If we're trapped up here, we can go down the other stair tower. There are two, you know."

"I know." And if their pursuer had half a brain, they'd walk down the other stairs and straight into the line of fire. "I've got a better idea."

They met a corner and turned right. The looms were on this end of the floor, Kieran remembered, beneath the clerestory windows that allowed the weavers to see their work better. A filament of moonlight leaked in, permitting him to make out the bulky shapes of the huge machines.

Against his left knuckles the wall changed from rough plaster to splintery wood. There.

He guided Margaret to the nearest loom and wrapped her hand around a metal bar. "Stay here, Maggie. You have to promise me, don't move!"

"Do you hear something?"

"Not yet."

Fleetingly wishing he had more hands, he tucked his gun back in his pocket and undid the latches that held together the big double doors. They swung wide, revealing a big square of cloud-striped sky.

Bile churned at the base of his throat. God, he hated heights!

The doors allowed the mill workers to lower crates of the finished product via rope and pulley, rather than having to maneuver bolts of cloth and spindles of yarn down the stairs.

Don't look down, don't look down.

Kieran took a good hold on the wood that framed the open doorway, leaned out, and snagged the sturdy rope that hung down from both sides of the pulley wheel.

He knotted one end of the rope around the loom, giving it a sharp yank to make certain it was stable. Then he went back to Maggie and enfolded her in his arm.

He wrapped her own arms around his neck, hooking his right elbow securely around her back. He grasped the rope firmly in his left hand.

"Maggie," he said quietly.

"Yes?" Here it is, she thought. The romantic, we're-going-to-die-any-minute declaration of affection. Though she appreciated the notion, she'd really rather not die to get it.

"For God's sake, don't let gooooo!"

17

She whimpered all the way to the ground. So did he.

Oh, she knew he would deny it, chalk it up to grunts of strain caused by having most of the weight of two whole people on one arm.

But later, when this was all over, that thought would comfort her.

As soon as they hit the ground, he grabbed her hand and yanked so hard it nearly sent her, nose-first, into the dirt. She stumbled after him, found her feet, and then they were off, hand in hand, racing for the trees.

She had to trust his ability to see through the darkness again. They bobbed around cottonwood trunks. Squeezed between twin box elders. Deeper into the grove, away from the river, away from the little cottage they'd searched the night before.

Her heart pumped. Her legs ached. Each breath seared her lungs.

Finally he stopped, hard up against the trunk of the biggest tree they'd passed. He pulled her to him, tucking her head along the crook of his neck.

"Shhh," he warned her.

And while he listened for danger, for the bullets that could end their life, she listened to the sound of his heart pounding sure and strong and wild. She felt the steady pressure of his hand against her lower back, the button of his shirt biting into her cheek, the push of her breasts against his ribs. The smell of the woods filled her nose, but stronger still was his smell, warm, male, and perfectly remembered.

"Is he following us?" she asked at last.

"No." His hand came up, stroked her hair. "We're safe."

Safe. Her lungs still bellowed air; blood still rushed in her veins. But, in that instant, all that fear and desperate, surging panic immediately transformed into something else. Something just as powerful, just as vital and overwhelming.

Passion.

Slowly she turned her head, touched her lips to where his pulse beat hard in his throat.

"Maggie." He gripped her upper arms, as if he meant to push her away, but there was no urgency to it, no insistence. Instead, he held her there, a little away from his body, caught between *should* and *want*.

"Kieran." She murmured his name back to him, a low, seductive word that was obviously an invitation, even a demand.

Her hands found their way beneath his duster and slid down his sides, gliding over ribs and muscle and man-warmed cotton. She felt him drag in a breath and, with it, struggle for control.

Control was the last thing she wanted. Instead she craved the elemental. Life, death, mating.

"We shouldn't . . ," His voice caught, trailed off as her hands reached his lower back and threatened to go farther. "Oh, God, not . . . now. We're *outside* . . . hell . . ." he managed.

"Yes, now." She gave him no time, no pause to think. He was the one who'd taught her this, how danger and its survival made the senses heighten and hunger. Now he'd help ease this, find expression for the celebrating, heady rush of being alive.

She dropped to her knees, there in the damp earth pricked with dried grass and twigs, and pressed her open mouth to him. Hard, full, over much-washed denim and the warm metal buttons that fastened it.

Even through the fabric of his pants, he could feel her, the steady demand of her mouth and a hint of her heated, moist breath.

He growled, a feral sound, dangerous, warning. But they both knew it for what it really was.

The sound of surrender.

He seized her by the arms and yanked her up, spinning, pushing her up against the trunk of the tree, one arm wrapped behind her back. Pain singed his hand—the rope burns, he remembered, but it was only another sensation, a less powerful one than the others he was now experiencing.

Fast now. Blindingly so. He rucked her skirts up around her waist, letting in a cool wash of night air.

"You want it?" His fingers brushed her once, quickly, grazing the dampened fabric of her drawers. She felt him fumble with his own clothing, and then the nudge of his erection against her right through the slit in her underclothes.

"You want it?" he repeated harshly. "Tell me you want it."

She brought her hands up and cupped his face in her palms, fingers searching out the precious features she couldn't see well enough in the darkness, tracing the outline of his lips. "I want *you*."

Another groan, another surrender; to emotion this time, instead of simply lust. He brought his mouth to hers even as he brought himself inside her.

But they were both too far gone to go slowly. Maggie pulled her legs up and wrapped them around his waist to urge him closer.

Hard and quick and deep. The bite of bark against her shoulders, the nip of his teeth against her lips, his fingers gripping tight beneath one thigh. And Kieran, always Kieran, stroking fuller, faster, until the world splintered around her and she cried out into the darkness, a call the grove's animals would recognize, the wild cry of the body giving over to its most primitive instincts.

"God, Maggie." He dragged air into his lungs, clearing his senses. "Are you all right?"

"I . . . think so."

He eased her legs down and himself out of her. Belatedly worried that he'd crushed her against the tree, he rolled with her so his back was against the trunk and he could pull her up to his heart.

But that was all his wobbly, stunned body could manage. Her skirts stayed wadded around her legs, his pants unfastened, while they waited for the world to stop spinning and sanity to return.

"I'm probably going to have the imprint of cottonwood bark on my forearm for a week," he said, faintly surprised the words had come out coherently.

She laughed softly.

"Maggie, do you know how long it's been since I . . . took a chance like—"

"Oh, Kieran!" She gasped, bringing her hands to her mouth in shock. "Your device, I completely forgot, I'm so sorry, I—"

"Yup, Maggie, it was all your fault. I tried to fight you off, I really did, but you were just too much for me."

"Kieran," she said, truly distraught. This is what came of her jumping in without caution, she thought. "I know how important it is to you, I don't know how to tell you how sorry I am—"

"Shh." He pressed his lips against her hair, breathing in the scent of it. "There were two of us here, remember? And besides, I told you I had everything we ever needed in my pocket, *didn't* I? I just couldn't think long enough to get it."

"Really? In your pocket?" If she'd have found his devices, back when she searched his things, she wondered what in the world she'd have made of them. Never in a million years would she have correctly guessed what they were for.

"Yeah." He rubbed her shoulders, her back; all the tenderness there'd been no time for earlier. "Maggie, you . . . *overwhelmed* me."

Warmth bloomed in her heart. "You don't regret it?"

"There is no living man on the face of the earth who could regret that," he said fervently.

Her conscience eased a little. "But what if . . . ?" She didn't even dare say it, for fear of tempting fate, that voicing it would make it happen.

"It's not very likely, just one time like that."

Someday they were going to have to move, Margaret thought. And walk, as impossible as that seemed right now. But please, not yet.

"We're both all grown up, Maggie. And we're not—" he stopped, swallowing hard "—otherwise attached. If it happens, we'll deal with it then."

He didn't sound too upset. Maggie was afraid to let herself even think about it, afraid she'd read things into it. Like the fact that he didn't seem too horrified by the idea that they might have made a child together, that there might be more for them than this.

She wouldn't let herself get drawn into those hopes, into believing there might be a future for them. She couldn't imagine him staying in

Redemption, any more than she could picture herself trailing him around the country while he chased lost causes and she tried to talk him out of it for his own safety and her peace of mind.

"Anyway," he went on, "we'll just have to be more careful the next time."

"The . . . next time?"

"Of course."

"I—I didn't think, this just *happened*, and I . . ." The words trailed off. How could she blame him for believing there'd be a next time? She'd been the seducer, twice; of course he'd assume she wanted a full-fledged affair with him.

"I didn't think," she repeated lamely.

"Maggie." He kissed her, so sweet, a kiss clearly meant to persuade and tempt. When he raised his head, her mind was fuzzy and dizzy and utterly without logic.

"I'm not going to lie to you, Maggie. When I find Melissa, and this is all over, I'm leaving. I have to; this is what I do, and I can't do it here."

He'd only said what she already knew. Damn it, it shouldn't hurt so much to hear it.

"But while I'm here . . ." His hands flexed against her back, drawing her closer. "I want you. We're good together. That doesn't seem so wrong, Maggie, not to me."

Is it wrong?

The hell of it all was she wasn't even sure any longer. Before Kieran, before all the excitement and upheaval and change he'd brought to her life, at least she'd always been sure.

The other times hadn't seemed like such a sin.

An experience, an experiment; surely God wouldn't begrudge her that once in her life? And this time—there'd been no decision here, just a raging, bursting release of too much emotion.

But to calmly, freely *decide*, to plan to have an affair with him, with complete forethought and her eyes wide open, knowing there was no future in it, knowing how it would surely end?

Somehow a calculated sin seemed far worse than an impulsive one. She should have been wise enough and strong enough to head it off.

If she'd learned anything the past few weeks, it was that some risks were worth taking. But others weren't. How did you tell which were which? This seemed such a big one to take, to indulge herself with him and risk being destroyed when he had to go.

She knew only two things.

When Kieran McDermott left, she would miss him. Desperately, quite painfully, whether they loved with their bodies again or not.

And that she wanted him with everything she was.

"You don't have to say anything now," he said, voice low in her ear, seductive as the brush of his hand along her naked thigh. "Your place . . . is the Perkins boy there all the time? Does he stay in the house?"

"No. He only goes in the morning and the evening, just to feed the animals."

"Good. Thursday afternoon, one o'clock. Will you meet me?"

"I—"

His mouth found her neck and she couldn't talk anymore. He skimmed his lips up, nibbled on an earlobe, and her legs went weak.

"Please come."

18

❦

After Lucy offered her room for Margaret's use, Margaret had invited the girl to have lunch with her the next day. Margaret always ate the noon meal alone, after the rush of feeding all the mill girls was over—they ate fast, rushing to gobble down their food before the bell called them back to work.

Margaret couldn't stand to have her lunch like that, so she waited to eat privately, or with Mrs. Clinghorn. She'd asked Lucy to join her as an expression of her gratitude; she suspected that unselfishly offering up her room for another's comfort was a big step for Lucy. But Margaret had been surprised when Lucy quickly accepted.

To Margaret's way of thinking, their lunch had been an awkward failure. They'd little in common, their conversation stilted and forced.

So it had surprised Margaret when Lucy asked what time to return to the boardinghouse for lunch the next day. And she'd seemed genuinely disappointed this morning when Margaret had told her that they'd have to skip it today, for Margaret had to take the rapidly healing Lily into town for an appointment with Dr. Ballard.

Dr. Ballard had been encouraged by Lily's progress; he'd even ventured the opinion that, though the motion in her right hand would always be partially restrained, she'd be able to use it for most anything but the finest activities, like sewing or writing.

They'd returned to the mill much earlier than Margaret expected. The trip had tired Lily out and she'd gratefully crawled back into bed. Especially, Lily had said, because she'd been having trouble sleeping—had Margaret heard the thunder, too? Her question had puzzled Margaret, until she remembered the shot Kieran had fired, and their pursuer's answering bullet.

Margaret assumed Lily would sleep for much of the afternoon.

Digging into leftover stuffed cabbage all by herself held little appeal. Margaret knew she'd just sit there, staring at her plate, and thinking about whether or not she should, or would, meet Kieran the next afternoon.

She'd already thought about it so much her head ached. And a few other parts of her as well, when she remembered the feel of him inside her. Mulling it over some more wasn't going to help anything. By now she'd looked at it from every darn angle there was, and she still hadn't come up with an answer.

All she'd done was miss out on a great deal of rest.

So she decided to go ask Lucy to join her for lunch after all. Anything was better than continuing to relive that last persuasive kiss in her mind. It would only get her body all heated up when there wasn't a darn thing she could do about it right now, and she still didn't know whether she ever would.

Rain smudged the horizon with deep blue; a storm would blow in later tonight, she thought. But the sun still shone over the mill. In the distance, the air whirred with the call of a prairie hen. Wildflowers dotted the deep green shortgrass: scarlet-eyed daisies; wild mustard; tiny pink, purple, and white anemones.

The outer office was quiet and still, lazily warm and empty. Just in case Lucy was in the back room, filing papers, Margaret knocked lightly on the door.

No answer. Perhaps Lucy had been called away on other business. Odd, because she never seemed to have all that much to do, though perhaps Walter or Benjamin had finally realized that and dug up something to occupy her.

Just as Margaret turned to leave, she heard a thump on the other side of the door, then a low moan.

A month ago, she would have hurried out and minded her own business. But how could she regard the inner office as private and off-limits when she'd already searched it in the middle of the night? She tested the knob, rattling it loudly. "Lucy?"

She heard nothing more. But trepidation prickled

the back of her neck. What if there was something truly wrong? Lucy might be ill, or injured. Or whoever had nearly caught them two nights ago could have come back and was holding Lucy hostage in the back room.

And where the heck was Kieran when she needed him?

Her shoes echoed loudly on the planks as she stamped across the floor and slammed the front door closed behind her. If someone was lurking in the back room, she didn't want them to miss her exit.

She glanced around. Near the mill, men unloaded a wagon of raw wool. They paid her no mind, and there seemed to be no one else around. Everyone should be too well occupied with their work to notice her.

She slipped around the corner of the office building, flattening herself against the outside wall. There were no other buildings at this end of the mill grounds; the only way someone would see her was if they came straight across the fields.

Bending over at the waist, she crept along, hugging the wall, placing her feet carefully. She crouched beneath the side window.

Fortunately, the window was open to the warm June breeze, so she'd be able to see in. Not so fortunately, there was nothing to hide her, either; if someone inside happened to glance at the window just when she looked in, they'd see her as clearly as the coming storm.

Another sound. The creak of the big desk chair,

she thought; she remembered it from when she'd sat in it herself.

Oh, well, Margaret thought philosophically. She was getting pretty good at running for it.

She poked her head over the edge of the window.

Lucy.

Margaret bit down on her tongue hard to stifle a gasp. The image seared itself in her brain: Lucy in the big desk chair, her head tipped back, her skirts up and thighs wide. A man, his back to the window, kneeling down between her legs. Details registered, a crazy-quilt of impressions—the contrast of his brown hair against the pale skin of Lucy's inner legs. The whiteness of his shirt pulled tight across his shoulders. Lucy's arm limp on the desk, her fingers ivory-pink on the dark brown blotter.

Breathe. Move. Anything!

But she stayed frozen, horror washing over her in sick waves.

Perhaps she'd made some noise after all, some involuntary gasp of shock. Or perhaps it was merely coincidence. Lucy's head lolled to one side, rolling across the high wooden back of the desk chair, and she opened her eyes.

Margaret knew immediately Lucy saw her there. Her eyes widened, her mouth parted on a gasp. Margaret waited for her to say something, to shout *stop*, to cover herself. Then Lucy's eyes chilled, a glaze of dissolute indifference hardening over her pretty young features. Deliberately, she rested her hand on her lover's hair, as if to call attention to him, closed her eyes, and let her head sag back.

Margaret didn't know what else to do.

She turned and ran.

Thwack.

Margaret centered another carrot on the wooden chopping block on the table before her, raised her big kitchen knife, and brought it down hard, neatly slicing off the carrot's pointy end.

The beginnings of a big pot of vegetable-beef soup simmered on the stove, richly scenting the room with bay and onion and meat. Sunlight streamed through the window, past the pot of ivy geranium on the sideboard and the bowl of raisins plumping in hot water for spice cake.

Margaret's first impulse, when she dashed away from the office, had been to run to Kieran. Only when she realized that by the time she hunted him down and dragged him back here, it would surely all be over had she reluctantly set aside that plan.

At a complete loss, except to realize that she should be where Lucy could find her, if she needed her, Margaret turned to the one thing she knew she could do to help her boarders: she cooked.

And she argued with herself.

She dug in the burlap sack of carrots at her feet, selecting a nice fat one.

She should have rushed in there and stopped it.

Thwack.

And then what? Lucy was her boarder, not her

daughter. And what if her lover was the Uncatchable
Man? And he had a gun?

Thwack.

She should have waited around to see who the
man was. She'd been too much in shock to focus
on him enough to identify him from the back.

Why? So she could get caught slinking around
outside the office? So Lucy could warn her lover
Margaret lurked outside?

Thwack.

She couldn't have stayed there anymore anyway,
not without giving herself away. For there was no
way on earth she could have sat quietly beneath
that window, waiting, knowing that, just on the
other side of the wall, that horrid man was doing
that to Lucy.

Thwack.

She could have left and fetched a gun. But for
what? So she could go charging to the rescue?

Maybe. If Lucy's lover wasn't the Uncatchable
Man, but merely some young man taking gross
advantage of her, a gun might be a very good idea.
A gun, and a wedding. And she could still do that,
if she decided that was the best plan of action.

First, though, she really needed to talk to Lucy.
Once she figured out what in the hell she could
possibly say to her.

Thwack. The stub end of a carrot flew across the
table, ricocheting off the big enameled dishpan she
used to hold chopped vegetables.

"I think you killed it, Miss Thayer."

"Lucy." Giving herself time to compose her face,
Maggie bent to pick up the piece of carrot. Careful,

she told herself. Lucy had come to her; the last thing she wanted to do was scare her away.

Lucy stood uncertainly in the doorway. Each hair, each piece of clothing was perfectly in place, as if she'd been very careful to make sure no sign remained of how she'd spent the last hour.

"I suppose I shocked you."

"Yes," Margaret said truthfully. "You shocked me."

"Oh." Lucy hovered, half in, half out, and finally turned to leave. "You're busy, I'd better—"

"Would you like to help me?" Maggie gestured to the chair opposite her. "I've another knife."

Lucy flinched, as if she'd expected Maggie to say something very different and she reacted automatically to what she'd anticipated, rather than what she actually heard. "I'm not much of a cook."

"This is easy." She hurried to fetch another knife and chopping block before Lucy could take it in her head to run away. Lucy eased into a chair, perching right on the edge.

Ready for a quick exit, Margaret thought. She had to go cautiously. But the fact that Lucy had come to her, so soon after, meant that now might be the best chance she'd ever have.

She piled a dozen carrots at Lucy's elbow, then took her own seat.

What now? The enormity of it welled over her; she was so far out of her experience. What did she know of troubled young women? What did she know of ruthless and conscienceless men who took sinful advantage of them?

She didn't know where to start, what to say, what to do. All she knew was no one else had a chance to do it. Only her.

God help her.

Lucy put a carrot on the chopping block, holding it delicately between two fingers.

"Not like that," Margaret told her, and showed her how to grip the carrot so the knife wouldn't slice her knuckles. "There, that's better."

Lucy bent over her task. Freckles peppered her nose. So young. She pressed her lips together in concentration, her mouth showing a poignant hint of vulnerability at the corners.

"Miss Thayer?" she said without looking up.

"Yes, Lucy."

"Are you going to tell someone?"

Margaret didn't want to lie to her; she suspected Lucy had been lied to enough in her young life. But she wasn't ready to commit to an answer yet, to make promises she'd end up compelled to break, not until she understood the situation better. "Lucy, whom would I tell?"

Lucy shrugged. "The other girls, maybe."

She looked up, chin high and defiant, as if daring Margaret to condemn her for what she'd seen. But shame lurked in her eyes, and Margaret's heart twisted. Lucy was too young to know that kind of shame even existed.

"It's not wrong," Lucy said boldly.

Tread carefully, Margaret reminded herself. *Don't frighten her off, stay accepting of what she says so she'll keep on talking.* "It's not?"

Lucy blinked; she'd obviously expected another

answer. "It's men. They'll either take it, or you can give it to them. Better to learn to use it, isn't it? At least you get something out of it that way."

Oh, God, Maggie thought. *What had happened to this girl?* "You're very young to be so . . . jaded." And so tragically bitter.

"I'm practical." Lucy painstakingly sawed off a coin-sized slice of carrot. "And I'm not so young. Lots of girls get married at my age."

"That's true." Carrie, her goddaughter, certainly hadn't been more than a year or so older than Lucy when she got married. But that seemed an entirely different thing, to go trembling and flushed with love to a bridal bed and a kind young man who felt exactly the same way. A world apart from allowing a man she wasn't promised to do such intimately sexual things to her in an office in the middle of the day.

So? her conscience whispered, the parts of her that had been well trained by Eleanor. *Is that so much better than inviting, insisting, Kieran to take you up against a tree? To revel in the equally intimate and shocking things he did to you? And seriously considering letting him do them again, and a whole lot more?*

But it *was* different, very much so. Margaret had nearly two decades of living and choices on Lucy. And she cared about Kieran, in a way she'd never expected to and could only be grateful to have experienced, no matter what it cost her in the end.

But Lucy, she was heartbreakingly certain, didn't care about her lover at all.

Maybe she didn't even care about herself.

Margaret fumbled for words. "Lucy, you have to . . . if you need help . . . you shouldn't . . ."

"I have to go." Lucy set down her knife and pushed herself away from the table.

Dear God, I'm losing her! I don't know what to say to her! "Melissa, don't go!"

She went absolutely still; the only sign that she was flesh rather than carved stone was the clenching of her fingers around the edge of the table. "What did you say?"

"I said . . . Melissa. Melissa Dalrymple. That's your name, isn't it?"

Lucy shuddered slightly. "I don't know what you're talking about," she said tonelessly.

"Please, Melissa, don't lie to me."

The girl eased back into her chair, letting herself down slowly as if she weren't sure where the seat was. "How did you know?"

"Kieran told me."

Blood drained from Melissa's face. "He knows?"

"No, of course not! Not that it's you. He just told me the story, and when I saw you . . . it was just a good guess. No one knows who you really are."

"Oh." Melissa reached for the knife, her hand trembling so violently that the blade wobbled, sending light slicing down the edge.

"Melissa, you're shaking. Please be careful."

"No, I'm okay." She grabbed a carrot and aligned it carefully on the block. "McDermott told you? I thought he jilted you."

"Yes, well . . ." She couldn't lie to Lucy. But she

couldn't tell her the truth, either. "It's a little more complicated than that. And he told me before . . . before everything happened."

"Oh." She began chopping the carrot.

"Melissa, you know why Kieran's here in Redemption, don't you? He's been looking for you for a long time."

"Don't you tell him!" Panic had Melissa quivering like a cornered doe, on the verge of flight.

"No! No, I won't, not unless you tell me it's all right to. I promise."

There, Margaret thought, I promised her. And how much am I going to regret promising that?

But what other choice did she have?

The edge of her knife angled against the board, Margaret scraped chopped carrots into a bowl. "Melissa," she said, trying to ease into a subject there was no easing into, "you know that he . . . the man you're with . . ."

"My lover?"

Margaret flushed, regretting that Melissa could say that word so baldly. She should be home, pampered and cared for and mooning over her first kiss, not talking bluntly about a lover.

"You know he's dangerous. He's not a good man, Melissa."

Melissa shrugged. "He's no worse than most. No worse than my father."

"He's done . . . awful things."

"Not to me."

Oh yes he has. Margaret checked herself just before the words burst out of her. And the worst thing he'd done was make Melissa unable even to recognize that he'd done terrible things to her.

"Kieran will catch him," Margaret said. "And then what?"

"No, he won't. No one will."

"You know who he is, then? What he's done?"

"Of course." Melissa giggled, a sound that frightened Margaret more than any she'd ever heard before. "I think it's exciting."

Exciting. She hoped the man suffered mightily in hell for this. "Melissa, he's hurt people. Hurt you."

"He hasn't hurt me."

Melissa worked faster now, slicing off thin bright orange disks that rolled away from her knife and across the table.

There had to be a way to get through to the girl. Margaret tried again. "Melissa, I know you're probably afraid to go home, after everything that's happened. But Kieran talked to your father, and it's okay. He's heartbroken, he doesn't care what you did, he wants you back—"

"I'll bet he does!" Her knife flashed, harder and harder, mangling the carrot into irregular bits. "What's the problem, Daddy getting tired of sleeping alone?"

The room whirled around Margaret, shattered, and she knew she'd never fit the pieces back into her ordinary life again. "You can't . . . Melissa, you don't mean—"

"You heard me." She looked up for a minute, eyes wounded, pleading, begging for something that Margaret was terrified she couldn't give her because she didn't have the experience, didn't have the knowledge, didn't know how, and oh God! She wanted to *help* her!

"How—" Margaret swallowed hard, fighting the nausea that pushed at her throat. She couldn't vomit now. Melissa's own father! "When?"

"It started when I was nine. Just after my mother died," Melissa said. She went on talking, dry-eyed and calm-voiced, chopping vegetables into mush. So calm; she'd used up all her tears on this already, Margaret thought, battling to contain her own tears and rage. Because she knew that if she let Melissa see one hint of the revulsion that churned inside her, she might think that the loathing was for her and not that monster—she wouldn't even allow him the name of father—and the vile things he'd done to the child he should have protected.

"So." Melissa brought the knife down hard, biting deeply into the wood. The blade stuck, quivering there. "That's it."

"I think you killed it," Margaret observed, a lame attempt to break the tension before it crushed them both, before she ran from the room to hunt down Melissa's father herself.

Surprised, Melissa glanced down, at the messy pile of smashed carrots, drops of juice smearing the cutting board. She laughed a little, with relief and surprise. "I guess it's not going in the soup, is it?"

"No."

Melissa looked at her curiously. "You surprised me. I thought you'd scream or faint or run away."

"I might have, once." Never in her life had she considered, never even imagined, that there were people in the world who did such unspeakably ugly things to their children.

She'd spent years a pawn in the war between her mother and her father. But they'd never tried to hurt her, not intentionally, reserving all their malice for each other. And she'd always known that they'd both loved her, with whatever remnant of emotion and energy they had left over after wasting all that hatred on each other.

But Melissa! Dear Lord, she prayed, *please help me make this right.*

"Why'd you tell me then?" she asked, trying to gain time to think.

"I don't know." Melissa picked up a towel and scrubbed at the orange staining her fingers.

Because you want out, Margaret thought. *And picked me to tell, to take the chance. I don't want to fail you!*

"Melissa." Margaret reached across the table and gently touched the back of Melissa's hand. "What your father did to you, it was a terrible thing, but that doesn't make what's happening now right, either."

Melissa shrugged. "It's not so bad. What difference does it make who does it to me? It's just my body. It's not me."

Margaret's heart was going to break. Surely it couldn't hurt this much and remain whole. "Talk to Kieran, Melissa. He can help you, he's good at—"

"No!" Melissa leaped to her feet. "You promised you wouldn't tell!"

"I know." But she couldn't do this all alone. Kieran would know what to do, she was sure of it, if she could just get Melissa to trust him. "But he's a good man, Melissa, he—"

"He's a man, isn't he?" Melissa cut in.

And, Margaret thought, as far Melissa was concerned, that's that.

19

"*I wasn't sure* you'd come."

"I wasn't sure, either," Maggie said.

She paused uncertainly in the doorway, sunlight silhouetting her in gold, and Kieran's breath caught. In truth, he hadn't even been positive whether he should hope for her to come or not, because he'd wanted her to far more than was certainly wise. It occurred to him that neither one of them might get out of this nearly as easily as they'd got into it.

Too late; there was no way he could deny himself now.

"I'm glad you did," he said, and he was. "Very much."

"Oh." She inched in and shut the door behind her. He'd closed all the curtains, so the only light in the room consisted of insistent sunlight filtering through the threadbare gingham, making the interior dusky and lazy-afternoon dim.

Her fingers knotted before her, she scanned the room, her gaze lighting everywhere but on him.

"It looks the same," she said.

"Did you think it would change?"

Maybe she had. She felt so astoundingly different than she had just a few short months ago that somehow she'd thought it would look different, be different, too, even after barely a week away.

"Do you miss it?"

"Not really," she answered, surprised to find it the truth. She'd thought she would. She missed a few things: the animals, the garden. But not the isolation. Certainly not the weighty memories.

He went to her, still standing only a step inside the door, and took her hand. "How long can you stay?"

"Oh." What was the matter with her, she wondered, that she kept saying "oh," like some foolish young girl tongue-tied in the presence of the first handsome man who'd noticed her? "Quite a while, I guess. Mrs. Clinghorn and I, we made an agreement. We both wanted some time off now and then, so we decided we'd switch off for one supper a week: I'd feed all her girls and she'd feed all mine. I'm supposed to have Friday off, and she Saturday, but I told her I wanted to switch to Thursday this week, because I'd been invited for supper at Martha Ann's."

Now that was much better, she thought, disgusted with herself. From "oh" to babbling about something he surely wasn't interested in.

"That's good." He drew her into the room. A crack of sunlight squeezed through a small gap between two curtains, fell in a bright bar on the bed. He'd turned back the covers already, rolled them all the way down to the bottom, leaving the sheets bare and white and very unsubtle.

"Would you like coffee?" he asked. "I made some before you got here."

"Coffee? I thought we were going to . . ."

He laughed softly. "We are. But you're nervous."

"I am not!"

"You're not? You can't even look at me."

Determined, she lifted her chin and looked him straight in the eye . . . for all of about three seconds.

"All right, so maybe I am a little nervous," she said, disgruntled. "But you don't have to sound quite so charmed by it."

"But I am charmed by it." And by her, by everything about her. By her fierce caution and the unexpected bravery she'd kept buried so deep. By her inability to turn from someone in need, and the way she tried to pretend otherwise. And by how her life had marked her, the wiry strength of her small body and the fine lines on her face that deepened when she smiled. "I don't understand why you're nervous, though. It's not as if we haven't—"

"I know that!" She fixed her gaze on his chin. "But, those times, I didn't have time to *think* about it beforehand. We just—"

"I can fix that." He swooped, bending, and straight-ened with her over his shoulder. Her head and arms dangled down his back. The room spun as he whirled toward the bed. She giggled, and he brought his hand flat on her rear. "Quiet, wench! And no thinking."

"Kieran!"

His shoulder jostled her stomach as he strode across the room. It would be so easy to let him do this. To let him sweep her away, allow him to overwhelm her senses and her mind. To let nothing else matter but the pleasures of the body.

Except she couldn't do it.

"Kieran, you have to put me down."

Alerted by her tone, he did so immediately, setting her gently on her feet beside the bed. "What's the matter?"

"I have to talk to you."

"We'll talk. Before or later. Your choice." He grinned, purposely winning. "Pick later."

"Oh, if only I could." She'd much rather put this off, because she knew how upset he was going to be with what she'd decided. She would rather let him love her first, just in case what she had to say ruined things between them. "But it's got to be now."

He sighed heavily. "I guess it's coffee after all, isn't it?"

Saying she'd done enough waiting on people lately, he made her sit while he fetched mugs and coffee. Seeing him so at home in her kitchen made her wistful, a little sad, and she resolutely pushed the feelings away. Soon enough to feel like that anyway; why do it before she had to?

"All right," he said, spinning a chair around and swinging a leg over it, crossing his forearms over the back. "What is it?"

The easy part first. She told him of Lily's accident, and the terrible working conditions at the mill. And of her confrontation with Benjamin Lessing.

She'd rather hoped he would be proud of her, standing up to Benjamin like that. *She* was. Instead, he brought his mug down to the table with a resounding thump.

"You did *what?*"

"I got what I wanted," she said. "Lily's going to be paid during her recovery. And there'll be a job for her when she's ready. Now if I could just get him to improve a few more things—"

"It's not your problem," he said flatly.

"Really?" Her temper rose, spurred by the impression that, for some reason, he apparently either didn't want her to or didn't think she *could* make a difference for the mill workers. "And I suppose all those lost causes you go chasing after, they're all *your* problem, too?"

He frowned at her. "That's different."

"And how is that?"

"It just is." Because it didn't matter what happened to him, he thought. While what happened to her mattered a great deal.

He sighed, knowing he'd lose this argument. At least, he would unless he told her more than he was yet willing to reveal. "So do you believe her, Maggie? Lily, I mean. About the child."

"Absolutely."

"So she's not Melissa. We know that for sure."

"No, she's not Melissa." And now came the hard part. "But I know who is."

"What!" He came halfway out of his chair. Ready to run off and do battle, of course, Margaret thought. "Who is it?"

"I—" She gripped her coffee cup, feeling the warmth through the mug, looking for strength. "I can't tell you that."

He stared at her in disbelief. "Tell me you don't mean that."

"I do, though."

Anger simmered in his eyes. "Maggie, you can't mean to—"

She placed a hand on his arm to still him. "Kieran, there's a lot going on here you don't know, you don't understand," she said urgently.

"So explain it to me. Make me understand."

"It's not my story to tell. I promised her."

He surged to his feet, roughly shoving the chair away. It clattered loudly, banged against the table, and Margaret flinched.

He stalked to the window, brushing aside the curtain so he could stare outside. Margaret looked at his back, at the fall of silver-brushed hair and the breadth of his strong, rigidly set shoulders, shoulders she remembered so well the feel of beneath her palms, and her heart twisted.

That was it, then. He was still in her house, but he'd already begun to leave her.

"If I know who she is, Margaret, I can protect her."

Margaret. It had been a long time since he'd called her Margaret.

"I know," she said.

"I could get her out of there, away from him."

"I know." She'd had this same argument with herself, a thousand times, since Lucy—Melissa—had told her everything. The fear that she would make the wrong decision had kept her up all night and still arrowed cold dread down her spine.

But the fact remained that Melissa had come to her, had trusted her. Margaret thought that Melissa desperately needed someone to trust, and that to destroy that now might mean she would never do so again.

Margaret went over to him, standing beside him as he continued to look out the window, his expression distant and angry.

"She's been here so long already." She had to try to explain it to him. "A little while longer surely won't make much difference."

"It might."

She'd agonized over that. If she was wrong, it would be something she'd mourn for the rest of her life; she knew that. But she didn't feel she really had another choice. Not yet. She'd made a promise, and Melissa deserved to have *someone* keep a promise to her, after her father had made such a hellish mockery of the promises implicit in parenthood.

"If you think the danger's increasing, I'll tell you who she is. I won't have any choice then." Dear Lord, he couldn't even stand to look at her, he was so angry. And that hurt, even though she thought she'd prepared herself for that possibility. She'd known what this meant to him, that these duties he took on were his life, and that by denying him information that might aid him she risked being cut completely out of that life.

But she hadn't known how deeply the pain would slice, that it would truly feel like her heart was splitting in two. "I tried to convince her to allow me to tell you, or go to you herself. I'll try again."

He didn't answer, just kept staring at nothing. Because he'd rather look at nothing than look at her, she thought.

"Well," she said helplessly, not knowing what else to do, the words hurting her throat as she said them. "I guess I'd better go."

"Go?" He whipped around, gaze settling on her immediately. "You're leaving?"

"I thought you were angry, that you'd want me to leave."

"I'm angry, yes." And getting angrier all the time, from the looks of it; his eyes blazed, a muscle twitched in his jaw. "Do I want you to leave? No."

"But . . . but . . ." She stuttered, then stopped trying to talk at all. She had no experience with this; she hardly ever argued with anyone. She'd listened to her parents battle endlessly and had decided long ago she would never do that. It wasn't worth the anger and energy it took, the way it consumed their lives. But there'd been an undercurrent of resentment between them, of disappointment and lost dreams, that didn't exist in this disagreement with Kieran. And that made it very different.

"I still think you should tell me. It would be safer, for her and for you." His shoulders relaxed slightly, and he circled one hand, the gesture encompassing the room. "But that has nothing to do with this. With us."

"Oh," she said in a voice as small as she felt. She'd leaped to conclusions, tarred Kieran with her father's brush. Believed that anger about what someone said or did necessarily spilled over into anger at the person who'd done it.

"Enough of that." Linking their hands between them, he smiled gently. "Is there anything else? Preferably something that can be dispensed with quickly."

She couldn't quite let it go. "You thought you knew who the Uncatchable Man is, you said. Maybe it won't matter, my keeping her secret for a while longer."

"I don't just think I know who it is anymore. I do know."

"You know?" she asked, surprised. She'd have thought that if Kieran had discovered that much, he'd have ended it all already. "How?"

Frustration ripped at him. "I saw him, in Red Fred's. We talked a moment, and he pulled out the pocket watch."

"The one we found at the cottage?"

"Yes. I'm sure it's the same one."

"But why haven't you—" She winced, wishing she hadn't said that as the rage visibly caught hold of Kieran again. His eyes hooded, his mouth thinned.

"Because I haven't got any goddamn proof, that's why!" He took a deep breath, raked his hair back with his hand. "I just can't make it all fit. There was something . . . obvious about the whole thing. Like maybe he wanted me to see the watch."

"But . . . why? Do you think he knew we were at the cottage?"

"Maybe."

"But wouldn't that be awfully stupid, letting you know who he is like that?"

"Or very arrogant. He seems to enjoy it, Maggie. The whole thing: fooling everyone, making sure his victims knew how badly they were taken in. If I confront him, he might think it was a huge game. He might like that, knowing I know the truth but am unable to prove it."

"So what are you going to do?"

"I'm going to wait," he said, and Maggie could see what that cost him. "I can't take the chance that he might simply decide to eliminate all leads to him and then disappear."

Eliminate all leads, he'd said. Sterile words that meant he'd kill Melissa. She thought of that girl chopping carrots across a kitchen table from her, with her innocent freckles and old, brittle eyes, and tears prickled. She blinked them away. Not now. Later she'd cry, if she needed to. Not now.

"Sooner or later he'll make a mistake," Kieran continued. "I can be patient, if I have to be."

"Really?" she murmured, moving close, pressing her body against his, letting her lips hover a few inches from his.

Quick as a blink, his mood changed. Exactly as she'd hoped. "About some things." He smiled slowly. "Are you trying to distract me?"

"That depends. Is it working?"

"Yes."

"Then I am."

"Good plan." He lowered his head and kissed her, deeply, with the sure familiarity of a man who'd kissed her before and so knew exactly how to angle his head, precisely where to tickle the roof of her mouth with his tongue to make her knees buckle beneath her.

Right up until this moment, until he kissed her, she'd wondered. Had a doubt or two about whether she was doing the right thing. She'd come only because she couldn't seem to stay away.

But, with the sweet pressure of his mouth on hers, all her doubts vanished. This could not be wrong. She could not regret this.

When he left, she would hurt. Dear God, she knew that well. But better to have this first, to have as much of him as she could, to fill herself with memories.

Lifting his head slowly, he smiled as he kissed her, with little nips and soft brushes, tracing his tongue along her lips, leaving her with a hint of what was to come.

He tugged her to the bed and sat on the edge of it, pulling her to stand between his knees. Tiny round buttons lined the front of her tucked shirt, and he started at the top, slipping the first one through its hole with a leisurely deliberation that had her pulse fluttering in her throat.

"Isn't it . . . awfully bright in here?" Despite the closed curtains, it was still afternoon, the muted light stronger than she would have liked.

"I like it light."

"I'm going to go check and make sure all the curtains are closed tightly."

"I already did that," he said, intent on his task.

"I'm just going to go check."

"Maggie?" His hands stilled. "What's the matter? Did you think someone followed you?"

"No." For an instant, that image came back: Melissa in the desk chair with a man's mouth on her. Margaret shoved the thought away. That had *nothing* to do with this. There were feelings here, and that changed something that could be profane into something very near sacred. "I was very careful. I checked behind me several times. And it's not like there's anyplace to hide on the way here."

"No. What is it, then?"

She couldn't tell him. He'd only laugh at her again.

But she should have known he'd figure it out.

"It's the light again, is that it?"

"I . . ." She knew what she looked like. Fine. Nothing special, certainly not ugly, just . . . fine. And, though she'd filled out a little lately, her breasts were still slight, her ribs visible. She'd feel better with the veiling of darkness.

"I told you, Maggie, I see real well in the dark. I already looked at everything."

"You keep saying that, but I don't think I believe you anymore."

"Really? I know you have a mole, right up under your—"

"Kieran!"

"Lord, I love it when you say my name like that."

"Like what?"

"Like you don't know what else to do with me, so you just snap my name out." His hands were busy again, down to the fourth button, and this time she allowed it.

"I'm sure I'll think of something."

"I'm counting on it." Two more buttons, and then: "Jeez, Maggie, there must be a hundred buttons here! Did you wear this on purpose to drive me crazy?"

"Yes," she admitted, smiling. Hard to remain concerned about how she looked or how attractive he'd find her, when he showed his pleasure so obviously. He undressed her with leisurely care, turning her this way and that to reach her fastenings, drawing off each garment slowly so that it whispered over her skin, a seduction all its own.

And then she was completely naked, still standing between his knees as he looked at her, his breathing coming hard, his eyes dark and glittering.

"Kieran?" she said. "Don't you want to get undressed, too?"

"Eventually." He reached out and cupped one breast, fit it right into his big palm. "But don't you like it like this? It's wicked, you totally bare, standing here for me to look at you, while I'm still buttoned up to my neck."

His thumb whisked over her nipple, and he watched as it beaded up beneath his touch. "There, you see?" he murmured. "But you're not blushing."

"Are you disappointed?"

"Yes," he said. "I guess I'll just have to try harder."

He bent his head, taking her breast in his mouth, his tongue hot and urgent. "*Kieran.*"

"Yes," he said again.

His hands went lower, and his mouth too, driving her up to the peak but not allowing her to fall over it. She clutched his shoulders to keep from falling to the floor, while his arm came around her rear to support her. The softness of his hair brushed her belly, and when he pulled away, trailing his slick mouth up her stomach, up her ribs, to find her breast again, she gave a soft sob of disappointment. "Please."

"Soon," he said against her skin. "It'll be better, for being on the edge for so long, remember?"

But soon was not enough for her. She jerked at his shirt, tearing it off him, searching for flesh. And then she found the attraction of daylight, of seeing him so clearly. His strength so evident, muscle roping his arms and rounding his shoulders.

His nipples responded to the graze of her fingers as readily as she'd responded to him. His belly clenched as she stroked her hand across it.

She fumbled at his waistband, at the fastenings of his drawers. That first night, she'd been too timid to touch him intimately. She did so now, reveling in the velvet-smooth skin and heat of his erection, the way it fit her hand. So hard, so smooth; she marveled at the differences between his body and hers, fascinated with the way he grew even larger beneath her palm. His breath hissed out of him, changed into a tortured groan.

"Serves you right," she whispered, satisfied that he suffered as much as she.

"Come here." He helped her climb up onto the bed and straddle him, her knees on either side of his hips, nudging against the wadded denim of his pants. He positioned her gently, lifting his hips so he could slide in a bare inch.

"But what about—" He rocked against her, and she gasped.

"What about what?" he said through gritted teeth.

"You . . . you said we had to be more careful."

"Oh. That." He threw his head back and his neck corded with strain. She kissed him there, tracing her mouth over the taut lines, his pulse beating hard against her tongue. "I will, later. I just . . . I've just got to feel you for a while first."

The world splintered as he surged upward. Light, sound, smell; they all faded. There was only Kieran, and those wonderful, wild things he made her feel. His hands clenched at her hips, guiding her, setting the rhythm, pushing her up and away, then bringing her back to meet him fully. He bent his head, temple bumping her shoulder, and she knew he watched them.

"Look at us, Maggie."

She wasn't going to, certain she couldn't survive doing such an incredibly wanton thing. But he urged her on, cupping the back of her head in his palm and tilting it down so she could see between their bodies.

Unable to look away, she did as he told her. Watched his dark, slick flesh sliding out of her, then in again. Joining, mating, coming together . . . all those words she understood now.

It was too much for her. Already so close to the edge, she cried out, pushed herself against him more fully.

"Maggie!" Kieran wrapped his arms around her, clutching her to his chest while she shuddered and shook in his embrace. He slammed his eyes shut, trying to hold on to that last shred of control, knowing if he watched her, her face twisted and beautiful in ecstasy, he would follow her over and the hell with promises he'd made to himself two decades ago.

Finally—oh, thank God—she quieted. He turned her in his arms, laying her gently on the cool sheets.

"All that," she mumbled, relaxed in the aftermath, "and we haven't even messed up the bed yet."

"We'll get to it," he promised.

His saddlebag was on the floor, near the side of the bed. He fumbled in it, swore, then got out of bed to search more thoroughly. There, near the bottom. He pulled out what he needed and quickly covered himself, wondering where in the hell in the territories he might possibly find more. At this rate they were going to need them.

Margaret's muffled shriek caught his attention. She'd sat up in bed, and her eyes were wide, focused directly on his crotch.

"Oh, my goodness!" A grin lurked at the corners of her mouth; he could see her pressing her lips together, trying to subdue it.

"What?"

Her eyes danced; under any other circumstances, he would have loved to see that expression on her face. But not when she was looking *there*. "It . . . it has a ribbon!"

He scowled. "I wore one before."

"But . . . but I didn't *look* then." She clapped a hand over her mouth, muffling her next words. "And the ribbon is *red*."

"Got to hold it on somehow," he groused, feeling himself flush. No wonder she hated it when he was always trying to make her blush. "What color do you think it should be?"

"Oh, I don't know." She tried to contain the giggles, but now and then one escaped, little explosions of merriment. "Black?"

"That's it," he said, and pounced. She shrieked as the bed bowed and complained beneath his weight. He settled himself over her, pinning her down with his body, looping her arms above her head, and entered her with one quick thrust. "If you think you can distract me by *laughing* at me, Maggie, think again."

Wearing the device had never particularly bothered him before. He'd accepted the necessity and gave it no more thought. Now, though, he wanted to feel her, just her, with nothing between them. Her heat and damp and the little ripples that gripped him when she found pleasure.

It had one small advantage, however; the muting of sensation allowed him to draw their loving out, lent him more control. He used that advantage ruthlessly, showing her no mercy, luring her, seducing her, pushing her into finding her pleasure, twice more, until she lay limp and trembling beneath him.

She opened her eyes slowly. They were glazed and hazy with passion, glistening with tears. And filled with tenderness. "Kieran."

A touch he might have withstood. A wanton smile, a tempting kiss. But he had no defense against tenderness. No armor against Maggie. And so it was his turn to cry out, to quake while she held him.

"Kieran," she said softly in his ear when he quieted, "when you're—" her voice broke, "—when you're gone, I'll miss you."

He squeezed his eyes shut but didn't answer. It wouldn't be fair to; he couldn't let her begin to think that he'd be anything more than he was. It was only much later, when her breathing had evened into sleep, that he whispered against her hair.

"I'll miss you, too."

20

⚜

    The Uncatchable Man stood in the middle of Front Street and studied the First National Bank of Redemption.

He liked the moniker the papers had taken to calling him, *The Uncatchable Man*. Others in his . . . profession had names that labeled their violence, appellations that played up the terrible things they did.

His, however, celebrated his achievement: his ability to outwit the best lawmen in several states year after year.

Mrs. Chaney, always curious about a stranger in Redemption, marched by him, staring. He tipped his hat, acknowledging her rude interest. She scuttled past like a startled beetle, and he had to struggle not to laugh.

The new disguise was working beautifully. He'd attracted a bit of notice, an unknown person strolling their streets, but no one had recognized him.

He greatly enjoyed this part of his career, creating characters, seeing how well they were received. He came by it naturally. His mother had been an actress, and he'd gone on the stage himself when the time came, to some modest acclaim.

But it hadn't taken him long to realize that the acting profession wasn't enough for him. Not enough money, not enough respect, not enough control over his own destiny. Not even a broad enough canvas for his skills. He relished performing on a wider stage, with proportionately higher stakes.

The bank was brick, of course. Banks should be brick, nice, sturdy, heavy buildings that gave the customers a sense of security. Elegant black lettering painted on the front plate windows spelled out the name.

He'd purposely avoided ever doing work in Dakota. This was his retreat, his stronghold. Someday, when retirement beckoned, he'd take his earnings and head someplace with more to offer. San Francisco, perhaps. Someplace his past could never catch up to him, and money and charm could carve him out the place in society he wanted. For now, Dakota had served him well.

Nodding to himself, he continued on down the street, his head turning casually, studying the familiar buildings as if he'd never seen them before. For, indeed, the character he portrayed today was viewing Redemption for the first time.

Perhaps he'd made a mistake. He'd worked in

every other region in the entire middle section of
the United States, and then some. His scrupulous
avoidance of Dakota might, conversely, point the
way here by its very oddity. No one would ever
expect him to pull a job so close to home.

Two little boys raced down the street, screech-
ing, chasing each other without looking where
they were going. He adroitly stepped aside and
continued on his way without breaking his
stride.

He returned to pondering the problem at hand.
Those two—McDermott and that annoying Thayer
woman. He'd not believed that everything was as
simple as it appeared between them, and congratu-
lated himself for his wisdom in not being taken in
by that jilting story that had whipped through
town.

He hadn't known for certain, though, until he
happened to catch a glimpse of her leaving the mill
today. Pure good luck, the kind he was often
blessed with. He might not even have noticed her
departure, except that she'd acted so oddly,
furtively looking behind her every few yards.

It had soon become clear that Miss Thayer was
heading to her house; there weren't that many
other places east of the mill to go. He'd held back,
taking no chances that she might see him, swinging
low to follow the river where there was cover.
More luck—taking that circuitous route was the
only reason he'd stumbled across McDermott's
horse, hidden below a cut bank a half mile from
her farm.

That had been enough evidence for him. He'd

headed home, certain that the two of them were still in league together, one way or another.

And so he had a problem.

Whistling, he swung the cane he'd affected today, smiling. Lovely day. Three different colors of spider lilies were in bloom, in the lushly disordered gardens that fronted Jamison's.

Problems didn't bother him. He often rather enjoyed the challenge. But this one—he supposed he'd have to get rid of all three of them. McDermott, Miss Thayer, and Melissa too. It would be the safest course of action, but it would also be extremely obvious. He'd be forced to leave Redemption permanently. And he really didn't want to do that yet.

Playing with McDermott had been a most amusing occupation. He could see the frustration build in the man as he ran around Redemption looking for answers. And then the certain knowledge in McDermott's eyes when he'd looked at him, and the wild, raging disbelief when McDermott had realized he couldn't do anything about it, not yet.

Unfortunately, he still didn't know what McDermott had told his colleagues. His disappearance or murder might bring an entire swarm of investigators to Redemption. If he killed McDermott alone, he'd still likely have to move on.

And Melissa. He had absolutely no fear she'd tell her new friend Miss Thayer about him. Oh, he knew about that, about the time the two of them had spent together, even though Melissa tried to hide it. But she knew better than to reveal anything about him—at least, not intentionally. There was no telling what she might let slip accidentally, however.

McDermott. Margaret Thayer. Melissa.

The link between the three of them was Miss Thayer, wasn't it?

He turned to look back at the bank building, substantial and reassuring in the bright sun, while possibilities played through his mind.

Then he tipped his hat at Mrs. Ballard, strolling down the street with her market basket over her arm, turned the corner, and disappeared.

They slept awhile, and loved again. They feasted on cold ham and bread and cheese, and listened to John Perkins come and tend her animals.

When John left, they dared to open a window, letting in a breeze and the sound of the meadowlark that haunted the dusk.

They lay on the bed, still naked, fitting together like spoons, Kieran curved around her back, thighs tucked beneath hers, arm around her side with his hand settled on her breast.

Even now, Margaret thought, there should have been some remnant of shyness or restraint or shock, to find herself in a wanton position like this. Instead, she was more comfortable than she'd ever been, relaxed, and thoroughly reluctant to move.

"I suppose we'd better go," he murmured against her hair.

"Yes," she agreed, but stayed put. "I'd better

get back and see if Lily needs anything. I feel badly about leaving her alone so much, but she insists she's enjoying the chance to catch up on her rest."

"She probably is." His hand flexed, squeezing gently, and any remaining inclination she'd had to get up fled. "You said she's doing well?"

"As well as she's going to do as long as she's apart from her son."

"And the boy's father?"

"I don't know. I got the impression he's long gone."

"Hmm."

"Don't get any ideas, Kieran. At least, not yet. Not until I have a better idea what the situation is."

"All right." Lifting her hair, he nuzzled her neck, and smiling, she pressed back against him. This was so sweet, to have the first overwhelming, mind-blotting rush of passion sated, to be able to savor and explore at leisure, to pay attention to each detail and sensation. To *play*, though she'd never thought of it that way before. "When can we meet again?"

"Not tomorrow. I've got several errands, and then I must fill in for Mrs. Clinghorn."

He groaned. "Too long."

"I could slip out for a few hours tomorrow night, maybe. You'd have to let me get some sleep, though."

"I'm not making any promises."

Silence descended. *I'm not making any promises*, he'd said. Though Margaret had known that all along, it was harder to hear it, laid out there plainly, stripped of possibilities and shadings. He hadn't meant it like that, but it was the truth all the same.

"Well." Kieran cleared his throat, breaking the awkward silence, and sat up. Immediately, Maggie regretted the loss of his warmth. Why couldn't they pretend for just a little longer?

Because neither one of them had ever been the type of person to indulge in fantasy. Even harmless ones, and this one, that this affair was not bound strictly to this place and time, was not harmless at all. For if she let herself believe it, she'd never prepare herself for what was to come, to guard against an eventuality that might otherwise destroy her.

"Could you hand me my shirt?" he asked.

She sat up and stretched to snag his shirt from the end of the bed, where she'd tossed it when she finally got it off him. "It's a little wrinkled."

"That's all right." He shrugged it on.

"You have the nicest shirts," she said. Talking about trivialities was easier than thinking about things she couldn't change. "Like they're made just for you."

"They are." He scooped a stray sock off the floor beside the bed. "I'll tell Mandy you like them."

"Mandy?" Darn it, she'd tried to sound more normal than that.

"Yes, Mandy." Shouldn't a man look silly, in only one black sock and an unbuttoned shirt? Instead, she was having a hard time remembering exactly why they had to leave quite yet.

"Is she . . . a good friend?" she asked, attempting

casualness and failing miserably, even to her own ears.

"A very good friend." He caught her around the waist and rolled to his back, trapping her on top of him, her legs falling between his. "And you're jealous."

"No, I'm—"

"I like it," he said, and kissed her beneath the ear. Against her belly, she could feel him stir and grow, and she wondered how long it could go on like this. So easy and joyful, with the passion between them always there, just beneath the surface, waiting, ready to be stoked with the slightest word or look or touch. "I've known Mandy for years. She's a wonderful woman. She is also deliriously happily married."

"Oh." Content, she laid her head against his chest.

"She lives in Minnesota, she and Jakob. I met them—oh, it must be at least ten years now. Maybe four years later, I was trying to locate a runaway husband. I found him, in a hole of a flat on the south side of Chicago. He'd had a woman with him, but she'd died a few months earlier. She'd had twins, from before—no idea who the father was. They weren't his, at any rate."

"How old were they?" she asked softly, touched to get this glimpse of a part of his life that she knew so little about.

"Two and a half, maybe three. He'd let them stay with him—a leftover shred of loyalty to the woman, I suppose—and threw some food their way once in a while, but not much else."

His hand stroked her hair, glided down her back. "I carted him back home to his wife—don't know why she still wanted him, but she did. Needed his pay, I suppose. But she sure as hell wasn't going to take care of his mistress's bastard children."

And of course, he'd taken it upon himself to make things right, Margaret thought.

"Didn't know what to do," Kieran continued. "It's not like I know a whole lot of nice families who are willing to take in a couple of lost children. It was going to have to be the orphanage, I figured, but then I thought of Jakob and Mandy. They'd raised his nephew, and her stepson, but they'd never been able to have children of their own."

His heart thumped steadily beneath her ear. And what a magnificent heart it was, though she knew he'd deny it.

"They love the hell out of those kids. Mandy's so grateful, she took it upon herself to see I was properly clothed. She sends me a new shirt every couple of months whether I need it or not. Got a whole drawer full back home." He chuckled. "Good deal for me."

A better deal for his friends because Kieran had the kindness and persistence and compassion to make sure of it. She lifted her head, propping it on her hand so she could look at him.

Evening shadowed his face, all angles and hollows. She fancied his eyes looked a little less haunted, a little less lonely than they had when she first met him. She hoped—oh, how she hoped—that she had something to do with it.

She kissed him softly, because she couldn't resist. "You really are the most amazing man, Kieran McDermott."

Aw hell, he thought. Now she'd done it. She'd gone and fallen in love with him, the foolish woman. He'd tried to keep this simple, tried to make certain he caused her as little pain as possible when he left. Tried to keep it about mutual pleasure, with messy and inconvenient emotions held far away. But now he would certainly hurt her, unless she could be made to get over her senseless delusions about the kind of man he was and would always be.

"Don't look at me like that," he said flatly.

"Like what?" she said, smiling at him, undisturbed by his change of mood.

"Like you've got that idiotic notion again, like you want to start pinning that hero crap on me."

"I can't help it."

"Well, you can just stop. I've done more than my share of lousy things in my life."

"Really?" she said, intrigued. "Tell me about them."

"No."

"Aw, come on. Prove to me how terrible you are. I'm not going to believe you otherwise, you know."

"Fine," he said, angry now. So she wanted to know, did she? Served her right to know the truth. At least it would get that look out of her eyes. "I killed a man."

He'd stated it baldly, daring her to react. Careful now, Maggie told herself. What she did now, the look in her eyes, could make all the difference.

"Just one?" she said lightly.

Only Maggie, he thought, furious and admiring in equal measures. Only she'd be idiot enough to say "just one?" as if she was vaguely disappointed in him, rather than being dismayed, shocked, and repelled, like she should have been. Like he'd intended.

"Only one that couldn't shoot back."

"What'd he do?"

"What'd he do?" Kieran repeated, rocked in spite of himself. People put their trust in him as a last resort, because they had nowhere else to turn. He'd always known he frightened them a little, too. But Maggie—this simple, unquestioning faith, her quick assumption that if he'd done what he said, murdered a man, he'd done it for a good and defensible reason . . . how was he to armor himself against that?

He felt old barriers crack inside him, shields that had served him well. Felt it, but he couldn't stop it. Didn't even want to. He dropped his head back to the pillow, stared at the ceiling.

"He killed her. Cynthia. He killed her."

"And you loved her," Margaret said as another piece of the puzzle clicked into place. The raw grief, the essential loneliness that could only be born of a great loss.

"Yeah, I loved her." Too much, though he hadn't known it at the time. Then, he'd been too caught up in it, in the dizzying miracle of that brand-new feeling. "This is a long story."

"I like long stories." She wasn't going to like this one, she thought. This one would hurt. But she wanted to hear it just the same, because she sensed that without knowing this, she'd never really know him.

The meadowlark called again, echoed keenly in the evening stillness. Kieran cuddled Maggie up against his chest, her head tucked beneath his chin. Easier to talk like this, to think of things he'd avoided remembering for years, with her sweet weight on top of him and her clean scent in his nose.

"I was . . . nineteen. My mother was a housekeeper by then, big fine house in New York. The guy who owned it—Jesus, Maggie, he was so rich! You can't even imagine rich like that. His name was Edward Sellington."

Even now, so many years later, Maggie could detect the clear and potent hatred in Kieran's voice when he'd said that name. And the scorching fury, muted by time but not dissipated.

"I was taking classes at New York University—"

"You went to college?"

"Amazing, huh?" His laugh held no amusement, just emptiness and self-recrimination. "Thought I was going to be something fancy. A doctor or a lawyer."

"You loved it," she said wonderingly, never having imagined him behind a desk, studiously poring over his work, turning that fine mind to the puzzles to be found in a classroom. Of course. She should have seen it before.

"Yeah. I did." He hadn't let himself regret that. There'd been too many other, greater losses to mourn than that young man who'd longed to be a part of a world he'd seen but never belonged to. "I didn't have much money, of course, so I was living with Mum. She had her own rooms, and nobody minded. I did day work at the mansion now and then, whatever they needed. An extra footman at a party, or a pair of hands and a strong back to help the gardener."

Margaret placed her hand on his chest, so she could feel his heart bump against her palm.

"He . . . he had a wife. Cynthia."

"Was she pretty?"

"Pretty." Though he hadn't let himself remember her face, not for a long time, he called up her image now. "She was dazzling. Slender, lovely, polished, with a smile that lit up a room. Everything the wife of a man like that should be. And kind, too; if I was working, and she passed by, she always stopped to talk. To ask how the work was going, what I was studying, if I needed anything."

"And you loved her," Margaret whispered around the lump in her throat, even as she tried to remind herself that she'd always known that Kieran McDermott was not for her, never would be.

"No, not yet." She felt him swallow and gently touch her hair. "I . . . admired her. The way you'd admire a . . . I don't know, a star, or a painting in a museum. Something beautiful you could look at but always knew would never be for you."

The words were too familiar to her own thoughts for Margaret to do anything but blink at the moisture gathering in her eyes.

"What I didn't know then was that Edward . . . he hurt her, Maggie. With his fists and his hands and his . . ." Even now, the anger surged in him, the blinding rage that Edward had done that to Cynthia. The wrath had fueled him for so long; he wondered if he'd ever be completely rid of it. And if there'd be anything left of him when he was.

"Then one day . . . I was putting some chairs away, after a party. There were rooms in the west wing that were hardly ever used, where we stored things. I found her there, curled up in an old rocking chair. She wasn't even crying. Just shaking, like she was outside in the middle of January. Except it wasn't cold."

He'd never said these words out loud, he realized. Never spoke of this to another human being, not the entire story. The telling of it brought it back, all the impotent fury, and the hurt—God, the hurt! And yet, it propelled him on, made the next part come out almost in spite of himself.

"She'd . . . he'd accused her of smiling at someone, at the party, that she wasn't supposed to. It had been a bad one that time, and she'd gone there to hide. We . . . I don't know why, Maggie, maybe she just wanted someone to touch her with caring. And I was too blinded, too bedazzled, to think of what would come out of what we'd done."

"And so you became lovers," Maggie concluded.

"Only that once. Even then, I knew it was too dangerous for her, and I knew I couldn't fight him. Who was I? Nobody. He was Edward Sellington."

But I should have fought him, Kieran thought. *Somehow, I should have found a way.*

"Then she found out she was going to have a child."

"A child?" Margaret lifted her head. "Your child?"

"No, not my child," he said, a lifetime of regret coloring his voice. "This was after we . . . too long after."

"Oh."

He cupped her head in his palm and pressed it back down to lie against his chest. If she looked at him as he talked, all that rich sympathy in her eyes, he'd never get through this. And now, once he'd started, it seemed important to finish. So she'd know who he was and what he'd done.

"He was better to her then, for a while. But we . . . we couldn't keep away from each other, not completely. I never touched her again, not that way, but . . . we'd meet. Talk, hold hands, just look at each other. That's all."

It had been so hard, he remembered, to leave it at that, two young people with all that emotion between them. But even that, apparently, turned out to have been far too much.

"He must have known, somehow. A week after her son was born, they found her at the bottom of the stairway one morning with a broken neck."

"Oh dear God." There should be more she could do for him, Margaret thought, even now. More than simply wrapping her arm around his chest and holding on.

"He killed her. I knew it, even then, but I couldn't prove it. Couldn't get to him. He was so well protected. He could have bought and sold half of New York. I couldn't get to him."

Outside, the sun had gone down, cloaking the room in darkness, filling it with shadows and memories and regrets.

"I'm sorry," she said.

"It—" He swallowed. "Never again. I'm never going to feel that again. I'll never let it happen."

And so he'd never allowed himself to love again. Had she been so foolish as to think that he might love her? She tried to deny it, but the ache in her heart wouldn't let her.

"I went away for a while, tried to forget." Against her back, his hand clenched into a fist. "Didn't work."

"And then?"

"And then I decided, if no one else would punish him, I would. I went back to New York, and I tried to find a way to get to him. But there were always people around him, and gates, and power. But I waited. He married again, and I guess he wasn't any better to her than he was to Cynthia. But she got away."

She tried to imagine Kieran then, young and powerless. That wasn't the man she knew. Only the pain was familiar, and the grief, the two things she'd seen in him from the start, the origins and depths of which she recognized only now.

"He couldn't let her go, of course. Not Edward. So he went after her, and this time he went alone."

"And you followed him."

"Yes. That was Mandy—his wife. That's how I met her. He found her in the little town in Minnesota she'd run to, where she'd met Jakob. I followed him all the way across the country, and when I found him . . . I shot him, Maggie. Right in the gut and watched him bleed. I tried to tell myself I thought he was reaching for a gun, but . . . I don't know. I don't know if I believed he really had one, or if I only gave myself that excuse. All I know is, when we searched the body, he was unarmed."

"Kieran." Her voice trembled with the need to soothe him, to make him understand that he was a young man who'd done his best, who'd loved too much and suffered for it and should now forgive himself.

It was all so clear to her. She wondered how much of it he knew, how much he realized about himself.

Kieran was no more naturally drawn to risk and danger than she. He was cautious and determinedly careful with others, intensely protective of everyone's life but his own.

He'd spent decades doing penance, chasing lost causes and saving people in trouble because he'd been unable to save Cynthia. And, because he'd failed to protect her, and because he thought he'd damned himself by shooting an unarmed man—however richly Edward deserved it—Kieran left himself open to punishment, took the chances that no other man would. He'd not cared about his life because he believed it already lost.

She raised up to look down into his face. Others might see only the harsh beauty of his features, even as she once had. Now she saw compassion, and grief, and a man who'd loved too well, too young. "I love you, Kieran."

"Don't," he said harshly.

"Too late," she whispered, and brought her mouth down to his.

21

Friday was payday at the Lessing Mill. So, on Friday afternoons, a steady stream of workers made the trip from the mill to town and back again, often skipping supper to get to the bank before it closed.

Margaret stopped at the office and asked Melissa to accompany her into Redemption. They'd not mentioned Melissa's revelations of a few days ago again, nor had Margaret had a chance to urge Melissa to break it off with her lover. It was as if, by unspoken agreement, they'd both decided they needed a few days to get their friendship on firm and familiar footing again before diving back into more difficult areas.

On the walk into town, worry lifted from Margaret's shoulders, as though the bright sunshine burned it off as easily as it had the morning's fog. Wild roses bloomed riotously along the roadside. A killdeer skittered across right in front of them, absurdly thin legs moving in a quick blur, and Margaret grinned.

"You're in a good mood today," Melissa commented.

"Who wouldn't be, on a day like this?" She reached down and plucked a wildflower she couldn't remember the name of, deep mauve with a golden ruff, and handed it to Melissa.

In truth, her good spirits surprised even her. Nothing had changed. Melissa was still troubled, Kieran would still leave soon, and Margaret was still in love with him. More deeply all the time. But somehow today seemed ripe with . . . potential.

And she had five whole dollars of her own in her pocketbook. Oh, five dollars was nothing, compared to the five hundred Kieran was paying her. She'd earned a little money before, here and there, selling eggs and knitted items.

But it had never occurred to her before that she had the skills to so easily find a job, one that would pay her a living, if hardly a luxurious, wage. A job she even enjoyed. It made her wonder what other things were out there in the world for her that she'd never considered before, either. However much she regretted the circumstances that brought it about, she couldn't regret the possibilities it had opened for her.

"Where do you want to go first?" Melissa asked as they gained the edge of town.

"I've Lily's money, too," Margaret said. "I promised I would send it to . . . her family for her, so I must do that at some point."

"I'd like to stop at Chaney's. I've got my eye on a new pair of gloves."

"The bank first," Margaret decided with a wry grin. "Then I won't be tempted to spend everything I have."

Even so, when they passed Chaney's Store, the front windows brimming with goods caught her eye. Having never had the extra coin to seriously consider purchases beyond the necessary, she couldn't resist stopping and taking a peek at the things displayed.

"There, Melissa—"

"Lucy! I'm Lucy now. Especially when there are people around who might hear."

"I'm sorry. Lucy, then. Do you see that Dutch calico there, in the far corner of the window? What do you think? I've not had a new dress for ages, and—"

Melissa gave her arm a pinch.

"Ouch! Lucy, what are you—"

"Shh! Look who's coming."

Kieran sauntered across the street, heading for the store. After all the time they'd spent together, shouldn't she be getting *used* to him? But even now, just watching him walk toward her, her heart gave a giddy little flip.

"Don't you look at him like that, Miss Thayer," Melissa hissed in her ear.

"What do you mean? Like what? I—"

As Kieran passed them, he gave a polite nod, flashing a grin that made her want to kiss him. She wished he'd grin like that more often, lighthearted, with his eyes as well as his mouth. A smile that clearly held memories of yesterday afternoon and promises of the night to come.

Melissa grabbed her by the sleeve and hauled her down the street.

"It's the bank for us," she said firmly.

"What's the matter?"

"The nerve of that man! Smiling at you like that after what he did to you," she fumed.

"Hold it right there." Margaret stopped in her tracks. "What he did to me?"

"The whole place is talking about it, how he used you and jilted you."

"You have no idea what you're talking about. I've known what I was getting into since the beginning. Well, almost," she amended. "Kieran hasn't done anything to me that I haven't wanted him to."

"You just like him because he's pretty."

"There is that."

"Now see here." Melissa stopped and jammed her hands on her hips. The sight of Melissa preparing to lecture her like a recalcitrant student made Margaret smile. At the same time it touched her that Melissa cared about her so much that she would insist on giving Margaret advice. "I know you're older than me, Miss Thayer, but I think I know more about men. Nothing good will come out of mooning over a man like that."

Margaret sobered. This had gone far enough. Glad as she was to see Melissa reaching beyond herself, trying to help another person, she couldn't allow the girl to continue thinking such things about Kieran. "Lucy, I've left this alone because I thought you wanted it this way, and I wanted to give you time to think it through on your own. But

Kieran's not going to give up. You can trust him, I promise you. If you'd just tell him who you really are—"

"He'll tell my father," Melissa said flatly.

"No, he won't, not if you tell him why."

"My father's paying him, isn't he?"

"I suppose so, but that won't matter. Not if Kieran knows the truth. I *know* him, Lucy, much better than you're giving me credit for. Do you think I would possibly suggest anything like this to you if I thought there was the slightest chance your father would end up anywhere near you ever again?"

"No." Melissa blinked rapidly. "I know you wouldn't."

"Good," she said gently. "Let's go find Kieran, shall we? You'll feel better when this is all over."

"I can't." Melissa tensed, her eyes glittering with emotion, so tightly wound that Margaret thought the slightest jar might break her. "I have to think."

"All right." She'd already pushed as far as she dared today. Margaret could only hope that it would be enough. "Promise me you'll think about it?"

"I'll think about it."

"Why don't we go along to the bank? And you are to watch me very closely, and make sure I keep out only enough money to buy that calico and deposit every bit of the rest. Otherwise who knows what I'll do when we go back to Chaney's?"

Melissa's laugh was a bit shaky, but it relieved Margaret just the same.

Most of the mill workers wouldn't be able to get into town for a few hours yet, so the bank was surprisingly quiet. A line of three people stood in front of the barred clerk's desk. Mrs. Heppelman was first, recounting the bills the clerk had just given her, but she turned to see who'd just entered. Margaret waved at her and re-signed herself to hearing all about Mrs. Heppelman's pansies.

They got in line behind a young man she didn't recognize. A cowboy, from the looks of him, who probably worked the open land west of Redemption. He smiled at Melissa, openly admiring, and Margaret edged over protectively.

The clerk finished with Mrs. Heppelman and called for the next customer. Mrs. Heppelman sailed on by with a cheery "so nice to see you, Margaret, I'd love to chat, but I've got tea with Reverand Parker in ten minutes."

"Nice to see you too," she said automatically.

"You don't have to look so relieved," Melissa told her.

"I didn't realize I was quite so transparent," she said, embarrassed to be caught out.

Sunshine poured through the bank's big front window, painting a golden rectangle on the highly polished wood floors. The door opened again, admitting another slice of light that slid across the width of the room before disappearing.

Another stranger, Margaret thought. Surprising; she hadn't heard there were so many new people in town. A large man, this one. Not tall, but bulky beneath the ample coat he'd, oddly, chosen to wear on such a warm day. A big, floppy-brimmed hat was jammed low over his forehead, and his head hunched low into his collar, like a turtle retreating into its shell, so she couldn't see his face. He wore spectacles, though; light glinted off glass when he turned his head.

He glanced around the room and shuffled two steps in.

The first person in line and the clerk held a low-voiced conversation. At her side, Melissa sighed, impatient to be gone. Anxious to get to Chaney's, most likely; even Margaret was beginning to get caught up in the fun of having money to spend.

The stranger straightened, his head rising out of his collar. A swatch of dark cotton covered the lower half of his face. For an instant, Margaret thought, Now isn't that strange? And then her heart seized the second before his hand disappeared into the folds of his coat and he drew out a gun.

"Melissa," she said softly, "get behind me."

"What?"

"Just get behind me."

Melissa's gasp told Margaret that she, too, had spotted the gun. The man had still said nothing, and the other three people in the room clearly had no idea anything was amiss. They chatted casually, and the young cowboy chuckled at something.

His eyes, shielded by thick lenses, met Margaret's. The thick curved glass distorted his eyes strangely, made the milky blue irises look outsized, bulging from his head. He seemed . . . amused by it all, by the secret that she and he knew that the others did not yet, that they were in danger and he was the source of it.

Margaret blessed the experience she'd received

the last few weeks with Kieran. That seasoning allowed her to remain calm, alert, senses and mind fully functioning. If this had happened to her six months ago, Margaret thought, she'd be on the floor screaming in panic.

Appearing completely at ease, he strolled into the center of the bank, right into the cheerful rectangle of melted-butter sunshine.

"All right, folks," he said, his voice calm, a clipped accent Margaret couldn't place, muffled only slightly by the cloth that covered his mouth. He spoke softly enough that seconds ticked past before the others realized what was happening, before the clerk's last instructions to his customer died off in a strangled wheeze.

"I bet you all can guess what this is," he said, his demeanor almost jovially friendly. "All of you"—he gestured with the barrel of the gun—"line up over there against the wall. I don't want any problems, now. And you folks don't either. I'd rather not have to shoot anybody, but I could change my mind easy enough."

The four of them—Margaret, Melissa, the cowboy, and the other customer—shuffled together as a group to the west wall. The fourth person, Margaret now saw, was Susannah Melman, a farmer's wife from south of town whom she knew only vaguely. Her disbelieving eyes squarely on the gun, Mrs. Melman couldn't see where she was going and stumbled into the cowboy's back. When the cowboy moved to catch her, the gunman tensed, ready to react immediately to any attempt at heroics.

"Now there, that's good," the thief said, when

they'd clumped in a huddle beneath the picture of President Grant that had been there since the bank opened. "I like it when people follow directions."

Margaret groped for Melissa's hand, giving it a reassuring squeeze.

The gun swung around fractionally to cover the clerk who stood hunched behind his desk.

"You there," the robber said. "I'm not going to come any closer, 'cause it's easier to cover everybody from back here. But you know I can shoot you just as well from over here as I could from ten feet closer, don't you?"

The clerk bobbed his head, jerking down a little behind his desk.

"Now, you're not thinking you're going to duck down there and hide behind that desk, are you? You know I'd have to come get you then. And to do that, I'd have to shoot everybody over there first, to make sure they didn't do something stupid while my back was turned. You don't want that, do you?"

The clerk shook his head.

"Do you?"

"No, sir," he croaked out.

"Good."

That quiet voice, Margaret thought, utterly calm, was a thousand times more frightening than he would have been had he shouted. It spoke of absolute control, confidence, and experience.

"Now, I want you to start filling up bags for me," he instructed the clerk. "Much as you can get in two big bags. I'm not greedy, and I can't carry much more than that by myself. But you be generous now, you hear?"

"Yes, sir."

Time unraveled slowly, each second yielding reluctantly to the next. Images caught, found permanent places in her memory. The nervous twitching of the clerk as he stuffed packs of bills into a canvas sack. The impotent fury of the cowboy beside her, awkwardly trying to soothe the whimpering Susannah. Melissa's unexpected calm, her hand warm and steady in Margaret's. And the eerie soft voice and still manner of the thief.

"That's as much as I can get in two bags," the clerk said.

"Are you sure?" Margaret thought she caught a hint of a smile behind the thief's mask, an upward wrinkle of dark fabric. This was about more than just money, she realized, her thoughts spinning, fragmented, trying to fit it all together.

"Yes."

"Throw it over here."

The clerk gave a heave, sending the heavy bags whipping through the air. The thief sidestepped gracefully and the bags hit the floor with a loud, depressing thud.

"Now, you aimed those at me, didn't you?" He *tsk*ed and scooped up both bags in his free hand. "You shouldn't have done that. Now somebody's going to have to pay for that."

"No, I—" He lifted his hands, attempting innocence, his Adam's apple bobbing wildly.

"Who should it be?" The gunman swung around, contemplating the four of them clumped by the wall as if selecting a chicken from the grocer.

The clerk found his voice and his bravery. "It's not their fault!"

"And I don't care."

Margaret knew the exact instant he settled on her. His gun lowered a fraction, and there was again the upward curve of the mouth beneath the fabric.

Something bumped her elbow hard. Melissa shoved past her and planted herself in front of Margaret, her arms wide, body shielding Margaret.

"You're not going to shoot her," Melissa said. "I won't let you."

Margaret saw it all. Saw the sun spilling through the window, the bright gloss on the floor. Saw the decision in those weirdly distorted eyes. Saw herself, desperately trying to pull Melissa aside. Saw the barrel of the gun move a fraction as the thief adjusted his aim.

She just couldn't move fast enough to stop it.

"NO!"

Kieran stepped out of Chaney's Store and let the door bang shut behind him. He paused, letting the sun soak into his shoulders.

And why not? It was a beautiful day. With an even better night to come, he thought, remembering the way Maggie had lit up when he met her on the street, gold glinting in the brown of her eyes, her little half dimple peeking out just for him.

He shouldn't be feeling this good. He was no closer to completing this job than he had been yesterday. And Maggie—if he had any sense at all, he'd be setting himself to making sure she fell out of love with him right quick, so she wouldn't be hurt too badly when he left.

So, while his body had every reason—many reasons, he remembered with a grin—to be pleased, the rest of him shouldn't be so lighthearted. But he couldn't seem to shake it, the giddy burst of warmth that had sparked in him when Maggie said "I love you, Kieran," and that had only been growing stronger ever since, every single time he thought about it.

Aw, hell. Whether he should or not, he felt good. Why shouldn't he enjoy it?

His stomach rumbled. He'd missed breakfast, he realized, and lunch too, so he turned and headed for Jamison's.

Behind him, he heard a muffled report.

"What the—"

He spun just in time to see a man burst through the front door of the bank, two bulging sacks clutched in one hand. A big chestnut horse had been left, ground-tied, just in front of the bank. He jumped on it, wheeled around, and spurred it down the street.

The bank door exploded open again. A woman dashed through, shrieking, her words garbled so Kieran had to work to decipher them.

"Robbery! There's been a robbery!"

"Damn it!" he shouted in disbelief. Who would have thought? How could he have misread it so completely?

Benjamin Lessing has just robbed his own damned bank.

Kieran took off running.

For it had to be Benjamin. Too much of a coincidence that another outlaw had found his way to Redemption.

Kieran had walked to the store, leaving his horse at the livery. By the time he got it saddled, he'd be maybe twenty minutes behind Lessing. Not bad, if he knew where Benjamin was headed.

Which he did not.

The woman was hollering again, this time: "Doctor! Get the doctor!"

The kind of fear Kieran thought he'd left behind decades ago knifed through his belly.

Margaret had been headed for the bank. He'd indulged himself by watching her through Chaney's front window, amused at how her friend had propelled her down the street. Saving her from Kieran, no doubt.

Far ahead, Lessing's horse charged on, almost out of sight. If Kieran was to have any hope of catching up with him, he had to go now. He'd been waiting for this chance for months, for the Uncatchable Man to make a mistake, to leave himself open to apprehension.

But Maggie might be in the bank.

Without even bothering to shoot another glance at Lessing's departing figure, he ran up the steps of the bank and through the doors.

A small cluster of people knelt on the floor. He saw the flutter of a petticoat against the wood, a highly polished black boot, and he stopped breathing.

And then one of the men shifted, and there she

was. Maggie, blood smearing her blouse, kneeling by Lucy's limp figure.

She looked up at him, her eyes huge, angry and terrified at once.

"He shot her, Kieran. He shot Melissa."

22

Minutes ground agonizingly into hours, accompanied by the too-loud ticking of the mahogany clock that was the only gracious accent in Dr. Ballard's decrepit front room.

Margaret perched rigidly on a frail-looking ladder-back chair, her hand clutched in Kieran's. They'd not spoken, just waited, their gazes glued to the door with its peeling green paint that led to the room where Dr. Ballard had taken Melissa.

They'd had a small stroke of luck in that the doctor had been in his office when Susannah Melman ran down the road hollering for help. He'd immediately grabbed his bag and rushed to the bank, and so was able to stanch the bleeding somewhat before Melissa was moved to his office.

They'd been here ever since.

Oliver Chaney had stopped by briefly to report that the sheriff had gotten up a group of men to chase after the mysterious bank robber. Kieran had little hope for their success—he'd met the sheriff and knew his post was purely honorary. Redemption hadn't needed any more law enforcement than that, until now.

Kieran hadn't told them that the man they sought was really Benjamin Lessing. He'd seen no point in it. He doubted they'd believe him, and he didn't have the energy or time to argue the point. He couldn't back up his story, not yet. Only Melissa Dalrymple could do that . . . if she survived.

Tick. Tock. Tick. Tock.

"I'm gonna throw that damned clock against the wall," he growled, immediately sorry when Margaret turned her strained, worried face toward him.

"Will it be much longer, do you think?"

"I don't know." Her hands were cold, and he rubbed them between his palms to warm them. "I should telegraph her father and let him know what's going on. I just don't know what to tell him."

"No, don't do that!" Her grip tightened. "Stay with me."

He couldn't say no to her. "All right."

The door opened and they both jumped to their feet. Dr. Ballard shuffled in, wiping his hands on a clean length of linen, his shoulders sagging with weariness.

"Is—" Margaret's throat froze; she couldn't force the question out.

"You've been bringing me an unusual amount of business lately, young lady," he told her. "Enough is enough. We got lucky this time, too, but I don't want to see you in again, do you hear me?"

"Thank God." She swayed, and Kieran's arm came around her for support.

"The bullet glanced off a rib, then lodged in her side. Didn't hit anything worth worrying about."

"What took so long?"

"Had to find it first. Then pick out a couple of little chips of rib bone. I had to stitch it up real neat too. Didn't want to leave much of a scar on a pretty young woman like that." He shook his head. "These girls, they get a mite upset about things like that sometimes. When you get to my age you know it don't matter a jot."

"Can we see her?"

"I don't see why not. She's kinda groggy; don't know if she'll stay awake long. But the first thing she asked me was if you were all right, Margaret, so I imagine she'll be glad to see you, all in one piece."

"Thank you."

She clung tight to Kieran's hand as they made their way to the back room. Just outside the door, she stopped and took a deep breath, trying to compose herself, smoothing the worry from her face. She didn't want Melissa upset by seeing her like this.

"Ready?" Kieran asked.

"Yes."

They tiptoed in, not wanting to disturb Melissa if she rested, but her eyelids fluttered open a thin slit as soon as they stepped into the room. Dr. Ballard hovered in the doorway behind them, to make certain they didn't tire out his patient.

Melissa lay completely still on a narrow iron bed that took up a good portion of the space in the tiny chamber. The room also held a white-painted metal cabinet, a basket of towels, and a tray of gleaming instruments that Margaret couldn't bear to look at; she wondered how Dr. Ballard managed to work in the tight quarters.

They moved to the side of the bed. Melissa's gaze flicked down, at their joined hands, and then up to Kieran.

"Why's he here?"

"He came with me," Margaret said, gripping his hand tighter.

"I can leave," Kieran offered quickly.

"No. He can stay."

Melissa's freckles stood out in stark relief, looking almost black against her bleached face, the skin paler than the pillowcase she rested on.

Tentatively, afraid the slightest jar would hurt her, Margaret laid her hand over Melissa's where it lay limp on the bed. "You saved my life."

"Did, didn't I?" she said weakly. "He . . . shot me. Never . . . thought he'd shoot me."

"Melissa." Kieran spoke from beside her, and Melissa's eyes flew open wide, accusing.

"You . . . told him?"

"No! No, I didn't, I swear. He knew, about Benjamin, and when you were shot—he just put the pieces together and figured out who you must be." Margaret forced a wobbly smile, trying to be reassuring. "He doesn't know the rest. I didn't tell him, I promise."

She met Melissa's eyes directly, clearly, willing her to see the truth, to trust. Finally Melissa sighed, going slack against the bed, and closed her eyes.

"You can tell him," she whispered.

"Are you sure?"

"Trust . . . you."

The tears Margaret had been battling all afternoon, the ones she'd tried to keep at bay because they'd do no good, caught up with her at last, welling in her eyes, spilling over the corners.

"What's she talking about, Maggie?" Kieran whispered in her ear.

"I'll tell you later," she promised, not wanting Melissa to have to listen to it, unwilling to upset her with bad memories if they could possibly avoid it.

"Melissa," Kieran said, his tone as soft and gentle as he could make it, "I know you're tired, but I have to ask—Benjamin, do you know where he could be?"

"Still . . . can't believe . . . shot me." Her voice broke. "Why?"

"Because you were the only one who could identify him before," Kieran said. "I'll catch him for you, Melissa, I swear. I'll make sure he never hurts you again. But anything you can tell me to get me going in the right direction would help."

"There's a . . ." She swallowed, tried again. "Soddy. Along another river. Other side . . . Missouri. Kept me there . . . for a while."

"How far away?"

"Two hours . . . maybe three?" The talking began to take its toll; sleep pulled at her, and she couldn't make her eyes open again.

"I'm afraid it's time for the two of you to go," Dr. Ballard said.

"Just one more moment," Kieran said. "Melissa,

do you know which river? Anything? It would give me a place to start."

"No," she said, tears gathering in her eyes and voice.

"Don't worry about it, Melissa. You just rest," he said. Though he spoke calmly, Margaret could see his determination. His mouth thinned, and his eyes narrowed, thick black lashes shadowing the light blue to steady darkness. Already he was focusing, preparing himself for the hunt.

"I'll get him for you, Melissa," he promised.

Dr. Ballard left them in the grim outer room and went back to watch over his patient, leaving them alone. Margaret, calmly as she could while the tears threatened again, told Kieran everything she knew about Melissa and her childhood and the things her father had done to her.

He didn't say a word. Just stood there, rigid, fists clenched, listening. But as she went on, she watched the flush of anger color his cheeks even as it froze his eyes to ice.

"I have to go," he said flatly when she was done.

"Wait!" She gripped the back of a chair, using it to hold herself up; the day had stolen all strength from her legs. "Take someone with you."

"It'll only slow me down."

Frantically, she tried to think of some excuse to give him, other than the truth. That she knew he blamed himself for not seeing through Melissa's father, for not protecting her from Benjamin. And that she was terrified that without her along to force him into uncharacteristic caution, he'd ride heedlessly into danger and get himself killed.

She had no doubt he would do what he'd said—make certain that Benjamin never harmed Melissa again.

She just didn't know if he'd come back from it.

There wasn't any way she could say that, though; she had a pretty fair idea what his answer would be.

It doesn't matter what happens to me. The only thing that's important is that Melissa is safe.

"Wouldn't it be better, though, to take a few other men along? To make certain you catch him?"

"It's only one man, Maggie. I don't need any help."

"Damn it, Kieran, you don't have to do this by yourself!" she burst out, fear giving volume to her words.

"Because I've done such a great job of it so far, you mean?" His eyes had gone flat, his face dead of expression. She wanted to shake him, to force him to understand, but she didn't know how.

"You know that's not what I meant!" Her hands tightened around the chair back until the edge of the wood bit painfully into her palm.

"But I did," he said. "I was so damn . . . arrogant. I thought I was such a good judge of people, and I let her father take me in completely."

"You did the best you could," she said, knowing it was weak, knowing he wouldn't accept it.

"Well, that was pretty damn pitiful, wasn't it?" A flicker of expression showed through his stony veneer then, and she almost wished it hadn't. Too much pain, too much regret; she didn't know how he'd survive it.

"Jesus, Maggie, what if I've been wrong all along, all these years? How much other bad have I done in the name of trying to help?"

"That's not true," she said softly, helplessly. She knew he was wrong, that he'd helped many people over the years, saved them. And he knew it, too; he just wasn't ready to remember it yet.

"Good-bye, Maggie," he said, and turned for the door.

"Kieran! How do you think I feel?"

He stopped, but his back remained to her. Just waiting. The vulnerable tip of his earlobe showed beneath the thick fringe of his hair. Those strong shoulders, the ones that took on more than their share, fit snugly into the shirt his friend had made him, and she wondered if she'd ever get the chance to run her hands over his shoulders again.

Sadness welled so deep she felt it might swallow her whole. *Dear God, he's going and I can't stop him. How am I ever going to live if he dies?*

"I knew, too," she said. "I knew who she was. I could have told you, I could have prevented this whole thing, and now I'm going to have to live with it. You don't get to own all the guilt, Kieran."

"But you didn't know," he said without turning around. "You didn't know what he was capable of, you didn't have any experience with situations like this. I did."

"You don't have to save *everybody*," she shouted after him. But it was too late.

He'd already gone.

*   *   *

It took Kieran two days to find Benjamin Lessing.

His tracking skills were rusty; he didn't get much call for them in the city streets where he usually hunted. Finally, on a clear, sunny day, he found the soddy, near a tributary of the Missouri called the Coyote.

The soddy was dug into the side of a massive butte that overlooked the river. It had to be the right one. There wasn't much else out there, and a big chestnut like the one Benjamin had ridden away from the bank on was contentedly cropping at the needlegrass nearby.

A light breeze rippled the grass seductively. Nearby, a fat, bright-colored pheasant he'd disturbed flew off to hide itself in deeper cover. A quiet, pleasant day.

Kieran pulled out his gun, tapped Charlie on the flanks, and galloped on in.

23

"I can't believe you let him shoot you!"

"Hey!" Kieran protested. "I shot him a whole lot worse than he shot me."

The glare he received told him in no uncertain terms precisely what Maggie thought of that defense.

"It's just a graze," he said grumpily. "Hardly even bled at all."

"Well, we'll just see about that soon enough, won't we?" she said, and continued to unwind the dingy strips of linen that bandaged his shoulder.

He hadn't killed Benjamin. After their skirmish—he was going to call it a skirmish, he'd decided on the ride back to Redemption, because he didn't think Maggie would much appreciate the idea of there having been a fight, however minor—he'd tied a sheet over Benjamin's bleeding thigh, loaded him up on the back of a horse, and delivered him to the authorities at Fort Pierre.

The fort's doctor had ventured the opinion that Benjamin would survive—at least until someone hanged him. As soon as the doctor patched up Kieran's shoulder wound, Kieran had headed back to Redemption as fast as Charlie could carry him.

After three days away, he'd been anxious to get back. To find out how everything had turned out in his absence, he told himself, and to make sure Dr. Ballard's prognosis had been correct and Melissa was recovering properly.

And maybe, he admitted to himself, he'd been impatient to see Maggie. Just a little.

But when he arrived he couldn't find her. He'd spent the morning in a state of agitated frustration. She wasn't at her house. Daisy had mooed at him when he looked in the shed, but it wasn't her welcome that interested him.

He'd checked Dr. Ballard's, thinking she might still be there, nursing Melissa, but the place was empty. He'd gone to his room at Jamison's and asked at the desk, but she hadn't left him a message.

Finally, he'd gone to the mill, thinking someone there might know where she was. And he'd found her in the boardinghouse kitchen, up to her elbows in bread dough.

It hadn't occurred to him that, with Benjamin captured and Melissa found, she'd keep on working at the mill.

It should have. He cursed himself for not immediately realizing she'd feel responsible for the girls under her care. And then he'd just plain cursed when she rushed to hug him and threw her arm right over where Benjamin's bullet had grazed him.

Not trusting some army sawbones' opinion, she'd wanted to drag him off to Dr. Ballard's immediately. He'd finally gotten her to agree not to, but only if he allowed her to check the wound for herself first.

And so he found himself, shirtless, sitting in a chair in the sunny, yeasty-smelling kitchen while Maggie fussed over his shoulder. Except now she was wrapping him up again, and her fingers kept brushing over his chest as she worked, and he figured this maybe wasn't such a bad deal after all.

He cocked an eyebrow at her. "Are we alone?"

"Everybody's at work."

"Even Lily?"

"Yes." She frowned, untwisting a strip of linen that wouldn't lie flat to her satisfaction. "She insisted on going back. But Walter put her to work inspecting finished flannel, so it's not too taxing."

"So we *are* alone."

"Except for Arne."

"He won't mind."

"You're hurt," she said flatly.

"I'm not *that* hurt."

Margaret tucked the last end of bandage firmly beneath the rest, finishing it off. "There." She stepped back, her hands on her hips, and eyed him critically.

Darn it, he thought. His plans for the rest of the morning were not looking too promising.

"You know this just proves that you're too old to be doing that anymore."

"*What?*" he said, almost strangling on the word.

"Gallivanting all over the countryside, charging in without thinking. Have you ever gotten shot before?"

"No."

"I didn't think so. I didn't see any other scars."

"Did you look?" he asked, intrigued.

"That's not the point," she said briskly, the shell of her ears pinking up nicely. "The point is, you're getting too old for it. Your reflexes must be slowing down. That's why you got shot this time."

"It's not because I'm getting old. It's your fault."

"*My* fault?"

"Uh-huh. Right before I went in there, I thought, 'If I get shot, Maggie's gonna be really, really mad at me.' Just thinking it slowed me down a fraction, and that's why he got a shot off."

Maggie opened her mouth, shut it again without saying a word. Now there was a first. He'd have to remember this one.

It would be so easy to go on like this. Light, teasing, pretending there weren't other worries and other barriers they'd have to address. Unfortunately, they'd avoided uncomfortable topics like the future and the many things unsettled between them for just about as long as they could.

The amusement died in Maggie's eyes, her expression sobering, and Kieran wondered if he'd ever again see her smile at him that way again, with the sparkle in her eyes echoing her smile. His shirt hung on the back of the chair behind him, and he reached for it and stuck his arm in, wincing when he stretched his shoulder farther than it wanted to go.

"Would you be careful!" Maggie said.

"It's all right." He looked up at her, only a few steps away, and he thought how easy it would be to take her hand and draw her down into his lap. How much he'd rather do that, to lose them both in passion, rather than begin sorting through the mess left in Benjamin's wake. "How's Melissa?"

"She's doing fairly well." Margaret wandered to the table and peeked beneath the cloth she'd used to cover the bowl of bread dough. It wouldn't be risen enough for hours, and she knew it, but it was safer than looking at Kieran—at least until he got his shirt all buttoned up.

"Is she still at Dr. Ballard's? I checked his office this morning and didn't find anyone around."

"No, actually, as soon the doctor said she was ready to be moved, I took her out to Martha Ann's."

"Martha Ann's?"

"Yes. I thought . . . in case Benjamin decided to come back, he wouldn't look for her there. And with Lucius and the boys around, it'd be safer."

"Good idea."

The chair scraped back. Kieran stood up, stuffing the ends of his shirt into his pants.

There, Margaret thought. She could look at him now, without being too tempted to throw herself in his arms, to forget once again that he was a man who thoughtlessly exposed himself to danger, who took extreme care with everyone else and none at all with himself.

"There's a few other things that happened while you were gone," she said, "that you'd probably be interested in."

"Yes?"

"Well, the sheriff went to talk to Ruth Lessing. She said she had absolutely no idea what her husband was doing. And she's absolutely mortified by the whole thing."

"Is she okay?"

"Oh, she's better than okay." A smile flirted with the corners of her mouth. "She's run off."

"Run off?"

The smile broke out. "With Stephen Dodge."

The laughter caught him, a blessed release. "Who would have thought it?"

"There's more. And you're never going to guess."

"More than *that?*" They'd been busy, while he was gone. Redemption would never settle down after all this excitement.

"Before she left, she signed ownership of the bank and the mill over to Melissa."

"Melissa?"

"Yes," Margaret said, thoroughly enjoying his surprise. Even Kieran couldn't have guessed how this would all play out. "Ruth cleaned out all their bank accounts before she left, hers and Benjamin's, and nobody thought to stop her. Since some of that money undoubtedly came from Melissa's father, I guess she figured she owed Melissa that much."

"An odd twist of conscience."

"It certainly is that."

He looked down at her, at the shining clean

sweep of her harvest-colored hair, her familiar features. There, right there, was where the delicious shy dent that accented her mouth hid, waiting for him to bring it out.

How was it possible he'd known her for such a short time? He had so much to say to her, so much to straighten out between them. But there were other things he must do first.

"I've got to go talk to Melissa."

"Of course." Tying up all the loose ends, Margaret thought. And then he'd go on to the next one, to the next lost and troubled person who asked for his help. "Let me go with you. I haven't visited her today, either."

"I rode Charlie over—I don't have the buggy with me today."

"I've got Gumbo here at the mill. I can ride."

"Gumbo? She'll collapse beneath you before we get a mile."

"She's tougher than she looks."

And so, to Kieran's surprise, was Melissa.

The Perkinses' original cabin had been added onto over the years, as their family grew. Melissa had been set up in Martha Ann's prized front parlor, on the crushed-velvet sofa that had been a wedding present from her mother.

Dread tightening his chest, Kieran cautiously stepped into the room. He'd expected to find Melissa sickly and weak from her injuries and wouldn't have blamed her a bit if she hated him for not preventing the whole stupid mess.

Instead, she was sitting up, her hair pinned on top of her head, and the ruffle of a fancy bed

coat peeking out above the quilt tucked beneath
her arms. She had one of the youngest Perkins
girls beside her—he never had gotten all their
names straight—and was reading her some non-
sensical rhyme from a book in a clear, strong
voice.

As soon as they stepped in, she glanced up and
her smile faded.

"Melissa." He cleared his throat. "How are you?
You're looking well."

"Thank you. I am well. Martha Ann is taking
extremely good care of me." Two bright flags of
color spotted her cheeks. "Did . . . did you catch
him?"

"Yes."

"Is he . . . is he dead?"

"No."

"Oh," she said softly, and he couldn't tell if she
was relieved or unhappy. "What happens to him
now?"

"I left him at Fort Pierre. I expect that a number
of states will be fighting for the privilege of getting
their hands on him first."

She carefully closed the book and handed it to
the little girl. "Take this back to your mother now.
I'm a little tired. We'll finish later."

The small, carefully decorated parlor brimmed
with vases and jars of flowers, cluttering every
table, even stuffed into every corner. A few of the
bouquets were simply masses of wildflowers; it
seemed as if every garden in Redemption must
have been stripped bare for the rest. "Looks like
you've had a few visitors."

"They're from Walter, mostly. I think he feels badly about not seeing what was right before him. He said he knew there was something odd about all the money coming in to the bank and the mill, but Benjamin told him it came from other investments, and he should just do what he was paid for, and he did."

Plenty of regret to go around, Kieran thought. And he'd best get on with his. "Speaking of which—Maggie, would you leave us alone for a little while?"

"I—" She started to protest, then caught sight of the expression on his face. "I'll just go say hello to Martha Ann."

He waited until she'd closed the double doors behind her, then walked over to stand at Melissa's bedside. She looked uncertain, maybe a little frightened. Well, he supposed he deserved that.

Where to start? He decided to ease into it. "I hear you've got yourself a couple of businesses?"

"Yes." She lifted her chin, met his gaze fully. "I suppose my father would say they belonged to him. Considering how much money Benjamin stole from him. Are you going to tell him?"

"No!" Is *that* why she'd looked at him so suspiciously? But then, she hardly had any reason to trust men, did she. Especially not him. He rushed to reassure her. "No, I'm not going to tell him. And, just so you know—I didn't tell him where I thought you'd gone, either, before I came here. I didn't want to get his hopes up. It took me nine months to track you and Benjamin down. I don't think there's a chance in hell he'll find you here."

Melissa sucked in a breath, let it out slowly. "Thank you."

"Don't thank me." The last thing she should do was thank him. "I'm so sorry, Melissa. Sorry I didn't get you away from Benjamin sooner. Even sorrier that I didn't see through your father, that I believed what he told me."

"It's all right." She cocked her head curiously, intrigued. Kieran had always seemed so certain of himself. So very male in that respect. She certainly hadn't expected an apology from him. Especially since she was hardly his responsibility. Perhaps, she thought, Margaret was right about him. She certainly hoped so. Because if he hurt Margaret, well . . . she'd just have to make sure he was extremely sorry, one way or the other.

She decided to reserve judgment. "It's not as if my father's not remarkably good at fooling people," she told him. "How do you think he made all that money?"

"I never heard anything about that. I checked him out before I said I'd help."

"No, because nobody knows. Everybody trusts him, he hides it so well. Like once—I listened in when I wasn't supposed to. He got all these people to invest in a mining operation, out west. He told them it went bust—they were happy, because he ever so kindly reimbursed most of their costs from his own pocket. They never found out that the mine actually paid off big. How would they? I don't think he even told any of them exactly where it was."

"Hmm." More to think about. He'd let it whir

around in his mind for a while. And this time, oddly, there was no more sting at misjudging William Dalrymple so completely. "What are you going to do? With the mill and the bank? Have you decided?"

"Not really." She settled back against the pillows, thin shoulders that didn't look as if they should have such responsibilities. But the light in her eyes said she relished them. "There's not much money left, to run everything on. And Walter says there's lots of improvements needed at the mill, to make things better for the workers. He promised he'd stay and help me. But if he takes over the traveling, meeting customers and suppliers, there's probably more than I can handle that would be left to me." Her mouth pursed, and he could already see she was considering the problems. "I don't know. William says we could bring in a partner if we had to, someone with money." She shrugged. "We'll manage somehow."

"You know, I might have an idea for you," he said. "But first, tell me more of what you know about your father's business dealings."

When he left Melissa, some time later, he found both Walter and Margaret right outside, arms folded across their chests, staring impatiently at the door.

"Oh, you're finally done!" Walter, clutching a fistful of droopy, wind-torn pansies, tore past him so fast he left a distinct breeze in his wake.

"Those were some pretty pitiful-looking flowers," Kieran said.

"I think it's probably all he could find. He's already given her all the rest."

"Has he been like this the whole time?"

"Pretty much."

She still had her arms jammed across her chest. Beneath the hem of her dark blue skirt, her booted toes jiggled. She was just brimming over with curiosity, and he wondered how long she was going to be able to wait to ask what he and Melissa had discussed.

"You think there's any hope for them?" He indicated the door. "Melissa and Walter, I mean."

"Not really," she said. "She's . . . she's got a really long way to go, Kieran, a lot of healing to do. But the mill and the bank are going to be very good for her, give her something to do, something real to accomplish that has nothing to do with . . . how she looks or whether a man wants her. And he'll be a wonderful friend to her, if nothing else. She needs that. Needs to find out that there are decent men out there like Walter, too, not just men like her father and Benjamin."

"Are you ready to go?" he asked.

"I suppose," she said, a little confused by the sudden change of topic. What had he needed to talk to Melissa about? Alone? She couldn't read anything, not in his eyes or expression or manner. That worried her; she'd gotten fairly skilled at reading Kieran.

"Is it all right if we go to your place? I'd rather not be interrupted."

Here it comes, she thought. *He's going to tell me that now with Melissa safe and everything fixed that it's time for him to go.*

On to the next lost cause or lost soul.

The only question was, would she let him do it? Walk out of her life so easily again? She'd learned a lot since the first time he did that, about herself and about life. She'd learned she could take a risk, if she needed to, and sometimes it was worth it. That feelings like this were precious and powerful and not to be given up easily.

She'd learned she could fight. For someone else, for herself.

But what would be the point? He knew how she felt about him. She couldn't imagine herself spending the rest of her life waiting around for him to come back from his latest job, worrying, wondering.

But she couldn't envision spending the rest of her life without him either.

"Let's go," she agreed.

Kieran was staring at her.

A fierce wind and racing clouds had chased them all the way back to her house. They'd made it inside just before the rain. It drummed on the roof now, ran down the sides of the house, and sealed them off from the world.

Inside, the light was dim and gray, softened by the storm. No thunder, no lightning, nothing that dramatic, just steadily thumping rain.

They'd settled at the table because there was

really no place else for them to sit. Well, the bed, but there was no way Margaret was suggesting *that*. Kieran had promptly set himself to studying her as if he'd never laid eyes on her before.

She figured he was trying to decide just how much of a fuss she was going to kick up when he told her he was leaving. The coward. He could stroll right into the line of fire, but he didn't want to watch her cry.

"What are you looking at?"

"You."

Looking at Maggie was an endless fascination for him. He wasn't entirely sure why. Perhaps because of the way her nose curved a little crookedly at the tip. Maybe how the soft light made her hair and eyes take on a richer brown, so different from the way they appeared in the sunshine, was what intrigued him.

Or maybe it was how she looked at *him*, the way it made him feel like a hundred-times-better man than he knew darn well he was.

"I know that!" she snapped. "But what do you see?"

"I see you," he said softly. "My Maggie."

Her heart missed a beat. Don't do this, she silently begged. Don't make me miss you more, I can't bear it.

"What are you thinking?"

"I'm trying to decide," he said. "I'm trying to decide if I should tell you something now, or if we should have a night of incredible, amazing, maybe-this-is-good-bye loving first."

"Tell me now."

He sighed. "I was afraid you were going to say that."

He reached across the table, linking her fingers with his. They fit together so well, his big brown hand and her smaller, paler one.

"What you said that day in Dr. Ballard's office, about my not having to save everyone—you didn't think I really heard you, did you? That I gave any thought to what you were trying to tell me?"

"No," she whispered, while a foolish, wonderful bubble of hope began to grow inside her.

"Well, I did." His voice grew low, urgent. "But I had to finish it, don't you see that? I'd begun it, I had to see it through."

She was afraid to trust it, what she saw in his eyes and felt in her heart. Because if she was wrong, she'd never survive it.

"I talked to Melissa. They need a partner in the mill, someone who can put in some money. Someone who's willing to travel, to work hard, someone with a lot of different skills."

"*You?*"

"I have some money." He ducked his head, as if the admission embarrassed him. "The people I help—they often want to send me something, a thank-you. Sometimes it's years later, but . . . what the hell did I need it for? I invested it, over the years, and—well, I learned something at the university, after all, I guess."

The hope grew, blossomed into happiness, enough to fill her whole heart, her whole life.

"I'm going to be doing most of the traveling. That way Walter can stay here and help Melissa, pretty much doing the same job he has been all along." Unable to stand the table between them any longer, he got up and pulled her to her feet. "That is, if my wife's willing to go with me."

"Your wife." So much more for her to say. But there wasn't room for it now, for words, even for thoughts. Only room for the joy. It encompassed everything, expanded until she thought it must fill the entire world.

"Maggie, if someone comes to me, if there's a problem—I can't promise you that I wouldn't try and help."

"I wouldn't want you to promise that," she said softly. It was part of Kieran and part of what she loved about him. But she'd be there from now on, to watch over him, to make sure he cared about himself as much as he cared for others.

She opened her mouth to say yes, but he laid one finger across her lips to stop her.

"One more thing." He moved closer until they were almost touching. "I love you, Maggie. I love you."

Too much. More than she'd hoped, more than she'd ever known existed. "I thought . . . I thought you didn't ever want to feel like that again. Would never let yourself love anybody again."

"I don't seem to have much of a choice in the matter," he said, linking his arms around her back, bringing her into his embrace. "I loved Cynthia, but that was—she obsessed me. It stripped me bare, made less of me. With you, Maggie, I'm *more* with you. More than I ever knew I could be."

She looped her arms around his neck, pulling him close. "Kieran?"

"Hmm?"

"I think we're going to have a night of incredible, amazing, this-is-definitely-not-good-bye loving anyway."

Epilogue

⛧

Six months later

Dear Margaret,
I was so pleased when Kieran's last wire said you'd be in one place long enough for me to send a letter. I have so much to tell you!

First, I got the copy of the Milwaukee newspaper Kieran sent, with the article about my father's fraud trial. Although I know he deserves it, my feelings are very . . . confused. For all he did, he was still my father, the only one I'll ever have, and it's hard for me to think about him in prison, even though there were so many times I wished him dead. I guess I'll have to think about this one some more.

Walter is spending most of his time at the bank, since I can't be of much help there. But he has his projects at the mill, of course. The newest one is some kind of fire prevention device. They've built cisterns on the roof and connected them to perforated pipes that run along the ceilings . . . that's when I stopped listening. You know how he gets about those things.

Margaret . . . I told him. About my father. I didn't think Walter could get so angry, but you should have seen him! I told him because I didn't want to get his hopes up— about him and me, I mean. But Walter says it's nothing for me to worry about now. I suppose it's unforgivable of me not to put him off completely, isn't it? But he's so sweet to me, and I kind of enjoy the way he looks at me. Never had a man look at me like that before. So who knows? I'm too busy to think about it more right now, anyway.

Things are running well at the mill— though tell Kieran if he makes any more sales the size of the one in St. Louis, we might not be able to keep up with him! I must have learned more than I'd realized all those months sitting in the office playing with pens. Especially with the new overseer Kieran found. Mr. Richards does more than his share. He says he knew Kieran from a long time ago . . . do you suppose we'll ever get to hear that story? I can't pry it out of him.

I'm taking good care of Arne for you. I even bring him into the office with me every day; he likes the windowsill behind my desk, and he's good company for me.

I've put Lily to work in the office with me. She's learning to write with her left hand. (I'm helping her; all those terrible handwriting lessons with the tutors must be good for something!) But do you know—she's wonderful with numbers! A great help to me. And here's the best part—you must let me crow, because I fixed this all on my own and I'm very proud of myself—I arranged for her son to come here! His name is John, and he's nearly two, and (you must never tell her I said this) he is the oddest-looking creature I've ever seen—too much ears and not nearly enough hair. But Mrs. Clinghorn absolutely dotes on him, and watches him while Lily is working. And Lily is so happy. I can see why Kieran did all those things; it's really a wonderful feeling to have had a hand in making something right.

Speaking of which . . . I got your letter with your news. Congratulations! You will be home right after the New Year, won't you? I want to tell you in person.

Tell Kieran he must take proper care of you, or he'll be hearing from me. And Martha Ann, too. (I see her often; she can't seem to get out of the habit of fussing over me.)

Melissa

Margaret folded up the letter and set it on the polished rosewood desk that sat before the broad windows. The door opened, and she smiled when Kieran entered the room, looking so incredibly handsome in his dark gray coat and striped tie that, even now, she could hardly believe he was hers.

"Are you ready?" he asked, crossing the room to her. "The wedding starts in half an hour."

"Almost," she said. He came up behind her, drawing her back against him, and rested his cheek on the top of her head. "How did the judge ever talk your mother into this, anyway?"

Kieran grinned and spread his hand over the dark blue watered silk that covered the slight mound of her belly. "He told her that would be a terrible example for her impending grandchild, to have grandparents that were living in sin."

"Ah, the old illegitimate-grandchild approach. Good tactic."

"He didn't spend nearly forty years in a courtroom for nothing."

"It was nice of him to let us stay here, even before the wedding." The judge's mansion fronted Lake Michigan, an imposing white three-storied house like none Margaret had ever seen, let alone ever thought to stay in. Their room, furnished with rosewood and touches of deep green, looked out over the sweeping expanse of lawn and lake.

"He never had any children. I think he's rather pleased with the prospect of getting an entire family in one swoop," Kieran said, sounding both bemused and a little touched by the thought.

Content, Maggie leaned against her husband. Outside, a savage winter wind howled, blowing fierce whitecaps on the glassy surface of the lake, throwing chunks of ice up on the rocky shoreline. Trees creaked under the strain, dark, stripped limbs bowing to greater force. The wind grabbed the thin, grainy coating of snow that covered the ground and battered it against the house.

"Looks like it's going to be one lonely night out there," Kieran said.

Maggie turned in her husband's embrace and smiled.

"Not for us."

Savor These Other Romances by Contributors to
HOMECOMING

TALLCHIEF by Dinah McCall

Ever since the night Morgan Tallchief lost the only woman he could ever love, he has struggled to seal away the past. But now Kathleen Ryder is back in his life, and Morgan is helpless against his own rekindled passion.

JACKSON RULE by Dinah McCall

After being released from prison, Jackson Rule finds a job working for a preacher's daughter. Jackson may be a free man, but Rebecca Hill's sweet charity soon has him begging for mercy.

TIMBERLINE by Deborah Bedford

Held captive in her mountain cabin by escaped convict Ben Pershall, Rebecca Woodburn realizes that the man's need for love mirrors her own. Even though Ben has taken her hostage, he ultimately sets her soul free.